D0201200

Speak Ill of the Living

By the same author

Spiked

Speak Ill of the Living

Mark Arsenault

Poisoned Pen Press

Copyright ©2005 by Mark Arsenault
First Edition 2005

10 9 8 7 6 5 4 3 2 1

Library of Congress Catalog Card Number: 2004114066

ISBN: 1-59058-139-3

All rights reserved. No part of this publication may be reproduced, stored in, or introduced into a retrieval system, or transmitted in any form, or by any means (electronic, mechanical, photocopying, recording, or otherwise) without the prior written permission of both the copyright owner and the publisher of this book.

Poisoned Pen Press
6962 E. First Ave., Ste. 103
Scottsdale, AZ 85251
www.poisonedpenpress.com
info@poisonedpenpress.com

Printed in the United States of America

For Jennifer, who inspires.

Chapter 1

Lowell, Massachusetts
Thursday, August 17

Resurrections are hot news stories. This one would be no different.

It began for Eddie Bourque with a ringing that would not quit. Eddie counted seven rings. Eight. Nine. Then he drifted off for a moment and lost count. The noise woke him again. He peered across his bedroom. Too dark to see textures. His room was a clutter of black walls and blacker shapes. His dresser was a rectangle. Square red numerals floating above it said: 4:14.

The phone jangled the sleep out of him.

Must be one of his students on the line, he thought. They always called on the days they had class. Somebody's dog ate somebody's homework. He started to drift off again, a new dream at the ready...

Big, fat, wood pulp-eating dog.

Riiiiii-ng!

"Cripes!" Eddie shouted, startled.

Some student's grandmother had died again. It was a fine excuse for skipping a class—upsetting for a day but not necessarily debilitating for the rest of the semester—and hard for a part-time professor to verify, or even to question, without seeming insensitive. Eddie wondered about the college record for dead grandma in one school year. Eddie's class had lost four before the mid-term exam.

Maybe a dog was eating them.

Riiiiii-ng!

He had shut off his answering machine before bed so the phone would be sure to wake him. Why the hell did he do that every night?

Work. A job.

Eddie lifted his head, blinked away the sleep. Students didn't call in the middle of the night, editors did. This was probably one of the wire services with an assignment. Such was the life of a freelance writer. When Eddie had quit *The Daily Empire*, he had expected freelancing to be just like working for a newspaper—except without a boss. What he had found was a life of late night calls, irregular paychecks, irregular hours, no health benefits. He was constantly living at the whim of the customer, getting paid only by the job, and then often forced to fight for his money.

Being a freelancer was like being a hooker, except you were on your feet all day.

When the newswires needed a good newsman fast in the Greater Lowell area, they called Eddie Bourque. Eddie needed the work, but the seductive pull of the warm pillow drew his head back down.

They'd have to dynamite me out of this bed.

Another dark shape, round-ish and blob-like behind Eddie's pillow, rolled over and stretched out with a quiver. Eddie felt the swish of a cat's tail against his cheek.

The telephone's electronic ring sounded like a robot laughing.

Eddie sighed. It wasn't going to stop until he answered. He reached across the emptiness on the other side of the bed and grabbed the phone. The cat chirped, annoyed.

"Yup," Eddie said, dropping hard on the pillow and closing his eyes, "it's Bourque."

"You up?"

"Nope."

It was Springer, the overnight assignment editor at the Associated Press. Eddie pictured him: six foot six, maybe a hundred seventy pounds, as pale and skinny as a young white birch. If Springer had a first name he never used it—unless Springer *was* his first name. He said to Eddie, "How'd you like to make a quick eight hundred?"

Eddie's eyes popped open. That could scrape a bill collector off his back, maybe two. But nothing meant more to him than a story. If the Associated Press was willing to pay that much for a few hours work, how big was this one?

"I haven't hung up on you, man," Eddie said, dryly. "Thrill me out of bed."

"Ever heard of Roger Lime?"

"Bank president carjacked last winter in his Audi."

"Six months ago, to be precise. What else do you know about him?"

"As much as anybody. A high school winter-track team found Lime's skeleton in the woods, in his burned-out car—what, maybe three weeks later? The bones were torched black. The crime's still unsolved. No witnesses. No suspects. They buried him in a lime-green coffin, so I guess somebody in the family has a sense of humor, though you wouldn't have known it from all the security at the cemetery."

"You have a good memory, Ed."

"I covered Lime's funeral as a freelancer for the *Times-Union*."

"Well, they need to print a correction," Springer deadpanned, "because Roger Lime isn't dead."

Eddie threw aside the sheets and sat up. The cat dashed off.

Lime? Alive? It wasn't possible. "Okay, I'm thrilled," Eddie said, trying not to giggle at how big *this* story might be. "Gimme more."

"There's a fresh picture of Lime with a recent newspaper—same tactics the kidnappers used six months ago. The cops want to get the picture out on the national wires as soon as possible."

"The cops are actually *helping* with this story?"

"They assume that somebody must have seen Lime the past half-year," Springer said. "It's hard to hide a man for that long and keep him alive. The mailman comes to your door every day, meter readers want to see inside your basement from time to time."

Eddie thought about how many strangers had knocked at his three-room cottage the past year. "Political candidates are always coming by harvesting votes," he said, "and kids selling waxy chocolate to pay for band or football, or some other part of school the taxpayers don't want to pay for."

"A bachelor like you must see the pizza guy about three times a week," Springer added.

"I guess it's logical for the detectives to get the photo in the news," Eddie said. He slid out of bed, stumbled over dirty clothes, patted the wall, found the light switch and slapped it on. "Except the story doesn't make *any sense*. The cops had Lime's dental records. The medical examiner matched them to the body. He was sure it was Lime."

"Now they're pretty sure it wasn't."

"What a fuckup!" Eddie howled. He pounded to the kitchen in his cotton boxers and clicked on his coffee pot, three hours before the auto-timer was set to brew a dozen cups of Blue Mountain Peaberry from Eastern Jamaica.

General VonKatz sprang onto the kitchen counter and rubbed his chin on the cabinet in which Eddie kept the cat food. The General's gray coat was shiny even in the dim light. He gurgled for his breakfast as Eddie flashed by, out of the kitchen.

Springer said, "The police have photo experts working right now to confirm that the pic is authentic, but their first impression is it's legit."

Back in the bedroom, Eddie dug through dirty clothes on the floor and salvaged a pair of crumpled tan chinos. *Wrinkle-free fabric? Says who?* He jammed one leg into the pants, held the cordless phone between his head and shoulder and hopped on one foot while he dressed his other leg. "How much do the kidnappers want for him? I heard that last time they asked for a quarter million, though I could never substantiate it."

"The police won't say. And they won't comment on any ransom note."

"So they want us to help them with the photo, but they won't give up any sizzle for the story?"

"Not unless you still have sources down there."

Eddie still had sources, especially in the detective's bureau. "I'll work my people at headquarters. What kind of story do you want from me?"

"I need copy to move with the picture. Maybe twenty inches of text. Just the new stuff and enough background so this story can play in Peoria. With Roger Lime coming back to life, I'm sniffing coast-to-coast interest."

Eddie buttoned the pants. He grabbed a white linen dress shirt from the bedpost. At least linen was *supposed* to be wrinkled. "Did you say this package was moving on the national wires?"

"Uh-huh. Your byline will be in half the papers in America."

Eddie pumped a fist in the air.

"Hang on a sec," Springer said. Eddie heard him begin a muffled conversation with someone in the Associated Press newsroom.

Back in the kitchen, the deep porcelain sink was cluttered with dirty coffee mugs. Eddie splashed one pint of Blue Mountain Peaberry into a giant two-pint Pyrex measuring cup. Steam fogged the inside of the clear glass.

The General sat up on the gold-flecked Formica and whined impatiently.

"Do you know what time it is?" Eddie said to the cat. "You don't usually eat for hours. I'll feed you when I get back from this job." Eddie hurried to the bedroom and stepped into black Doc Martens shoes with frayed and knotted laces.

He thought about angles for the story. If Lime was alive, that meant somebody else's bones were in his grave. Who was *that* person? How did they get into Lime's burned out car? And how did the medical examiner make such a blunder with the identification? It was great follow-up material, he decided, but the first-day coverage had to focus on the new evidence that Lime was alive. It was a resurrection story, in a sense. Eddie Bourque had never written anything like it. But how many writers had, in the past two thousand years? *A reading from The Gospel according to Eddie.* He quivered with delight.

Springer got back on the line. "Bourque? We just got confirmation—police experts have verified the photo of Roger Lime. No doctoring, it's the real thing. They're showing the picture at a media availability in thirty minutes."

"I'll be there."

"I'll need a story thirty minutes after you see it."

"How about sixty?"

"Thirty-five"

"C'mon, Springer! I type with two fingers."

He groaned. "You're one of *them*. Forty-five minutes, Bourque. We have afternoon papers to feed. Their morning deadlines are getting earlier all the time."

"We'll make it." Eddie clicked off the phone and flung it on the bed.

He stuffed his laptop computer into its case, grabbed his keys and started for the door.

My caffeine!

Eddie whirled and hurried to the kitchen. General VonKatz was reaching a paw into Eddie's coffee. The cat slapped three times into the cup, then shook the wet paw, splashing Blue Mountain Peaberry over the wall.

Eddie sighed. He fetched a peel-top can of sliced beef and giblets from the cupboard. "I don't want to know where that paw has been," he mumbled, and then downed the coffee in six hot gulps.

◇ ◇ ◇

Outside, Eddie's Pawtucketville neighborhood was still. His three-room cottage, with its sloping roof and rough asphalt shingles, was unique among the houses around it, yet blended perfectly. Pawtucketville was a mish-mash of building styles:

two-family duplexes, triple-deckers with clotheslines strung between the porch posts, square little single-family homes with steep roofs—all built on lots barely bigger than the buildings. The neighborhood was so compressed that if you didn't like your neighbor, you could spit out your window and into his. The streets were narrow, choked even further by parked cars that formed tunnels through which two drivers could not pass in opposite directions. Utility poles in front of every third house strung webs of black spaghetti over the sidewalks and across the roads. The closeness of the buildings blocked the view of everything beyond the next street, where the homes rode higher on a little hill like houseboats on the crest of a wave.

Eddie glanced to a house on the next street, just visible between two duplexes. At this hour, the peak on Phebe Avenue looked to be just a sharp gray triangle, but Eddie knew it to be light blue, lighter than the sky. He knew it as a former home of Jack Kerouac, the founder of America's Beat Generation writers. Kerouac had a brilliance that any city would be lucky to see one time in its history.

The Kerouac family had lived all over Pawtucketville in the 1930s and 1940s. They had moved to that house on the next street in 1932, when Jack Kerouac was ten years old. Eddie nodded to the peak, his way of being neighborly to genius.

The Mighty Chevette was parked on the street. Eddie's fifteen-year-old Chevy ran like a cheetah—it could reach sixty miles per hour in a short burst, then needed lots of rest. The Mighty Chevette was at one time yellow, and parts of it still were, but now the dominant color was rust. Eddie yanked the door open with a jarring creak and stuffed his laptop under the seat.

He steered the car through streets laid out in a senseless tangle, and then drove onto Riverside Street, past a concrete university building that reminded Eddie of a futuristic prison for comic book villians. He followed a divided boulevard along the north bank of the churning Merrimack, traveling northeast with the river around an elbow bend where the Merrimack widened in the heart of the city, and then southeast to a bridge of red iron lattice, one of six bridges that suture the two halves of the city divided by the river. Other than a few delivery trucks and a pair of fresh-water anglers with fishing rods in the back of their pickup, the Chevette was alone. Eddie pulled up outside the 1970s-style concrete police station and parked at a meter. He jogged across a plaza of scattered trees and flagpoles, and up the stairs between two illuminated blue globes that each read: POLICE.

Inside, a paunchy middle-aged officer directed foot traffic outside an interview room the size of an average bathroom, as reporters and photographers squeezed in two at a time to view the evidence that Roger Lime was still above ground. Eddie could see from the hallway that the police had displayed the photograph from the kidnappers in a plastic zipper bag, taped to the cinderblock wall. Two TV photo crews were inside, shooting film of the picture on the wall.

"You two, next," the cop said, pointing at Eddie and another scribe, whom Eddie had never seen before. "You get two minutes once these clowns are done." He had the bedside manner of a mugger.

The reporter paired with Eddie was short and slightly built, in his early fifties, with an inch-long gray goatee. Two silver hoops pieced his left earlobe. He dressed in black, including a felt beret. His press pass, dangling from a paperclip threaded through a buttonhole, identified him as Lewis Cuhna, editor of *The Second Voice*, Lowell's weekly alternative broadsheet.

Cuhna wore a digital camera on a cord around his neck, and a tanned messenger bag on a strap. His notebook was a full-sized lined pad. He scribbled on it with a dull green pencil that looked like eyeliner. Eddie couldn't help notice what he wrote:

"I'm next...two minutes."

Then Cuhna crossed out what he had written and below it printed in jittery letters: *"Not important...no need to note."*

He sighed and crossed *that* out. Then he read over the four-paragraph press release from the police again.

He seemed so nervous. Was this his first major cop story? At his age? Eddie said to him, "Timing sucks, huh?"

Cuhna shook, startled, and pointed the tip of his pencil toward Eddie, as if to defend himself with a tiny spear. He looked Eddie up and down, recovered, exhaled heavily, doodled a swirl on his legal pad, and then sputtered, "What do you mean…the timing?" He sounded suspicious.

"I meant this timing is no good for your weekly deadlines," Eddie explained. "You guys are on the newsstands on Thursdays, so you must put the paper to bed on Wednesday nights. It's too bad the cops didn't get this photo a couple days ago. You could have made this week's paper."

Cuhna's shoulders slumped. He shrugged listlessly. "I try to tell them we shouldn't chase stories like this if we're going to get beat by a week, but they don't care."

"Who's they?"

"Sometimes I don't even know," he said. He sketched a question mark on his legal pad, and then crossed it out. Cuhna had melodrama in his voice, as if he was reporting on the approaching end of the world. "That's the problem when you're owned by a media chain—new supervisors all the time. My latest boss is in Salt Lake City. Do you think she cares if I get scooped in Lowell?" His voice rose as he worked out some pent-up anger. "And the office they rent for me? They knocked down the wall between a former greasy spoon and a bankrupt laundromat. Stinks like pork sausage and lemon Tide."

Eddie hid a smile behind his hand. For Cuhna, this seemed like serious stuff, and Eddie didn't want to make an enemy out of him.

"My lease says that I have to let the people who live upstairs use the giant washing machines in my office anytime they want," Cuhna said.

"Crazy."

"Now the family upstairs has started making evening meals in my kitchen on deadline, and I can't find anything in the lease that says they can't!"

"Whew."

Cuhna groaned. "Not that it matters to my H.Q. Sometimes I feel all they want from me is to gray-up the white space around the ads." He looked Eddie up and down again. "You're still in the eighteen-to-thirty-five demographic, right?"

"Barely."

"You're supposed to be my target audience, but I bet you don't subscribe."

"Actually, no," Eddie admitted. He quickly added, "I pick it up on the newsstand sometimes, but I only have time in the morning for the *Washington Post*."

"The *Post*? It's darn near impossible to get that delivered up here. You a diehard Redskins fan?"

"No, I'm a fan of the help-wanted section. Lot of people advertise for freelancers there."

"Freelancer, eh? Must be nice to have no boss, but I'd wager the corporate newspaper boys screw you as hard as they do me."

"Amen."

Bitching about the business side of journalism is the universal sign of fellowship among scribes. Eddie introduced himself and they shook hands. Cuhna's hand was small, sweaty, and stained black with ink.

Eddie felt bad for him. Media chains are sometimes more concerned about stockholders than readers. They cut spending on their newsgathering to show more profit on Wall Street. Teeny editorial budgets at many weekly papers make for low pay and small staffs; sometimes the reporters have to sell ads or design pages in addition to writing.

The straight newsweeklies have it the toughest; they can't compete with the dailies on breaking news, and they don't pay enough to attract experienced writers who can produce the thoughtful pieces. They survive by thinking small, offering news the dailies don't bother with—school bus schedules and lunch menus, Little League and bridge club scores.

Entertainment weeklies do better with younger readers. They give more movie and concert news, and sometimes offer political analysis with attitude.

The Second Voice was a mix of the two styles, so it did nothing particularly well. The paper was forever clouded in rumors it was about to fold.

The TV guys had finished and they bustled out of the room. Their aluminum tripods bounced and clacked as they carried them.

The officer called, "Next!"

Eddie let Lewis Cuhna go ahead of him. Cuhna got three steps into the room, looked toward the picture on the wall and stopped. He wiped a hand over his face and then slowly stepped toward the photograph.

The picture was standard print size, about four-by-six, in color. The man in the picture was trim and healthy, probably in his early fifties. He sat at attention, holding the top half of a newspaper, at the edge of an oddly shaped coffee table, five-sided, made of blonde wood.

The picture looked to have been taken in the basement of a very old house. The lighting was uneven—the light source off to the side somewhere, out of view—and the man and the newspaper cast long black shadows on the fieldstone wall in the background. Eddie had never met Roger Lime, but he had seen other photographs of the bank executive, and he recognized Lime's thinning orange hair, his pointed chin, long Roman nose, and the wind-burned complexion of a competitive yacht racer.

In the photo, Lime wore a navy polo shirt with the collar turned up, tan drawstring pants, and no shoes or socks. The expression on Lime's face drew Eddie's attention. He looked tight-lipped and tense, like he was seething. Eddie interpreted the expression as rage and disbelief, as if this executive had found himself inconvenienced by ignorant little people. A thought-bubble above Lime's head could have shouted: "Don't they know who I am?"

The newspaper he held was ugly and gray, no photos above the fold.

Eddie gasped in surprise and lightly slapped his own cheek.

Lime was holding *The Second Voice*. Eddie looked to Cuhna, who was red-faced and engrossed in his note taking.

The paper's banner headline was readable in the picture:

```
SHAKESPEARE FESTIVAL
OFF WITHOUT A HITCH
```

Eddie puzzled over the headline. *Without a hitch?* Was that a Shakespeare pun? No, he decided; the line was merely a cliché. Either way, it wasn't exactly true: a drunk driver had rammed the stage during Act II of *As You Like It*, sending Rosalind and Celia sprawling through a mural of the Forest of Arden. Eddie had gone for a beer during Act II, unfortunately, and had missed it.

Cuhna was sniffling and writing furiously. "This is bad," he muttered to himself. "Bad. Bad. Bad. I don't need this."

Eddie's competitor on this story was also a source of information. "Lew," he said. "I gotta ask, what edition is that?"

Cuhna sighed. He opened his bag, rooted around inside and shoved a newspaper at Eddie.

It was the August 3 edition of *The Second Voice*, two weeks old. Eddie smoothed the wrinkles from the page. The Shakespeare story carried Cuhna's byline. Eddie skimmed the text. Cuhna had buried the news about the car crash in the twelfth paragraph, but at least he had it in there. Below the fold, the paper had run a black-and-white picture from a summer youth basketball league, a folk music concert review, and four government stories generated from the meetings of city boards and commissions.

Pretty dull paper.

But the kidnappers had verified Lime's state of being with the local weekly, and that was dynamite stuff for Eddie's story. Maybe it meant that Lime was still in the area, perhaps held captive nearby for six months. It meant that the kidnappers had been in Lowell within the past two weeks to buy the paper, unless they had an out-of-state subscription.

"So tell me, Lew," Eddie said, "do you mail many copies of *The Second Voice* to subscribers from…"

"We don't mail any at all," Cuhna snapped. He whipped his bag open, stuffed his legal pad inside and hunted around in the mess. "Ah!" he said, when he found what he wanted—a roll of antacid tablets. He peeled back the foil, pried up a tablet with his thumb.

"It's just that…"

"I know what it is," Cuhna said, interrupting again. He ate the tablet, chewed and talked: "It's part of the story—I know that. But I don't need this negative publicity. Things are tough enough. And I can't lay off any more staff because I don't have any more."

Eddie glanced to the paper Cuhna had given him. "Judging by all these different bylines, you have a big staff for a paper your size."

Cuhna grimaced. "That's all a ruse. Those people are all me."

Eddie looked to the paper again. "You're Amanda Collar?"

"Yes. And I'm Paul Alan, okay?"

"Is that ethical?"

"Too late for ethics, Bourque—I have no goddam staff. Nobody wants to read a paper written by one person—it looks cheap and not worth their time. I do *everything* on the news side—write the stories, edit my own goddam copy, write the headlines. I empty my own trash can, and once a week I gotta run the press, by myself!" Cuhna wiped his hand over his face again. He glared at the picture of Roger Lime. "And now I have to deal with *this*…" He trailed off.

Eddie might have pulled a useable quote from Cuhna if he had invested the time, but decided he couldn't afford it. He wanted to visit someone else who could help with the story, if she was on duty so early in the day.

He left Cuhna and hurried through the halls of mint-colored cinderblock, toward the detective's bureau. He couldn't understand why Cuhna was so upset. Publicity was exactly what *The Second Voice* needed, and rarely in publishing was there such a thing as bad publicity.

The detective's bureau was a long room with desks arranged like two lanes of gridlocked traffic. Half the ceiling lights were off at this early hour and gloom hung over the space. Several doors led to offices and small interview rooms in which investigators would speak to potential witnesses. Calendars, street maps, and crime prevention posters covered the walls of the bureau. Just inside the doorway was a glass-topped wooden counter display-ing stacks of official forms, for members of the public to fill out whenever something bad happened to them.

A middle-aged clerk in jeans and a fleece sweatshirt—the uniform of the third shift—was typing handwritten field reports into a computer at a desk beyond the counter. She smiled and lifted her head, to invite Eddie to say what he wanted. That's when Eddie smelled her perfume. Spicy, very nice. She shed ten years before Eddie's eyes.

"Is Detective Orr around?" Eddie said.

The woman looked away in thought for a moment, then pressed a button on her speaker phone and said, "Lucy, there's somebody here to see you."

A tinny voice came from the phone, "Who is it?" The woman lifted her head to Eddie again.

"It's Bourque," Eddie called out.

"Eddie?" squeaked the phone. "Before breakfast? Tammy, you can send him down here."

The woman directed Eddie with a long index finger. "Last door," she said.

Eddie passed three detectives on the night shift typing at keyboards, irradiated in blue by their computer screens. The last door swung in to the narrowest office Eddie had ever seen. Inside were two wheeled chairs on either side of a desk. The chair closest to Eddie was turned sideways and jammed against the left-hand wall, so the door had room to open. There seemed to be no way to get to the other chair, except by climbing over the desk. The office was windowless, painted burnt-orange, and lit by a buzzing fluorescent doughnut on the ceiling.

Detective Lucy Orr, in the chair across the desk, stood when Eddie came in.

She grinned and shook his hand. "I've been following your freelance work in some pretty fair magazines," she said.

"My work has been rejected by all the prestigious ones."

They both laughed and sat down.

Detective Orr was about forty. She had a squat build and powerful shoulders, like an Olympic swimmer from an old Soviet-bloc country. Her hands were rough, her nails unpainted and bitten down below the fingertips. Her hair was pulled back in a tight bun, which was impaled by what looked like two chopsticks.

Eddie checked his watch. He didn't have time to warm up the conversation before he asked for what he needed. "As a matter of fact, I'm working today," he said. "Hard news, deadline stuff."

She squinted at him. "Are you on the Roger Lime story?" She didn't wait for the answer. "Well, you can forget it, Ed, because I can't help you."

"Just a couple questions," Eddie pleaded.

"It's not my case."

"Then what are you doing here at quarter past five in the morning?"

She frowned at him. "Maybe I was bored."

Maybe she was. She lived alone. Maybe she was alone and bored. Eddie felt a sting of regret for asking the question. He pressed on. "Lucy, this story is huge. You must have heard something." Eddie felt no guilt over trading on his friendship with Detective Orr to get information. The woman could not be manipulated or corrupted, and she'd cheerfully throw Eddie out of her office if she thought he was out of line. "There has to be some inside noise on this case," he said, leaning against her desk. "Just one scrap of red meat to set my story apart from the rest."

Orr lowered her voice. "This investigation is all buttoned down."

Eddie leaned back. The lowered voice was the tip-off—she had decided to help him. The opening she had given him was big enough for one question. He had come here hoping to peek at the ransom note, but that seemed like too much to ask. He'd have to be satisfied with something smaller. Eddie closed the door. He whispered, "At least tell me why you're so sure the photo is legitimate. Any digital photo can be manipulated by a chimp with a laptop."

She looked him over and laughed. "You don't give up, Ed. It's what we have in common."

"It's why you like me so much."

She shook a finger at him. "Now cut that out," she scolded. "I'm not helping you because you tricked or flattered me into it—I want you to understand *that*."

Eddie held up his hands. "Perfectly understood." He readied his pad and pen.

"The photo," she said quietly, "came to Lime's wife as the single exposure on a roll of undeveloped film—we processed it and made the print ourselves. At first, we considered that the picture might simply be a close-up snapshot of a digitally altered photo, but the experts at our lab don't think so."

"How do they think the photo was made?"

"Somebody pushed a button on a camera and nothing more," Orr said. "They think it's an un-doctored picture of Roger Lime."

Eddie made some quick notes.

"So how are your aunts?" Orr asked.

"Fine."

"Good to hear it. Now if anybody asks, we can truthfully say we've been in here chatting about your family." She smiled.

"Check." Eddie got up to leave.

"Make sure you camouflage where you got the fact."

"Check."

"And Eddie," she said, in a sober voice, "stay out of trouble. You nearly got yourself killed the last time you crossed the line between investigative journalist and *investigator*."

Eddie's hand unconsciously reached to his head. He passed a thumb over the scar tissue on his ear where the bullet had cut a notch. He winked at her. "Thanks, Lucy. I've got no personal stake in this—Roger Lime's reappearance is just a damn fine tale."

Detective Orr gave the infuriating fake smile she used whenever she didn't believe him. Eddie pretended not to notice, and hurried out of there.

Outside, the air was cool, the sky clear. The stars were gone. A far-off orange glow, behind a four-story brick office building, hinted at dawn. A long, sputtering cloud to the east had been un-spooled across the sky and brushed with gold.

Eddie dashed to the Mighty Chevette. Time was his enemy. He grabbed his laptop and then ran a block toward the brightest light in downtown Lowell, the Perez Brothers restaurant, a silver-top diner that never closed, and always smelled of coffee and bacon. Eddie pushed through the glass door. There were two pairs of customers in the diner's two booths, shoveling mounds of cholesterol into their mouths.

A heavily muscled man overfilling a white t-shirt was wiping down the aluminum counter with a rag. He looked up and shouted: "Eddie! Where have you been the past few months?"

"Been trying to quit my breaking-news habit," Eddie said, "but I'm off the wagon today." He headed for the last stool. It was covered in a marbled green and black vinyl.

"Just made a fresh pot of Columbian," said the cook.

"Set me up and leave the pot, Bobby. I got thirty minutes to file this story."

Eddie powered up his laptop. Bobby Perez's coffee was scalding, as if drip brewed by atomic fission. A long splash of cold milk coaxed out the coffee's mellow flavor.

Eddie stared for a moment at the blue screen. Where to begin?

News writers can't afford writer's block; it's a luxury for people without deadlines. Waiting for the muse is for poets. Reporters on deadline *write*; the muse can pitch in or get the hell off the keyboard.

Eddie typed:

> Bank executive Roger K. Lime may have missed his
> own funeral.

A little flip. Too bad. No time to fool with it. Eddie kept
typing. He wrote about the photograph, how the cops had displayed it for the media. He wrote about the tip from Orr, and
that the police refused to comment on any ransom demands.

He guzzled coffee and added background about Lime's kidnapping, and how it appeared that Lime was murdered last spring
after his wife, Sandra, had gone to the police. He wrote from
memory about the funeral, the green coffin, and the security
that had kept the press away.

He wrote until time was up.

"Gotta send it, Bobby," Eddie yelled.

Bobby Perez pulled the telephone off the wall of the diner.
Eddie threw him one end of a modem cord, which Bobby
plugged into the jack. Eddie's computer dialed the Associated
Press, connected with a hiss of static to the correspondent's queue
and dumped the story there.

He verified electronically that the story had arrived, emailed
his cell phone number to Springer, in case a desk editor had
any questions about the story, and then rested his head on the
keyboard.

"More coffee?" Bobby asked.

"Amen, brother."

"And how about breakfast?"

"Something fast, Bobby. I gotta teach class and I don't have
a lesson planned."

◇ ◇ ◇

The letter arrived four days later.

It was in a long white, number-ten envelope, hand-addressed
in dark pencil to Edward Bourque at his cottage in Lowell's
Pawtucketville neighborhood. The postmark was from upstate
New York. The back of the envelope was stamped in red:

"THIS CORRESPONDENCE ORIGINATED
AT A FEDERAL CORRECTIONAL FACIL-
ITY. ITS CONTENTS HAVE NOT BEEN
CENSORED. THE SENDER IS NOT AUTHO-
RIZED TO ENTER INTO FINANCIAL CON-
TRACTS."

The return address was one word: Henry.

Eddie's brother, Henry Joseph "Henry" Bourque, twenty years Eddie's senior, had been jailed all of Eddie's life.

For murder.

The envelope sat unopened on Eddie's kitchen table. Eddie stared at it. General VonKatz lay belly-up over Eddie's lap, front legs swung to the left, hind legs to the right. Didn't look comfortable, but the cat seemed to like it. He purred, eyes slowly closing, on the edge of a nap. Eddie rubbed the General's head absentmindedly.

Eddie Bourque had never met his brother. Never heard his voice. The words on the envelope were the first Eddie had ever seen printed by his brother's hand.

He knew little about the atrocity Henry had committed, more than thirty years before. Something about an armored car, a robbery, a guard killed during the crime, a wife widowed, children left fatherless. Painful things, about which Eddie's parents had told him little before they stopped speaking to each other, and then divorced. Eddie barely spoke to either of them anymore. He had always meant to look up the news clips about the robbery and Henry's trial, but that had always seemed like a project for later.

Why are you writing me now?

What could Henry Bourque want? Money? *Money for what?* Was he dying? Did he have some terrible disease? Was he writing to apologize? To make amends? Or did he just want to meet the brother he had never known? Why did the letter look so fat? How much did he write?

For a second, Eddie considered throwing the letter away. He looked to the trashcan. Then to the sink, in which he could burn the letter safely.

Why don't I just read it?

He slapped his hand on the envelope and snatched it up. General VonKatz jumped away, startled. Eddie tore open the message.

A wad of newsprint was folded inside. He unfolded a page torn from an out-of-state newspaper. The folio at the top of the page identified the paper from the suburban Buffalo, N.Y., region.

It was Eddie's story on Roger Lime that had moved over the national wire and had been picked up and published by this paper in New York. The paper had also printed the photo of Roger Lime that Eddie had seen in the police station. The paper's local editors had headlined the story: "Dead and Alive? Massachusetts Bank Exec Again Held Hostage."

Eddie's byline had been circled in pencil.

The words "Held Hostage" in the headline had also been circled. An arrow drawn from the circle pointed to five words scrawled down the left margin:

I
know
who's
doing
this.

Chapter 2

The Mighty Chevette murmured along the Massachusetts Turnpike, west, toward New York. The morning sun glared in the rear-view mirror. Cars, buses and garbage trucks blew past Eddie in the next lane, but he wasn't in a rush. He had budgeted six hours for the three hundred mile drive, and six hours back.

The Chevette's radio played only white noise. To help pass the time, Eddie had only the scenery, and little of it. He passed woods and sound-dampening fence, and sheer cliffs of sandstone still striped with blasting holes five decades after the rock was dynamited to cut a path for the road. He drove past signs for western Massachusetts towns he had never heard of, passing the backsides of suburban malls, and identical rest stops, spaced a half-hour apart, selling the same brands of gas and fast food, as if these plazas had been replicated along the highway with the copy/paste function on a computer.

He thought about Hank's message.

I know who's doing this.

How could he know? He had been locked up thirty years. What could he know of Roger Lime? Was this a psychotic joke?

Eddie's back grew damp against the seat. He drove past a sign for an upcoming exit. He thought about turning back. What would he lose? A few hours on the highway. A few hundred miles on a car that had precious few miles left.

Could he live without knowing what Henry had meant in that message? No, no way. He smacked a palm on the steering wheel and settled the argument. "Keep going," he muttered out loud. He was going to see Henry Bourque, his brother, the killer.

◇ ◇ ◇

The prison was down a winding street, outside of a village that was nothing more than a service station, a post office, and the intersection of two roads that led to more interesting places.

For a federal pen, it wasn't imposing. It was a one-story modern building made from tan and yellow brick. Concrete walkways wound from the parking lot through rolling lawn and perennial gardens encircled by spilt-log railings. Take away the guard tower and the twenty-foot chain fence, and the place could have been a community college campus.

Eddie climbed out of the car and stretched. He was stiff from the ride, dry mouthed and dehydrated. Just behind his eyes, he felt the early rumblings of a caffeine withdrawal headache. His stomach filled with cold anticipation.

Inside, a guard in a gray uniform gave Eddie a clipboard and a one-page form. Eddie stopped at the question: "Relationship to Inmate_____ ." He felt his face flush with embarrassment.

He printed: "None."

The guard gave the paperwork a nanosecond's review, tossed the clipboard on a desk, and waved Eddie along.

Security for a prison visitor was no worse than at the airport. A second guard ran a metal-detecting baton over Eddie, and then x-rayed his shoes. He led Eddie through a sliding steel door, six inches thick, like the hatch to a vault filled with gold, and then into a security airlock. There was a similar door on the other end. The door he had entered thundered shut behind him, and the other door opened.

The visiting room was just like the movies. Ten chairs faced ten windows, which looked into a mirror image room on the other side of the glass. Telephones were mounted to the wall. The visiting area was beige and olive. The hard gray tile floor had been buffed to a wet shine and Eddie's shoes squeaked against it.

There were no other visitors here.

"Sit at number six," the guard said, pointing to a chair. "It has the best phone."

Eddie nodded and slowly stepped to the chair. The guard left, letting the door slam. Eddie jumped, startled.

He sat. The room was cold, like the frozen food aisle in the grocery. Eddie had worn a polo shirt and dress slacks. Gooseflesh roughened his bare arms. He rubbed the goosebumps away. The glass barrier between Eddie and the other side of the room, where the prisoners sat, was spotless. Eddie reached to it. Twice tapped a finger on. Felt the glass there. Heard the thump, thump.

What will the face of a killer look like?

A door opened on the other side of the glass. A man with a scarred face shuffled in. He was tall and broad, mountainous in the upper body, sharply tapered to a narrow waist, and then wide again in the thighs. He wore a tan jumpsuit, silver hand-cuffs and high-top canvas sneakers. His ankles were shackled. His head had been shaved recently, maybe two days ago; there was five o'clock shadow on his scalp.

Eddie had prepared for an older version of himself, but this man was not his doppelganger. He had the same pointed French-Canadian features, and similar deep-set dark eyes. But Henry Bourque's face was longer, his complexion lighter, his nose wider and slightly bent. His skin was deeply lined around the eyes. He had a familiar look, but not like a twin. More like an older uncle.

Eddie's eyes went to the scar on Henry's face, an arresting, hook-shaped gash. It started at the left corner of his mouth and ran up his check, just outside his eye, then slashed up and across his forehead in a curve, ending above his right ear. The scar was muddy red, and no hair dared grow near it. How could a man survive such a wound? Goosebumps raised again on Eddie's arms.

Henry stood and looked Eddie over, too. His lips bent into a tiny smile. The crow's feet around his eyes exposed themselves as laugh lines.

Henry Bourque eased into the chair, and then nodded to the phone. They both picked up. Eddie listened. His brother's voice was low and whispery, encrusted with nicotine: "Have you been to the mountains?"

Not what Eddie had expected to hear. "Huh? I don't…"

Henry's voice sank lower. "The mountains, man. Haven't you been this summer?"

"Once, to the Whites in New Hampshire."

Henry smiled. "Ooooo, the White Mountains," he moaned. "Tell me about them."

"I thought you wanted to tell me—"

Henry's eyes widened and Eddie stopped in mid-thought. Henry looked like a madman. Red veins squiggled through the whites of his eyes. He said, "The mountains, little brother, tell me about them." His head weaved, as if he was fighting a stiff wind on the other side of the glass.

Little brother?

"I dunno," Eddie said. "They were great. I climbed Mount Adams, solo."

Henry rolled his eyes and rapped the telephone receiver twice on the glass. "No, man," he said, exasperated. His voice got raspier. "You're the fucking writer. Tell me like a writer."

Eddie stared into his brother's eyes. Maybe they were not the eyes of a madman, maybe they were just desperate.

Eddie nodded, looked away for a moment to gather his thoughts, and then spoke slowly, "At twilight I threw down my sleeping bag under an old beech, gray, the color of an overcast sky, climbed into the sack and burrowed myself in the goose down. Dry leaves under me crackled whenever I moved. The day had been humid and I could smell the ground, kind of peppery."

Henry Bourque closed his eyes and listened.

"I had a flask with me," Eddie said. He laughed.

Henry smiled, said nothing, kept his eyes closed.

"I took two shots of bourbon. And God*dam*! That Kentucky corn whiskey burned on the way down, like drinking pure steam. But it spread its warmth over me. As I closed my eyes I could hear a few raindrops flicking off the leaves of that beech tree. I waited for a drop to strike my face, but one never did.

"In the morning I hiked past sugar maple with deep ridges in their bark. I saw a doe watching me through a hobblebush, but I pretended not to notice it. The trail cut higher, over boulders, slick with dew. A spruce grouse, fat and brave as hell, fluttered down right in front of me. It was slate gray with a red patch over one eye, like a pirate. It tilted its head at me. I tilted my head back at him. He lost interest and waddled away, into the balsam trees."

Henry leaned forward and rested his head against the glass. His eyes squeezed tightly closed.

Eddie paused, recalling more details from his hike.

"At tree line, about four thousand feet, I climbed into a cloud. I couldn't hear anything except my own boots on the rock, and my own breath, panting. I couldn't see much beyond the next boulder, just white fog. I scaled a steep talas field, following the painted blue blazes on the rock, scrambling on hands and feet like a bug. I could smell my sweat. Green lichen speckled the granite."

"How'd the rocks feel?" Henry asked, eyes still closed.

"They left my bare hands rough."

Henry rubbed his hand together.

Eddie continued, "There's a sign on the peak, a wooden marker nailed to a shaved log, and wedged in a cairn. I couldn't see the sign through the fog until I could nearly touch it. The mountain was fifty-eight hundred feet high, it said. Wind was rushing over the summit. It was cold on my face. I stood on the highest rock, the peak of the peak. And then the fog grew brighter, and suddenly the wind pushed it all away, like somebody had thrown a switch. I could see for miles, and from my perch I looked *down* on a hawk circling the valley."

Eddie was finished.

Neither brother said anything for a minute. Then Henry pushed away from the glass and looked at Eddie. "I can see it," he whispered. "I'm there, on the mountain." His head weaved again, like a cobra charmed by a flute. He gave a contented little smile and said in a jolly voice, "That's how I travel, do it all the time. My wife gets sick of describing things for me."

"You're *married?*"

Henry held up his left hand. "Not allowed a ring in here."

"But...how?"

"Lonely people outside these walls are looking for conversation, for someone to listen to them, for a husband who will be wholly devoted to them, whatever his circumstances." He smiled. "They can be sure we're not cruising the bars when they're out of town."

"Can't be much of a marriage."

Henry knocked a knuckle on the glass. "World's best birth control," he said. "It was a quick courtship. Got married last May, right in this room, on the thirteenth." He looked sly and smiled. "We're having a party next month. Are you free that day, little brother?"

"Do you have to call me that?" Eddie snapped. Why did Henry address him like they were so familiar? *Why does that piss me off so much?* "Until I got your letter, I wasn't even sure that you knew I was born. You're a stranger, nothing more."

Henry's eyes widened again. He turned the scarred side of his face toward Eddie and broke into a tight-jawed grin that raised another wave of gooseflesh on Eddie's skin.

Henry's hard whisper came from a reddened face: "You *know* me better than you think." The muscles in his neck tensed. He looked like he was about to crash through the glass. Eddie leaned away from him. Eddie's hand unconsciously tightened around the phone, as if claiming it as a weapon—closest thing he had to a club—to defend himself.

This is foolish. He can't reach me through the glass. He can never get out of this prison.

Eddie willed himself calm. He paused for a deep breath, then said in a breezy voice: "I don't know much about you. I know you were an athlete before you came here, a good one."

Henry's face instantly relaxed. There was no trace of rage in him. He asked, "Do you know how the universe was made?"

Another sudden change of direction? "Sorry, I wasn't around for Genesis."

"Genesis? So you say God made the world?"

Eddie shrugged.

Henry leaned back, looked around the room. He seemed indifferent.

The sonofabitch is mirroring my emotions!

Was that a game for Henry? To read what another person was feeling, amplify the emotion and turn it back on them? Was that what thirty years in prison did to a person? Eddie wanted to talk about the note Henry had sent him, about who kidnapped Roger Lime. Henry was acting crazed, but Eddie didn't believe it. There was something in Henry's face that revealed a calculating intelligence behind the non-sequiturs and eccentricity. Henry Bourque would come to the point when he was ready.

Eddie played along. "Where do *you* say the universe came from?"

"There are scientists who have developed marvelous theories of the origins of the natural world that do not have to include a god," said Henry.

"The Big Bang theory?"

"A child's guess in simpler times, in comparison to the thinking of today—there's too much luck involved. Did you realize that the ratio of matter and energy in the universe is perfect? Had that ratio settled more than a quadrillionth of a percentage point either way, the universe would be too compressed, or too spread out, for life to begin?"

"I guess we're lucky."

"Maybe not. There are other theories."

"What's your favorite?"

"Imagine a mother universe polluted with points of infinite mass and no dimensions," Henry said. "The unthinkable gravity of these points bend the space around them, until they snap off into another dimension, and create a new daughter universe with unique physical laws. Imagine that happening trillions of times, until, as chance would eventually determine, one of those daughters develops the right ratio of matter and energy for life. It's called the multi-universe theory. I didn't think it up, though I wish I had. Isn't it lovely? A theory of creation that doesn't rely on luck or on the Almighty?"

Eddie's eyes traced the scar on Henry's face. The edges were jagged, as if the wound had been carved with a dull knife. "That's a weird concept of the universe," Eddie said. "It's weirder than God."

Henry smiled. "Occam's razor."

"The simplest answer is usually the best."

Henry's finger rubbed the ridge of scar beside his eye. "Wasn't long ago that skeptics used Occam's razor to *disprove* the existence of God."

"As you said, the universe was simpler back then." *Where is he going with this?*

Henry shifted his weight in the chair, rolling his massive shoulders. He said, "When you play chess, do you prefer the white pieces or the black?"

Here we go again.

"The black."

Henry snapped his fingers. "Yes, I knew that." He looked Eddie hard in the eye and asked sharply, "And which do I prefer?"

Eddie thought about how Henry had controlled their encounter, from the mysterious letter to his disjointed questions. He answered, "The white."

Henry laughed and banged a palm on his knee in delight. "That's right! Can you tell me why?"

"Because white always moves first. You like to have the first move of the game."

Henry's eyes closed for a second, as a smile spread over him. With playful sarcasm, he said, "I feel like you're the brother I never had."

Eddie imagined himself looking through Henry's eyes, seeing another human life end by his own hand. What weapon had been in that hand? A gun? A knife? A club? Eddie didn't know. He imagined a blurry gray object of death at the end of Henry's arm. He saw an armored car driver on the ground begging for life. Saw the begging stop and the blood begin. Saw meat and bones on the ground, and then the widow in black. The thoughts enraged him.

Eddie blurted, "You're so smart, how could you have been so fucking stupid?"

Henry raised an eyebrow. "Easy, easy," he cautioned. "If you went back in time to save me, you'd destroy yourself."

"What the hell are you talking about?"

Henry sighed. The telephone crackled. He switched it to the other ear. "Your kidnapped bank president is pictured sitting on a five-sided table made entirely of poplar, assembled in traditional method with white glue and pegs—not a nail in it anywhere."

"How do you know that?"

Henry winked. "Because I made it."

"You? But you're—it's been thirty years."

"I built it to last, little brother."

Eddie felt his reporter's skepticism bubbling up. He turned on his bullshit meter. "Can you prove it?"

Henry gave a pained look. "I got angry during construction—the wood wouldn't behave," he said. "The left front leg would show the results of that anger. Look closely, see for yourself."

"Fine, let's say you made the table. You didn't kidnap Roger Lime. Who did?"

An intercom burped to life and a voice of tin screeched, "Aaaangem-up!"

"What's that?"

"We're out of time," Henry said. "We gotta hang up."

Eddie jumped from the chair and slapped a hand on the glass. "Who's doing this?" he cried. "You said you knew who's doing this to Roger Lime!"

A guard appeared at Henry's shoulder, tapped him twice.

"I gave away the table I made," Henry said, "to my partner's old lady."

He hung up.

◇ ◇ ◇

Eddie's foot mashed the accelerator to the floor. The Mighty Chevette whined and shuddered, like it might to fly apart on the trip back to Lowell. Eddie steadied the wheel with one hand and one knee, and dialed the Associated Press news desk on his cell phone.

He asked for Springer, waited for the transfer.

"Need a favor," Eddie yelled to Springer over the wind roaring through the windows.

"Sure, Ed. Where the hell are you?"

"My car."

"Sounds like you're *under* your car."

"Just bear with me. Can you get the photo of Roger Lime that the cops released the other day?"

"Yeah. It's been scanned into our archive. Gimme a sec to call it up on the computer."

Eddie yanked from his pocket the newspaper clip Henry had sent him. The newsprint photo reproduction was muddy. He couldn't see anything on the table legs.

"I got it," Springer said.

"Zero in on the lower left quarter of the photo," Eddie said. "The table legs. Can you enlarge it?"

"Lower left…yep…okay. Now what?"

"The table legs, man. Look closely. Notice anything, uh, unusual?"

"Seems pretty ordinary…well, there's a half-dozen marks on one of them—curved lines, crescent shaped."

Eddie felt rising tension, like his stomach was being pumped full of helium. He knew the answer, but he had to ask: "What would you say made those marks?"

"I dunno, Ed," Springer said. "Looks like somebody got pissed and whacked the thing with a hatchet."

Chapter 3

Eddie burst into the classroom, ducked under the mysterious gurgling pipe, glanced at the clock, slapped his briefcase on the gray steel teacher's desk and grabbed an eraser.

"Sorry I'm late," he announced as he obliterated the chemical formulas left on the blackboard from an earlier class. Eddie had been obsessing over his visit with Henry, and had struggled to plan his lesson before class. He despised being late and was embarrassed to face his students. He felt like he had cheated them out of ten minutes of learning, though Eddie suspected that his ten remaining class members would rather chat with each other than listen to Eddie Bourque.

In large, squeaky chalk letters, Eddie printed the evening's lesson: "ON AND OFF THE RECORD."

He dropped the chalk in his shirt pocket and turned around. Five blank faces looked back at him.

"Oh," Eddie said, suddenly realizing he was missing half his flock. "Where's the rest of the class?"

The mysterious pipe made its disgusting sucking sound, like a plunger in a bucket of worms.

"Eeeew!" said the class, as they always did.

Eddie frowned at the pipe and waited for the noise to end. It usually stopped after half a minute.

Another great moment in education.

When he had applied to teach this community college course, Eddie had come to the school with lofty images of the academic world. But "Introduction to Journalism" had been assigned a windowless, raspberry-red basement classroom, sectioned off from the boiler room by a cinderblock wall. The mysterious disgusting pipe, about five inches thick and made of unpainted steel, ran down the middle of the room at about six feet off the floor—just low enough for Eddie to scuff the top of his head on it. The pipe had nearly scalped him a dozen times, until Eddie had become programmed to automatically duck when passing from one side of the room to the other.

Nearly halfway through the semester, Eddie was wondering if agreeing to teach the course had been a mistake. He had applied for the job because he needed the money. At his interview, he had to overcome a lack of classroom experience, and to convince the college administration that money had nothing to do with it; he was just desperate to share his knowledge of journalism and practice the world's noblest profession—teaching. In convincing the administration, Eddie had convinced himself.

Lately, though, he was dripping with doubt. He had expected his students to be raw in the beginning, but they didn't seem to be getting any better. Actually, it was almost as if they were losing knowledge. And whose fault was that? An even worse sign: the class didn't seem to care that they weren't learning anything from Eddie Bourque.

They're killing their grandmothers to avoid my lectures.

"I heard that the two Irish lasses who sat in the back dropped this class," said Gerard from the front row. He was around fifty, round-shouldered and potbellied, with dark eyes that looked frightened while he was listening but demonic when he was speaking; it was something about the way his eyebrows rose and fell. With a phony British accent he used from time to time, Gerard suggested, "Maybe you were too tough on 'em, Mr. Bourque, and their fair stock couldn't handle it."

That got a laugh from the class.

"Are you calling them sweet girls *stocky?*" demanded Margaret, a chain smoker with a cheese-grater voice who had already lost two grandmothers that semester. "Because we girls don't like being called stocky."

Gerard shot her a frightened glance, then turned away and mumbled devilishly, "How about *livestock.*"

Margaret squealed, "*What'd* he say?"

Eddie spread his hands and smoothed the tension out of the air. "Okay, now…"

The pipe made its other noise, the slurping, like somebody vacuuming live squid in a flooded basement.

"Eeeew!"

Eddie pinched the bridge of his nose a moment, and then slowly opened his briefcase. Two more students had dropped the class? That made eight—eight students who had signed up for Introduction to Journalism had decided to quit before the semester was over. Eddie couldn't wait until after mid-term exams—no more refunds for anybody who dropped the class…assuming anybody was left by then.

Don't let them smell fear.

He fished the chalk from his pocket. The instant the slurping stopped, Gerard asked, "When are the mid-term papers due?"

"Good point," Eddie said. He reminded the class, "Your mid-term assignment is due by email next week. Those of you who still have living grandmothers might want to turn it in early, just in case something happens." He lifted an eyebrow and glanced around the room. Half the class refused to look him in the eye. "It's a straightforward assignment. Just attend any meeting of any public board or commission in your home towns and write up a news story based on what takes place."

He pointed to the blackboard and plowed into his lesson: "Which leads me to the point I'd like to discuss tonight. Public officials often try to go off the record. Can anybody tell me what it means to be *on* the record?"

"Like my band, man," said Ryan Daniels, a twenty-something kid in all black. His right nostril was pierced with a nut and bolt from a hardware store, his head shaved to the scalp except for patterns above each ear that resembled a fist extending a middle finger. "We're cutting two tunes this weekend for an e-p recording next December." He gave the devil horn sign with his fingers. "It's a heavy metal Christmas, baby."

"That ain't what he means," scoffed Margaret. "Your garage band ain't breaking any sales records. I doubt you'll sell ten of those things."

Eddie ducked under the pipe. "That's not what I mean," he said.

"See?" said Margaret.

"Elvis has the record," another student said. "Or The Beatles."

"No," argued Ryan, "Pink Floyd."

"What does *the term* on the record mean," Eddie said, voice squeaking.

"I believe the sales record for a musical recording," said Gerard, rubbing his chin, "is held by that Brazilian gentleman who plays the pan flute."

Another student offered, "He means public records."

"Public? Like free downloads?" Ryan asked, incredulous. "No way, man. If it's good enough to listen to, it's good enough to buy."

"What the hell is the pan flute?" asked Margaret.

"People!" Eddie pleaded.

"I've never heard of anybody downloading music from that pan flute dude," said Ryan.

Gerard shook a finger at Ryan, saying in his British accent: "That's probably why the gentleman has the sales record— nobody listens for free."

Ryan nodded slowly, impressed. "Yeaaaaah!"

Margaret repeated, "What the hell is the pan flute?"

The pipe made its sucking sound.

Without meaning to, Eddie pulverized the chalk in his fist.

Chapter 4

General VonKatz walked on the piano keys, from the low notes to the high, sounding, in Eddie's imagination, like a tone-deaf elephant turning into a pixie.

Eddie opened his eyes. He had fallen asleep in the recliner again. He stretched, felt the knots in his back. The clock said seven-thirty in the morning; it felt much earlier. After class, Eddie had swallowed two jiggers of scotch and an Advil to help him sleep, but he had spent a restless night replaying the conversation with Henry in his mind.

I gave away the table I made to my partner's old lady.

Was Henry saying that this woman kidnapped Roger Lime? And which partner?

For a moment, Eddie considered telling Detective Orr about the table, and what Henry had claimed. But Eddie resisted. The story was so outlandish, the proof flimsy. Henry might have seen a better copy of the Roger Lime photograph in some other paper, and had concocted that detail about damaging the table leg.

He doubted that finding this woman—his partner's old lady—would even lead to Roger Lime. Even if Henry were telling the truth, what's to say this woman even had the table? She could have left it at the curb for junk-pickers ten years ago.

Eddie also was uncomfortable with the notion that his brother, the killer, might have given Eddie something of value.

He hoped that Henry was wrong—that it wasn't his table, and that he had nothing to do with Roger Lime.

The General walked back down the keys. He stopped, looked at Eddie and whined. Eddie laughed. "All right," he said, heaving his body out of the chair with a groan. "Let's eat."

The refrigerator held wheat bread, cottage cheese, eleven Rolling Rock beers, still left from the case he had bought a month before, and two dozen foods from the goop group: spreads and dressings, mustards and marinades.

"Nuts," Eddie said. "Not much here."

Hmmmm. *Nuts?* He checked the butter dish for a bag of slivered almonds he vaguely recalled. Nope. Long gone.

The General whined more intensely at Eddie's feet. There was better fortune in the cupboard—a can of white tuna. Eddie spooned half the fish into a bowl for the General. He ate the rest himself from the can, and then had two pieces of bread; it was like eating a sandwich one component at a time.

With more than twenty coffees to choose from in his freezer, he picked a Guatemalan he liked for the chocolate undertones.

Eddie went to fetch his *Washington Post* while the coffee dripped.

What the hell?

The paper was spread across the tiny patch of lawn between Eddie's rented house and the street. He recovered the news, metro and sports sections, and then gave up on finding the rest and went back inside.

Bad night's sleep, bad breakfast, bad newspaper. If my coffee is bad I'm going back to bed.

The coffee was never bad. Crisp. Nice acidity. Hard to believe something so good was legal. The caffeine jacked him to a higher level of awareness, like smelling salts for the soul. He read what little he had found of his paper, and barely missed the rest of it. The national news page had a short update on Roger Lime—essentially that the police had no new leads.

The General had finished his food. He swiped against Eddie's legs, whining for something else.

"How about some TV?" Eddie said.

He fed a videotape into the VCR and turned it on. The house filled with chirping and fluttering, as the television showed close-ups of wild finches jockeying for space on a crowded birdfeeder. The General hopped on the coffee table to watch. The cat's eyes darted over the TV screen.

"When you're sick of the birds, I'll put in the garden moles," Eddie promised. He owned a half-dozen videos from the "Small Prey Series for Indoor Cats." The tapes cost twenty bucks each, for sixty minutes of backyard animals scurrying around; it was an absolute goddam rip-off, and it *killed* Eddie that he hadn't thought of it first.

Springer called during Eddie's third cup of joe. "You working today?"

Eddie had planned to do research, to see if he could identify Henry's old partner. But it was hard to turn down a paying job, especially on a story with national interest. "I wouldn't mind another piece of the Lime story," he admitted.

"Work the coroner angle," Springer said. "The police have determined that the quack who mismatched Lime's dental records to the bones from the car fire is named Crane."

"Yeah, Alvin Crane," Eddie said. "Been in the medical examiner's office a long time. I've covered a zillion trials where he was the expert witness."

"Well, he hasn't been around the office since the photograph of Lime turned up. Called in sick, and hasn't been back."

"Is he sick? Or did he just misidentify his office?"

"Ouch," Springer said. "Head over to his place and see if the doctor is in."

◇ ◇ ◇

Dr. Crane lived in a development of suburban mansions, each home identical except for details like brick face or stone face, pebble driveway or concrete. The developers had clear-cut a hardwood forest to build the homes, preserving little stands of mature white birch here and there for decoration. Crane's place was the only finished home on a cul-de-sac. Three dirt driveways stemming from the circle of asphalt led to fields of turned earth and weeds, for which the developer had not yet found buyers.

The house was two-toned, brick and yellow stucco. It was huge and attractive and unspecial at the same time. The black driveway smelled liked it had recently been treated with sealer. A silver Buick sedan was parked there. Eddie could see an unpainted, two-story barn out back, still under construction, stacks of clapboard on sawhorses outside it.

There were no cars going by, no children chasing each other around the neighborhood. Just the sound of the breeze sweeping across the lawn. People like Dr. Crane paid a lot of money for that kind of silence. Eddie found it creepy.

Eddie peeked in the mailbox—empty, so it seemed that Dr. Crane hadn't left town.

The doorbell was an orange dot lit from behind by a bright little bulb. Eddie rang it, heard the sing-songy chime from within the house.

Nothing.

He rang it again, waited, and then rapped the horseshoe knocker. He waited some more. He couldn't hear anyone moving inside.

From behind the house, a door slammed.

Eddie strolled across the front grass. "Dr. Crane?" he called out. "Dr. Crane?" Eddie felt like a trespasser on the lawn. He called out again, to announce himself, "Hello? Is Dr. Crane around?"

He walked down a lush side lawn that sloped gently away from the house. The lawn abruptly turned to dirt at the property line. Red brick paths wandered through the backyard, around rock gardens garnished with leafy ferns and smooth silver driftwood. Somebody had begun applying clapboard to the unfinished barn. A circular saw lay on the ground, still plugged into an extension cord that snaked through a window into the house. There was a hammer on a sawhorse beside a coffee can full of nails.

"Dr. Crane?"

A back deck on the house led to a sliding glass door, which was open. The breeze tugged at the curtains. That door could not have made the noise Eddie had heard.

He looked over the barn. The twin roll-up garage doors were down. The side door was closed. There were no windows to peek through.

Eddie went to the side door and tested the knob—unlocked.

He pushed the door open. It led into a tiny vestibule, and then, through another door, into the barn. The inside was nearly black.

Does he think he's developing film in here?

Eddie could make out a workbench, scattered tools, a lawnmower.

"Dr. Crane?"

He's got to be in here…he's not sick, he's working on his house.

Eddie stepped into the barn. "Dr. Crane, it's Eddie Bourque," he said, as he walked, arms feeling for objects in the darkness. "I'm a reporter, and I'm doing a story for the Associated Press today. I'd really like a word with you."

Eddie recognized the "A"-shape of a six-foot stepladder. He walked around it, toward the garage doors, where the light switch probably would be.

On the other side of the ladder, he walked into something with a thwack on the bone above his right eye. "Ow," he muttered, rubbing the tender spot.

Eddie frowned. Did he smell urine? He grabbed at the dark shape in the air.

Thin, narrow, smooth, leathery.

A shoe.

A leather wingtip and it was full.

Oh, Jesus.

Eddie dashed across the garage, stumbling over boxes and a bicycle. He felt along the wall, found a conduit tube, followed it up, found the switch, turned on the light.

"Oh Jesus!"

The body hung by the neck from a green and pink braided nylon rope, the kind of happy rope you'd use to hang a little girl's tire swing.

Eddie had disturbed the body by touching it. It slowly rolled a quarter turn to the left, paused there, then rolled the other way.

He hadn't seen Dr. Crane in more than a year, but there was no doubt this was he—silver haired, slight paunch, close to seventy years old. He was wearing denim overalls under an unbuttoned white painter's coat. His face was swollen and purple, hard to look at. Eddie got another whiff of urine. What he had read was true; people piss themselves when they hang.

Eddie wanted to run. But he couldn't. For there was something in the chest pocket of Crane's white smock that grabbed Eddie's attention and wouldn't let him leave. A sheet of paper, folded once lengthwise. Something had been typed on it.

A note. A suicide note.

Part of him—the better part—knew that he should dash right out of there, get his telephone from the car, call the police and wait for them on the street. But then the police would seal the barn. They would take the note. And they wouldn't show it to Eddie Bourque.

It would only take a moment to read it. What would it hurt?

The rope had been looped over a crossbeam near the top of the twenty-foot peaked roof; Crane hung high off the floor. Eddie steeled himself with a deep breath. He put his clammy hands on the ladder and stepped up, up, up, to the third rung. He looked the body in the small of its back. He still couldn't reach the note.

The feeling of trespassing was back, a thousand times stronger, like Eddie had crossed some line between trespasser and grave robber. He reached for the paper. A drop of sweat ran down his underarm with a cold tickle. Still couldn't reach the note; the body was facing away from him.

With just a finger and thumb, he pinched a tiny fold of the dead man's smock, and tugged. The body slowly rotated. Eddie stepped one rung higher. The body turned toward him. Another whiff of piss. Eddie kept his eyes off that purple face and snatched the paper from the pocket. A dark urine stain had spread across the front of Dr. Crane's overalls.

Eddie read the typewritten lines:

> *The district attorneys are fighting the good fight!!!!*
> *When they needed me, I was THERE.*
> *For what THEY needed. Told them what they*
> *WANTED to hear.*
> *I never meant to hurt anyone.*
> *I just wanted to HELP put the monsters AWAY!!!*
> *It grew out of my control, like a thing of its own*
> *mind!!!!*
> *Forgive me, these FORTY years.*

The letter was unsigned.

Eddie's hand trembled as he slid the note back where he had found it.

Dr. Crane had been falsifying his reports. Cutting corners to help prosecutors close their cases.

Eddie had never heard his police sources chatter about Crane— nobody had ever suggested that Crane's work might have been suspect, except defense lawyers. But they got paid to discredit the state's witnesses; they'd do it to their own mothers.

Forty years? How many bodies were in the wrong graves? No, to hell with the graves—Crane had been an expert witness at *thousands* of criminal trials over the past four decades. How many innocent people had he helped put away?

The body rocked back. Eddie smelled the stench. He grimaced at the stain on Crane's overalls.

Wait… his pants… still wet?

Eddie grabbed Crane's hand—cooler than the living, but still warm.

Holy Jesus, this just happened!

Eddie threw himself down the ladder and sprinted out, slamming the door behind him.

He ran toward his car.

The slam echoed in Eddie's mind.

Who made the door slam when I first got here?

Not Crane—it had been barely two minutes between the noise and the moment Eddie opened the door to the barn. Even if the rope had been ready, would Crane have had time to hang himself dead? Eddie couldn't say.

Was somebody else here?

Chapter 5

The police arrived in their Ford Crown Victorias, white with blue and gold stripes. A belligerent lieutenant named Brill wanted to hear Eddie's story again.

"But I told you guys everything," Eddie protested. He looked down Dr. Crane's driveway, past the barrier of police tape, and saw a television news van pull into the cul-de-sac. Word of Crane's death had leaked.

This is crazy. I'm the only reporter with the full story, and I can't get away to write.

The lieutenant was short and built like a power-lifter. His shirt collar dug deep into his thick neck. "So why were you in the man's garage?" he asked.

Eddie started to sigh, but stopped himself. No sense aggravating this lieutenant and dragging out this interview longer than it had to be. "I heard a door, all right?" Eddie said, "I went looking for Crane. Found him hanging in the garage. Ran to my car. Called you guys."

"Uh-huh. So you heard a noise and then broke into the garage," the detective paraphrased, scratching notes on a pad.

"Don't write it *that* way," Eddie said. "The door was unlocked. I just went in."

Lieutenant Brill looked up from his notes. His eyes were the lightest blue Eddie had ever seen. "Doesn't really matter, under the law."

Eddie sighed. Couldn't help himself. "Somebody else was here," he said. "That's the person you ought to be interrogating."

"Crane lived alone," the detective said. "There's no evidence anybody else was here, except you and him."

"I'm telling you, I heard somebody."

The lieutenant went back to writing. "Mm-hm," he said.

Eddie felt the sudden stab of caffeine withdrawal. It quickly grew worse, as if his skull was a diving bell that had gone too deep.

Another voice said, "When I heard that a reporter found the body, I hoped it wouldn't be you—"

Eddie turned. It was Detective Orr. She looked ticked.

"—but I *knew* it would be, Eddie."

"I explained everything three times already," Eddie said. "I need to go."

Orr ignored him. She nodded to the lieutenant, and the two of them walked out of earshot. She murmured to Brill, he mumbled to her, and then Orr came back alone to speak to Eddie.

"Crane left a note," she said.

Eddie shifted his weight from one foot to the other. He didn't say anything.

"Did you read it?"

A second TV news van pulled into the cul-de-sac. The reporter from the first van was taping her report with police cars and the house in the background. Eddie's skull felt like it was about to buckle.

Eddie asked, "Is that what Brill was busting my balls about?" He shrugged, irked that TV news was beating him on a story he had cold. TV should *never* beat print. He felt like he was letting down the brotherhood of ink scribes. "What do you think, Lucy? Of course I read the goddam note."

Orr gave a disapproving little grunt. "I wish you could have told me differently." She pointed in the lieutenant's general direction. "Brill wants to arrest you for interfering with a police investigation."

"Oh, come on," Eddie complained, "That's a bullshit charge." His head was in a vise. His temperature was rising. Why couldn't *somebody* make a caffiene patch or some gum for coffee drinkers who needed help between cups? He said, "The investigation didn't even start until I called you."

"Of course," she said. "But Brill can keep you in lockup, force you to pay for a lawyer—they ain't cheap—make your life hell for twenty-four hours or so, till the charges are dropped."

She was right. Eddie calmed himself with a deep breath. He said, "Look, I'm not proud of what I did. But this is a big story—Crane admitted that he *made it up* as he went along for forty years. All those cases? When the district attorney hears this, he'll shit his liver."

"He already has," Orr said quietly.

They stepped out of the driveway, to let the black hearse drive by.

Orr said, "In light of the Roger Lime fiasco, I've been assigned to investigate Crane's death, and to determine what evidence there is that he falsified his reports."

Eddie whistled. "A big job."

"The lieutenant said that you heard something, before you found the body?"

"He said that? I didn't think he cared about what I heard."

"He doesn't, but I do." She squinted at him.

Eddie told her about the sound that he heard. She took notes. Then they retraced Eddie's path around the house, to the back deck, and then into the barn. Detective Orr timed it at two minutes, fifteen seconds, give or take.

"Nobody chokes that fast," she said, more to herself than to Eddie.

"I thought hanging was instantaneous—broken neck."

"Only from the gallows, when the body can drop six feet or so—and even then it's not always instant," Orr said. "No, Dr. Crane suffocated at the end of that rope, and that would have taken longer than two-fifteen. Hard to pinpoint time-of-death with body temperature on such a warm day, but he was probably alive within the hour you found him."

They walked back to the driveway. The pressure on Eddie's head had stabilized. He liked Detective Orr's methodical style. She was the constant drip of water that eventually wore away a stone. Eddie had more information that any other reporter on the story. If he could get a cup of coffee and a telephone line in the next thirty minutes, he'd be okay.

"So either I imagined a door slamming," Eddie said, "or somebody ran out of the garage when I came calling for Crane."

Detective Orr was quiet a moment. Then she said, "Could have been neighborhood kids, here to steal a bike."

"You don't believe that."

She gave him the fake smile he hated.

◇ ◇ ◇

The TV was on in the Perez Brothers diner. The place was packed with the lunch crowd, mostly third-shift factory workers ordering their first meal of the day: cheese omelets and Budweiser. Four men were engaged in an animated argument in Spanish, either about Massachusetts politics or the metric system—Eddie wasn't sure.

He pounded the story into his laptop.

Bobby Perez refilled Eddie's coffee mug. "How can you write with all this noise, man?" he asked.

Eddie kept his eyes on the keyboard. "Deadline makes me deaf." He typed some more, and then added: "This place is peaceful compared to the newsroom I used to work in."

"Oh yeah, you worked for *The Empire*, man, that rag."

Eddie finished a final sentence, and then cracked, "I was young, I needed the money." He smiled and handed Bobby the modem cord.

After he transmitted his story, Eddie relaxed with coffee and a rumpled newspaper left behind by an earlier customer. It was the current edition of *The Second Voice*, gamely reporting the reappearance of Roger Lime, a week after every other paper in

America had the story. Lew Cuhna had run the photograph the kidnappers had released, under the double-decked banner:

Thought to be Murdered Last Spring
Bank President Held for Ransom

The story was a week late, but at least Cuhna had used his own byline on it, and had done a competent job with the writing.

The noon news was starting on TV.

"Could you turn this up, Bobby?" Eddie asked. "That's my competition."

Eddie had little tolerance for local TV news, and the noon broadcasts were usually the worst. The TV anchormodel teased the rehashed material from the night before—a bar stabbing, a man who found his class ring twenty years after he had lost it down the toilet, and the Red Sox rain-out in Texas. Then she began a breathless reading of the morning's one fresh story:

```
Local coroner Dr. Alvin Crane was
found dead at his home this morning,
the victim of an apparent suicide.
Crane has come under fire in the past
week over his misidentification of the
skeletal remains of kidnapped financier
Roger Lime…
```

Bobby Perez pointed to the TV. "This your story, Eddie?"

"Yeah, but they don't have half the material I have. They'll be updating their six-o'clock report with my exclusive stuff."

```
Sources close to the investigation
say that evidence found at the scene
suggests that the doctor was despon-
dent about his mistaken work on the
Lime case, and perhaps other cases
going back forty years…
```

Eddie clapped his hands on his head.

How did TV news get that info?

Eddie was the only reporter to read the note.

Lieutenant Brill!

He knew Eddie was about to break the story, so he leaked Eddie's scoop.

```
    Dr. Crane was pronounced dead at the
    scene, after a local freelance jour-
    nalist, Edward Bourque, discovered his
    body while at the house to ask Crane
    for an interview…And now a check of
    the weather…
```

Eddie was slack jawed. Most reporters despised becoming part of a story. Those who didn't became columnists. Eddie had never wanted a column. If Eddie became too closely identified with the death of Dr. Crane, no news organization with any ethics would pay him to write about the case.

Bobby grinned and slapped Eddie on the shoulder. "You're famous, man. So you found him, huh? And the old man—he was dead?"

Eddie frowned and then downed his coffee. He thought about the noise he had heard at Dr. Crane's place. His palms grew damp reliving the feeling of Crane's skin, the fading warmth left behind by a life that had hastily departed.

"Yeah, he was dead, all right," Eddie grumbled, "though just barely."

Chapter 6

Eddie's *Washington Post* was a mess again in the morning, parts of it missing. He made a mental note to call the delivery service. He often made mental notes about trivial items, and rarely followed up on them. He could never remember mental notes. For important stuff, he wrote real notes. A mental note was Eddie's way of telling himself that an inconvenience wasn't important enough to do something about. A few more days without the classified section, and he'd write himself a real note.

General VonKatz was at Eddie's feet, screaming about the dry kibble in his bowl.

"I've got nothing to share," Eddie told him. He leaned over and showed the General his breakfast plate—a mound of fried red cabbage with Velveeta. "See?"

The General sniffed Eddie's food. Satisfied that nobody was eating better than he, the cat crunched his cereal.

The bag of cabbage discovered in the crisper drawer had been three days past its expiration date. It still went well with a quart of Hawaiian Kona coffee. But, really, what wouldn't? Eddie would happily wash down a plate of potting soil with Kona.

He had planned to dedicate the day to running down the tip Henry had given him. But he found himself loitering over the box scores, unable to start his research. The thought of his brother left Eddie uneasy, and he wasn't sure why.

He pushed the newspaper away and grabbed for the telephone, determined to unscramble Henry's tip. There was just one place that would have all the information he needed. He dialed a local number.

After three rings, a deep, rumbling voice answered, "*Daily Empire*, news library."

Eddie whispered, "Durkin? It's Eddie Bourque."

"Bourque? That can't be right. That chicken shit little bastard don't work here anymore."

Eddie laughed. "You're still campaigning for an ass-kicking. Why don't I come down there and apply one?"

Durkin roared. "That's a good crack, Bourque. The next crack outta you will be your tibia, when I snap it like a candy cane." He laughed like a dragon on a new pile of gold. "Been a long time, Bourque. What can I do you out of?"

"Same shit as always. I need to see a file."

"Ooo. You heard the new rules? Employees *only* down here in the library. And that would go triple for you, considering all the trouble you caused this place when you left."

Eddie was shocked. "Since when do *you* listen to any rules that weren't chipped into stone on a mountain?"

"You're right—there's only ten rules in the world, and there's nothing in them prohibiting a favor for an old friend. I was just softening you up for what you gotta do to get in here without security calling the cops."

Durkin chuckled. Eddie got a mental picture of the dragon's grin before he sprayed fire. "Here's what I want you to do…"

◇ ◇ ◇

The truck needed shocks; it bounced over pitted streets toward the *Daily Empire* Building.

Or that's where Eddie assumed it was going. He couldn't see a damn thing from the back of the truck, sealed inside a fifty-five gallon metal drum, which, according to its label, was supposed to hold newsprint ink.

This is crazy. Durkin is crazy. I'm crazy.

The big diesel slammed over a large bump, and Eddie's chin clacked against his knee. His lower legs were going numb.

How much air is in one of these barrels?

He took comfort from the tiny hole in the lid that shone like a star. The truck driver, a buddy of Durkin's from their service in Vietnam, had assured Eddie that plenty of air could squeeze through that pinprick. It was supposed to be a short ride on the flatbed truck with the barrels of ink, but Eddie began to wonder if the driver had taken a wrong turn. It started to get warm inside the barrel.

Finally, the truck stopped, idling. Eddie heard the driver's door open and then slam. And then a muffled conversation:

"S'pose to be seventeen barrels on this truck."

"That's what I brung you."

"You got three rows of six, that's eighteen."

"Eighteen, huh? And you're complaining?"

Muffled laughter.

"Okay, you're fine. Bring 'em in."

The truck door opened and then slammed again, then the diesel growled and jerked forward. Eddie could feel the truck angling down a ramp. It leveled off, then stopped, and the engine shut off.

Chains rattled. Bolts were thrown open. An electric motor hummed. Eddie's barrel shuddered and clanked into its neighbors. His head banged the steel. He cringed silently and rubbed the spot. He heard a beeping, felt motion, assumed that a forklift was unloading the pallet of ink barrels. The forklift slammed the barrels down and motored off, doing more work nearby. Eddie rubbed his numb ankles. He was supposed to wait in the barrel for Durkin to let him out, but how long could he stand being squished in there?

Soon, the forklift finished and drove off. He heard the truck start again. It snorted and went away. A metal door slammed. And it was quiet outside the barrel.

The pinprick in the lid glowed more dimly than before. Eddie was inside the the *Empire* building, probably in the production warehouse room.

He waited, waited, waited, hearing nothing. After what seemed like half an hour, but probably was less, Eddie felt a wave of claustrophobia. The air inside the barrel grew steamy. Where the hell was Durkin?

Screw it. I gotta get out of here.

Eddie reached his hands to the lid. It was warm. He pressed, gently at first, trying to be quiet. The lid was stuck fast. He pressed harder, as hard as he could. No good. Eddie pounded the lid with the heel of his hand. It made a dull sound that vibrated around him. The lid wouldn't budge.

What if Durkin forgot?

Durkin would never forget.

But what if he got delayed somehow? What if he had a blackout? Or a heart attack?

What if he went out for a sandwich and—by a case of mistaken identity—got arrested for a crime he didn't commit? And then was hauled off to the police station while screaming nonsense about his friend stuffed in an ink barrel. And what if it took the police and a dozen lawyers a week to sort out the facts? Eddie would be decomposing by then. He thought of the perfect headline:

```
STINK FROM INK
IS MAN IN CAN.
```

Eddie sighed.

Stop thinking stupid stuff.

What if Durkin just forgot?

A door slammed nearby. Eddie held his breath. He thought he heard the clip-clop of metal crutches on the concrete floor. He was about to call out for Durkin when the barrel tipped over.

"Whoa!"

The barrel rang like a gong when it hit. And then it rolled. Eddie slammed around inside like a pair of sneakers in a clothes dryer, until the barrel crashed into a wall and the lid popped off.

Eddie dragged himself out, to a blast of hoarse laugher.

"Goddamit, Durkin," Eddie said, staggering to his feet, "I'd give you that ass kicking right now, if my legs weren't numb."

Durkin laughed even harder. His huge shoulders jiggled. He balanced on his one leg and pounded his metal crutches on the floor. He looked different than when Eddie had last seen him. Same big square head, same silver hair, but his goatee had spread to a full white beard. His diamond stud earring had been replaced by a humble paperclip, threaded through the hole in his earlobe.

Eddie stamped his feet. They erupted with prickles as the blood returned. Durkin's laugh was so hearty, so long-lasting, that even Eddie had to smile at the prank.

Durkin balled his massive fist. "Anytime you think you're man enough, Bourque," he said.

"Someday," Eddie promised. "I'm a lot younger than you. You won't be bench-pressing four hundred pounds when you're eighty."

Durkin laughed, thrilled by Eddie's threat.

"So don't be surprised," Eddie warned, "when I sneak into your nursing home and push your wheelchair into traffic."

Durkin slapped his thigh in delight. His need for combat was satisfied, and he was ready to be helpful. "It's been too long, Eddie," he said. "Whadda you need from me?"

◇ ◇ ◇

Down in the *Empire's* basement news library, Durkin lorded over a dimly lit world of unlabeled file drawers, stacks of newsprint and cobwebs. His AM radio was tuned to conservative talk radio, his desk littered with empty paper coffee cups and motorcycle magazines. Durkin had lost his left leg in an explosion in Vietnam when he was just nineteen, but he moved with grace on his crutches, like a hulking Minotaur through his labyrinth of file cabinets.

The file on the crimes and trial of Henry Bourque was more than thirty years old. In it, Durkin's predecessors had dutifully filed news clippings of every story published in *The Daily Empire* that had mentioned Henry Joseph Bourque.

"Is this an uncle of yours, or something?" Durkin asked.

Eddie didn't want to answer, and couldn't decide why. He trusted Durkin, who was risking his job by letting Eddie into his library. So why didn't Eddie want to admit the truth? Why was his first instinct to lie? He forced out the words, "Not an uncle. My brother."

Durkin frowned. "But Ed, this guy's gotta be at least twenty years older than you."

"Twenty years and a few months," Eddie said. He sighed, then explained: "My folks married young and planned to have one kid—that was Henry. He was a genius—I've heard—and an athlete, with a room full of trophies. My parents were devastated when he got arrested, and they decided to—uh, well, they decided to start over. My mom was in her forties when I was born. They thought I'd be another Henry, except with a clean record." He chuckled at the dark humor. "Didn't work out that way. Henry's conviction took too much out of them. They blamed themselves, of course, for raising him wrong, and then maybe they tried to be too perfect with me. I dunno—I've given up trying to analyze it. They split when I was a kid. Don't hear much from either of them anymore."

"I wonder sometimes what makes a family," Durkin said.

"So that's the legacy of Henry Bourque," Eddie said. He tapped the file folder on Durkin's desk. "As well as whatever atrocities are in this file."

Durkin studied Eddie's face a moment. He looked away, leaned against his desk, stroked his beard three times, and then said quietly, "When I got home from the war, I didn't see outside of my hospital room for three months." He smiled out of the corner of his mouth. "Shrapnel fucked me up all over. I'm lucky I kept the leg that I got." He slapped that leg. "What kept me going were the visits from my brother and from my fiancée."

"I didn't know you were married."

Durkin's brow wrinkled like a package of hot dogs. "I ain't," he said. "Don't jump ahead. Anyway, the reason I *ain't* is because after my brother and fiancée visited me, they were visiting each other."

"Oh."

"Yeah."

Eddie felt uneasy hearing of the heartbreak of someone so physically imposing as Durkin. He figured that Durkin would despise being the object of pity. Eddie asked, "Did you break his neck?"

Durkin shrugged. "I got over it."

"What? You had to be furious."

"Oh yeah? I had to? Says *who*?" He looked at Eddie. There was no answer, but Durkin let the question hang there a while. Then he said, "I don't gotta be anything I don't want. I didn't have to hate him." He pushed himself suddenly away from the desk. "I'll be in the back. Scream when you're done."

Eddie watched him clip-clop away. He had known Durkin for years, but was beginning to doubt that he had ever known him well.

Eddie turned his attention to the file folder on the desk. It was layered with a fine grit of paper dust. The file tab was labeled in red ink: "Solomon Co./armored car heist." A list of cross-referenced subjects written across the front included: "Henry J. Bourque trial/sentencing." There were other names printed there, too, which Eddie did not recognize.

It struck Eddie odd to see Henry's name on the file; a myth from his childhood had been proven true. Henry Bourque was real. It was like seeing the Loch Ness Monster at the aquarium.

The stories had been filed in chronological order, starting with the earliest:

```
ARMORED CAR ROBBED
 Three Guards Missing
 $600,000 in Cash Stolen
```

The Daily Empire had done a competent job on deadline covering the morning robbery. From the story, told in straightforward, declarative sentences, Eddie learned that the armored truck from Solomon Secure Transport Company had reported by radio that a broken-down car was blocking its path on a back road in Tyngsboro, the tiny town to the north, on the New Hampshire border.

That was the truck's last message.

When the transport company couldn't raise the driver by radio, it called the police.

The cops found the truck in a hayfield two hours later. The armored car's guards, locked in back with the money, had been under a policy to never open the truck in a robbery, but the truck was empty. The driver, the two guards and the money were gone. The paper reported the names of the missing men: Dumas, Forte and Nicolaidis.

The names had long been out of the news, and they meant nothing to Eddie.

His eyes lingered over one detail in the story—the police had found blood in the back of the truck.

Oh Jesus, Henry.

Henry's crimes had always been an abstract. Now they were becoming real. Eddie felt a nervous flutter. He suddenly noticed that Durkin kept the basement too warm. He unbuttoned his shirt collar.

God, I need coffee.

"Durkin? Hey Durk!"

He heard clip-clop, clip-clop in the darkness, and then Durkin appeared. "Done already?"

"You got any of that industrial waste you like to brew?"

He chuckled. "Didn't learn your lesson last time, eh? Fine. I can make a pot." He went off. Eddie left Henry's file alone while Durkin brewed the java. He had decided not to look at the file alone. On his expedition into his brother's criminal past, Eddie wanted somebody with him to watch his back.

Durkin returned in a few minutes with two paper cups of steaming black sludge. "Don't spill any," he said. "This stuff stains."

Eddie sipped and flinched at the bitterness. "Like licking a car battery," he said. "I love it."

Durkin laughed and turned to leave.

"Hang on a sec," Eddie said. "This murder case—my brother's case." He sighed. "I guess I could use a hand going through this stuff." He smiled. "I could take your crutches away, I suppose. But I'd rather you just offered to help."

Durkin looked at him. Eddie readied himself for more verbal combat. But Durkin didn't want to fight. He sat at the edge of the desk and flipped open the file.

"What I remember best is that they never found the money," Durkin said. He searched through the file, pulled out a story about the missing money and flipped it on the desk for Eddie. "And they never found the guards' bodies, either."

Eddie blanched. "Three murders? I didn't know it was three."

"Naw, just two," Durkin said. "Nicolaidis survived." He tugged out another story for Eddie:

```
MISSING ARMORED CAR DRIVER ALIVE
Ralph V. Nicolaidis escapes captors
```

"The guards were tied up in a basement somewhere," Durkin explained. He gestured to a head and shoulders photo of a thick-necked man with heavy black eyebrows. "They blindfolded this guy, Nicolaidis, and brought him out into the woods, out in Tyngsboro somewhere, probably to shoot him. But he managed to run off."

Eddie scanned the story. The driver told police he had escaped in darkness and wandered through the woods for hours, until he heard the sound of traffic and staggered out onto a road.

Eddie was thrilled to learn that Ralph Nicolaidis had lived. Nicolaidis was just twenty-two, the paper had reported at the time. He had a mother and a stepfather. He had been accepted into the police academy. He played the drums.

In one sense, there was little difference between two murders and three—one man escaping didn't make Henry any less of a killer. But the difference of one life was infinite.

"So how did they catch them?" Eddie asked.

Durkin pulled out another clip. "Partial fingerprint in the truck. They finally matched it to a punk stickup man, who was doing life in prison on the installment plan—a year or two at a time." He pointed to a mug shot of a young man with sharp, bony features. "This is the dude, Jimmy Whistle. He helped your brother pull off the heist."

Eddie stared at the picture. He whispered, "My brother's partner."

I gave away the table I made to my partner's old lady.

"Once the police nabbed Jimmy, he turned on Henry Bourque—fingered him as the mastermind and the trigger man who killed the guards, Dumas and Forte," Durkin said. "Your brother admitted he had helped Whistle hold up a convenience store a few months before the armored car robbery, but he denied any involvement in the Solomon Transport murders. The jury saw it otherwise."

Eddie read the story. In exchange for testimony against Henry, prosecutors had offered a plea bargain for James J. Whistle: parole in thirty years.

"He'd be out by now!" Eddie shouted.

Durkin read over the story. "I guess, assuming he stayed out of trouble. Cripes, imagine that—going into prison in your twenties and getting out at my age. That's a lot of life to miss."

Eddie flipped through the file. "Something doesn't make sense," he said. "Without the guards' bodies, and just the testimony of a convicted felon, how did the state stick the murder charge on Henry?"

"Blood evidence, if I recall," Durkin said. He explained as he searched the file for the right story. "They found blood on his shoes." He found the clip he was looking for and scanned it quietly for a minute. "Yeah, the cops found bloody sneakers in your brother's closet. Henry tried to say it was his own blood—and he did have a cut on his hand at the time. But you can't run from science. This was long before DNA testing, but an expert matched the blood types on the shoes to the missing guards."

"How could they do that?"

"They knew from Army records that Dumas was blood-type B-negative," Durkin explained, reading from the story. "Forte was AB-positive. Both types are rare—just two percent of the population is B-negative, four percent is AB-positive. Your brother is O-positive, which is common. But they didn't find any type O on his shoes—they found *both* of the rare types. It's pretty hard evidence."

He offered the story to Eddie.

Durkin was right. Considering that Henry had tried to claim it was his own blood, the scientific conclusions were solid evidence. Beyond a reasonable doubt, for sure.

A name in the story leapt out at Eddie. He stood and read it again.

Dr. Alvin Crane.

"Holy shit—Dr. Crane testified at my brother's trial."

"Crane? The guy who hanged himself yesterday?"

"Yeah…" Eddie read on. "He did the blood-type matching. It looks like he was the only expert to testify for the state."

Durkin frowned. "Eddie, man, what the hell?" he said. "You're turning white."

Eddie's eyes raced across the text. "Jesus! He was the only expert to testify *at all.* The defense didn't even offer a counter expert."

"That was the public defender, back thirty years ago. What do you expect?"

The district attorneys are fighting the good fight!!!! When they needed me, I was THERE.

He sputtered, "Alvin Crane…he went to the rope a *liar.*"

Chapter 7

Leaving the *Empire* library was a lot easier than getting in. Security didn't care who broke *out*. Eddie had studied every story in his brother's file, and by the time he left the *Empire*, night had fallen.

The night was unusually cool for August. Eddie stuck his hands in his pants pocket and walked toward his car, which was tucked discreetly in the parking lot of one of the city's historic mills. The mill buildings were monsters of red brick that seemed too big to have been built in the century before modern machines. It seemed more likely that the mills just pushed themselves out of the ground the way mountains do. Some of the mills had become luxury apartment houses, others had become museums. They were the centerpiece of the city's tourism economy, a marketing plan based on America's industrial history.

Eddie squinted and scanned the field of dark asphalt. The Mighty Chevette was alone, deep in the parking lot. He listened to the knock of his shoes on the ground. He felt the breeze on his face. Simple details from everyday life, inaccessible to his brother. To live in such a way for thirty years seemed impossible. Eddie thought about goldfish that grew only as big as the bowl you kept them in. That must have been how Henry handled prison.

He fished his key ring from his pocket and felt for the ignition key. Headlights came on across the parking lot. Eddie held up his keys to the light and found the right one. He listened to an engine revving, from the car across the lot. He wondered if Henry could still drive a car after three decades in jail. Would he even know how to change the TV channel by remote control?

Eddie creaked open the car door and looked inside. The headlights from across the lot were coming toward the Mighty Chevette from the rear, and they illuminated the interior of the car. Eddie gave the back seat a quick inspection in the light. Finding Dr. Crane's body had been unnerving. The memory gave his mind plenty of raw material to imagine a killer hiding in his car. But there was nothing there but a few hand tools for the garden he intended to grow someday, two dozen empty Dunkin Donuts cups, and potato chip bags.

An engine gunned. Tires scrubbed the pavement. The headlights swerved toward Eddie. He saw the outline of a van.

This guy drunk?

The van lurched forward with a roar and the high beams bore down on Eddie.

Eddie froze for a moment in amazement.

He's running me down.

No place to run.

He dove into the Mighty Chevette a split-second before the van strafed the car with a screaming metallic crunch. The Chevette rocked and groaned, the driver's door was shorn clean off its hinges. Eddie heard it crash and skid away.

He looked over the dash, disbelieving what had just happened.

The van's brake lights came on. It was slowing down.

He's coming back.

Eddie fumbled with his keys, dropped them, snatched them up and tore through them. He looked up. The van made a hard U-turn. Eddie jammed the ignition key home, stomped the clutch and prayed as he turned the key.

For once, let it start the first try.

The Mighty Chevette coughed to life. The van came at him again, slowly this time. Eddie flicked on his lights, saw an arm sticking out of the van's window, a gun in the hand.

He popped the clutch and the Mighty Chevette jerked forward.

The gun flashed and banged.

The Chevette's windshield crackled in a spiderweb pattern, just below the rear view mirror.

"Jesus!"

Eddie drove straight at the van's headlights, then veered hard left at the last second and passed the van on its passenger side. He slammed the gearshift into third and floored the accelerator, aiming across the parking lot, for the street.

With no driver's side door, the pavement raced by close enough to touch. In one quick motion, Eddie reached his right hand over, dragged the seat belt across his body and clicked it into place.

Headlights filled his mirrors. The van was giving chase.

The Mighty Chevette zoomed onto the street, its engine high and whiny. Who was doing this to him? How did they find him? They must have followed him from Pawtucketville, and waited all afternoon in that parking lot for Eddie to get back from the *Empire*.

The wind whipped inside the Chevette. The speedometer reached fifty. Eddie watched the van in the mirror. One silhouette behind the wheel. The van was gaining. The arm snaked outside the window again.

Bang.

The back windshield cracked around a tiny hole. The bullet thumped behind the passenger's seat.

Get small.

Eddie hunched low against the wheel, close enough to bite it.

The road merged ahead with a busy urban thoroughfare. The Chevette weaved into traffic. Horns blared. A sedan with four people swerved out of his way into the breakdown lane.

Traffic was slowing for a yellow light. Eddie twisted the wheel left. The Chevette's tires squealed over the median line, through the intersection toward oncoming traffic. Those drivers slammed their brakes and darted left and right, looking for a safe spot out of the way of the madman in the little yellow Chevette. Eddie threaded through the jumble at forty miles per hour, then yanked the wheel hard again and got back in the right lane.

In his rear view mirror, the van was trying a copycat move, but it was bigger, couldn't go as fast through the maze of cars, and Eddie pulled ahead. He glimpsed his own face in the mirror— jaw clenched, eyes bugging out, hair matted with sweat.

Typical rush hour commuter.

The steering wheel felt slick. He gripped it with all his strength; veins on the back of his hands bubbled against the skin.

To the left was a public park, dark at this hour. Beyond it, twinkling between the trees, were the lights of a shopping district. A blue flash caught his eye—a police car, across the park, probably responding to the chase through downtown Lowell.

The van was growing in the rear view mirror.

The shortest distance between two points...

Eddie wrenched the wheel left, thumped up the curb. The car answered with a pathetic rattle. Two hubcaps shot off like UFOs. Eddie raced the Chevette over the grass into the darkened park. The ground was soft, the wheel unsteady in his hands.

Please, don't get stuck out here in the mud.

The headlights in the rear mirror bounced up and down, as the van pounded over the curb. Eddie watched it. Still gaining. But the far edge of the park was coming up. He turned toward the store lights, racing up a little knoll.

Suddenly, ahead of him appeared two teenagers holding hands.

Oh fuck!

Shocked by the car, the teens stood paralyzed in Eddie's path, horror on their faces.

Eddie pulled hard right. The Mighty Chevette plowed into a giant puddle. Muddy water splashed over the windshield. The car slowed to nearly a stop. Water poured in the open door. Eddie slammed into first gear and gunned the engine. The car wailed in pain, tires spinning. For a moment, Eddie considered abandoning the machine and running for his life, but the Chevette seemed to sense the urgency and it struggled to dry land. A sickening sweet friction smell filled the car.

The van was nearly on him.

Bang.

The slug clanged near a rear wheel.

Eddie had no choice—there wasn't time to turn around—he sped away from the van, away from the storefront lights and the police, toward an industrial area of windowless warehouses. The Chevette rocked over the curb, back onto the street, and Eddie pounded the pedal to the floor.

The van barreled from the park a moment later and roared after him.

Will this guy ever give up?

The streets of the industrial park were wide to accommodate the tractor-trailers that serviced the warehouses there. Eddie aimed the Chevette down the center of the road. White aluminum buildings flew by on both sides. The street was lit in eerie yellow from curbside utility poles.

Eddie had the pedal buried, but with a newer, bigger engine, the van overmatched the Chevette and grew huge in Eddie's mirror.

Eddie had driven through this warehouse district a few times on assignment for *The Daily Empire*. He tried to picture it like a map. Where were the turn-offs? Which exit roads led back downtown?

The gun barked.

A tire exploded.

The Chevette bucked as if possessed by a demon. Eddie fought the wheel—no use, the car skidded toward a light pole. Two wheels bumped over the curb. Eddie heard a thunderous *wham* as the car ricocheted off the pole. The world outside the windshield flipped violently on its side. Over the scrape of hot metal, Eddie heard his own scream. The car slid across the tar. With no driver's-side door, Eddie's face was inches from bare pavement and a blast of white-hot sparks. He closed his eyes and wrenched against the seat belt.

Then, in an instant, the car stopped and everything was quiet, except the feeble squeak of a single spinning wheel.

Dazed, bruised by the seat belt across his chest, but not seriously hurt, Eddie tried to reconnect with reality.

The car had rolled onto its left side, in the middle of the street.

Eddie was still buckled in. The Chevette's engine had died. The van had swerved around him. Eddie saw its brake lights, some sixty yards down the street.

He's coming back to finish me.

Eddie slammed his fist on the seat belt release. It let go and he dropped to the pavement. It was hard and cold. The passenger's door was facing straight up. He struggled to his feet, put his shoulder into the door, pulled the handle and shoved, trying to open it like the hatch of a submarine. The door wouldn't budge. He tried to roll down the window; the handle snapped off in his hand.

Eddie smelled gasoline.

There was a twelve-inch dandelion puller at his feet, a tool he had left in the car months before. Eddie snatched it up and smacked it backhand against the windshield. In the tiny confines of the Chevette, he couldn't get leverage and the weapon glanced meekly off the safety glass.

I'm trapped in here.

The van's headlights swung back toward the Chevette.

A rivulet of gasoline flowed down the street, away from the Mighty Chevette. Eddie's car was hemorrhaging fuel.

The van pulled up in front of the Chevette and stopped.

Eddie felt as if he could choke on the ball of nerves in his throat.

The driver of the van wore a black ski mask. He got up from his seat and disappeared into the back of the van. A moment later he reappeared with what looked like a stick of dynamite—a road flare. He unscrewed one end of it, held both halves out the window and struck the two parts together, like lighting a giant match. It erupted into blinding red light.

This is the end.

Eddie waited for the man in the mask to meet eyes with him at least once before he dropped the flare, but he didn't. The son-of-a-bitch just dropped the fire into the river of gas, and then peeled away in the van without a glance.

Flames rose from the street. They spread in seconds around the little Chevette. Eddie had the point-of-view of the woodpile at the start of a bonfire. Smoke drifted into the car. Eddie felt the heat and the hopelessness.

He wasn't scared in a traditional way. He was furious with terror. Of all the thousands of miles he had safely driven in his Mighty Chevette, the little yellow car he had bought used for eight hundred bucks was about to become his coffin. He was supremely frustrated that a man *who wears a ski mask in August* was cheating Eddie Bourque out of his life, and of all that he would have become. Eddie didn't even know why the man had murdered him.

He slammed the lawn tool on the pavement in frustration.

It clanked, metal on metal.

Eddie sunk to his knees, coughing in the smoke, and studied the ground. Sweat dripped from his nose and his chin like raindrops. The Chevette had skidded to rest above a manhole. The steel cover was about thirty inches wide and marked:

City of Lowell—ELECTRIC.

The electric service on this street was underground.

Hopelessness fled instantly. He dug the dandelion tool in a notch between the cover and the rim of the manhole, and pried. The cover lifted an inch. Eddie grunted and growled and wormed the tool in deeper. Musty air poured out.

At least it's not a sewer hole.

The fire filled the field of view outside the windshield.

Eddie gagged, choking on smoke. His eyes stung and filled with tears. Working furiously, muttering curses, he wormed his fingers under the steel cover and lifted. It must have weighed more than a hundred pounds, but Eddie's muscles were supercharged by adrenaline, and the hole yawned open. He could see the first step of a ladder on the side of the hole.

Eddie wasted no time backing down the passage. Standing on the fourth rung, he tried to lower the cover slowly, but unbearable heat stung his face. He yelped and ducked deeper into the hole.

The cover slammed above him and everything was dark and cool.

He heard a whoosh as the car flashed over in flame.

Chapter 8

Eddie sat on the bumper of a red fire-pumper truck and sipped bottled water. The scene smelled of diesel exhaust from the six idling emergency trucks, and charred vinyl and seat foam, scorched paint and wiring, and burnt rubber from the Chevette, no longer Mighty.

Detective Orr was red-faced, as hot as the car.

"Tell me again, Eddie," she demanded, "why you drove through a public park, nearly running over two Lowell High kids on their first date?"

"I missed them by ten feet."

"That was an hour ago. What have you been doing all this time?"

Eddie went through the story again, slowly this time, with all the details. "And then when I got down into the manhole, I tried to call the police station, but my cell phone couldn't get a signal underground."

She looked skeptical.

"It was the first chance I had to call," Eddie insisted. "It's hard to dial and drive for your life at the same time."

"Uh-huh."

"So then I had to feel my way through a conduit pipe on hands and knees for, oh, maybe two hundred feet, until I found another manhole and was able to climb up. It's slow down there, believe me—if you're not bumping your head into junction boxes, you're worried about getting electrocuted any second."

She looked to her notebook. "This van—did you get the license number?"

"No Lucy—I mean, *detective*, uh…" Eddie thought back and pictured the van. "The front plate had no light, now that I think about it, and I never saw the back of the van clearly. But I'm pretty sure it was cream colored, maybe a Ford. Hmm, I guess I'm not sure of that." Eddie was embarrassed; as a journalist he was supposed to be a professional observer.

The fire department had arrived by the time Eddie had gotten out of the manhole. They had quickly doused the visible fire in the car. Several firefighters had torn out what was left of the seats, to drown the tricky fire that could smolder in the flammable foam cushioning. Police investigators were taking photographs and measurements. Two officers bagged the spent road flare.

Eddie sighed. The Mighty Chevette was his only transportation. It had been an old junker, but Eddie had respected how the car carried on long past retirement age. He felt as if an old friend had died. He tried not to think about his own close call, but the smoldering car and the smoke stench in his clothing kept reminding him. Eddie's legs went rubbery every time he thought about his escape, and he felt a tingle of nervous electricity in his gut.

A young firefighter, barely eighteen, brought Eddie the Chevette's steering wheel. "We saved this," he said. "Thought you might like to have it."

The firefighter had a tiny hint of smile on his face, and Eddie wasn't sure if he was being ironic. No matter—Eddie wanted the memento. "Thanks. I'll take it."

Detective Orr had a few more questions, about the route Eddie had driven, the speeds the chase had reached. Eddie answered honestly and as fully as he could.

When Orr was finished, she snapped her little cop notebook shut and wrinkled her brow at Eddie. She scolded, "Where did you get this knack for nearly getting killed?" It was a question from a friend, not an investigating officer.

Eddie held up the steering wheel and shrugged. There was no answer.

"I need ten more minutes here," she said, "and then I'll drop you off at your house."

Detective Orr walked away. Eddie sipped more water. He had been calm the entire time he had been crawling through the electrical tunnel, and when he was being interviewed by police. But now, as he looked at his charred car and smelled the poison smoke, his hands were trembling.

His cell phone buzzed in his pocket. With great difficulty, he retrieved it and checked the caller ID number. Local, but not a number he recognized.

"Hello?"

"Professor Bourque?" The idling fire trucks were noisy and Eddie wasn't sure he had heard what he thought he heard. He looked around, to see if anyone was playing a joke on him. "This is Eddie Bourque."

"Ay, Professor! It's Ryan, from Intro to Journalism, man! I have a question about the mid-term assignments."

Eddie rolled his eyes. "Oh, hell, Ryan. Can this wait? You caught me at a bad time."

"I can see that, that's why I'm calling. What did you have? Some kind of accident? The TV news says you drove through the park. That sounds fucked up to me, man, because you don't *sound* drunk."

Eddie stood. "I am *not* drunk." He looked around. "Where are you?"

"At home. You're on TV. I'm looking right at you."

That's when Eddie saw the news van parked down the street. *When did Channel Eight get here?*

Closer to the action, in the shadows near the sidewalk, he saw that a camera crew had set up a tripod. The camera was pointed straight at Eddie. His stomach tightened. He pictured the driver from the van at home, relaxing after a good night of killing, maybe eating crackers and wombat pâté, or sipping blood from a skull—whatever—and watching Eddie Bourque on the eleven o'clock news.

Now he knows he failed. He knows I escaped.

He had no idea what the driver looked like. In Eddie's imagination, the man went to bed in a ski mask. Eddie stared into the camera; he couldn't look away. He felt a paralyzing anxiety, as if his insides had suddenly liquefied and gushed out his feet, leaving a hollow tin replica of himself.

"Oh, dude! You're looking right at me," Ryan said. He laughed. "That's creepy. Whoops! Now you're gone. They're onto the sports. Awwww! The Red Sox got *bombed* tonight."

"So why are you calling, Ryan?"

"Well, dude—professor!—I was thinking that you might have undergone some sort of trauma in this car accident, and if that was the case—I mean, like, we *hope* it's not, but *if*—would the mid-term papers still be due next week?"

Eddie watched the TV news crew break down their equipment. "They're due," he said.

"Aw man, it's just that I'm having a hard time finding a public meeting to go to, and, um…"

"Just find a city board dealing with a topic that interests you and you'll be fine."

"That's the problem, professor!" Ryan said. "The only thing that interests me is *music*."

"Try the liquor licensing board," Eddie suggested. "Nightclubs go before those commissions to get permits for live music. Happens all the time."

"You mean government controls our nightclubs?"

"Find the conflict," Eddie told him, thinking about the conflict he had just escaped. "And tell both sides."

◇ ◇ ◇

The next morning, General VonKatz planted his hind legs on Eddie's forehead, boosting himself to get a better look at whatever he was meowing at out the bedroom window.

Eddie had a feeling he would be sore from the car crash, and that it would hurt to move. He stayed still in his bed and moved only his eyelids. The room was dim; it was too early to get up. A gray tail swished above his face.

"General," he mumbled, "the human head is not a stepladder."

Eddie heard a rustling from the front yard.

"Stupid raccoons."

The General soon lost interest in whatever was outside, and jumped down.

"Thank you."

Eddie woke sore a few hours later, like a runningback the day after a punishing game. His chest hurt from where he had slammed against the seatbelt. He swallowed five ibuprofen, set the coffee maker to brew his darkest Italian roast, and went out in a t-shirt and boxers for his *Washington Post*.

The air was cool and a steady breeze bent the top branches of his neighbor's sugar maples. Again, the paper was a mess, and Eddie wondered if raccoons could be destroying his morning read. He picked up what he could find of his *Post* and brought it inside.

At least I'm still around to read it.

He discovered a can of mixed grill in gravy in the cupboard, emptied it on a paper plate and set it on the kitchen table for General VonKatz. Usually, the cat ate on the floor, but what did it matter today? During the minutes Eddie had been trapped in the burning Chevette, he had thought he'd never see the General again.

Today's newspaper scavenger hunt had yielded sports, life-style and the main news section. The metro and classified were missing. He daydreamed through the paper, distracted by the memory of the man in the ski mask. Who was he? And why had he come after Eddie Bourque with such ferocity? Was it a case of mistaken identity?

Who the hell did he think I am?

Halfway through Eddie's second cup of coffee, he noticed the General staring at the front door. A second later came a lyrical knock, to the rhythm of "Shave and a Haircut—Two Bits!"

Eddie pattered in bare feet to the window, in time to see a yellow taxi drive off. He went to the door and opened it.

The woman on the top step was maybe forty-five, slim and attractive, but a little gray in the face, as if she had lived a hard life. She had high and prominent cheekbones, and dark green eyes outlined in black pencil and highlighted with aqua-green smears on the upper lids. Gray streaks ran through her wheat-colored hair, which was long and straight, hanging halfway to her waist. She wore new blue jeans, a wide black belt, cream-colored high-heeled shoes, and an orange tiger-striped blouse. A pink duffle bag was at her feet.

"Hi there!" she squealed in a cartoon voice an octave higher than Eddie might have expected from her tired, serious face. "I'm Bobbi." She looked Eddie up and down. "Oooh! Look at them knees—bony as a pony! Does that run in the family? Dear gawd, I hope not." She laughed.

Eddie looked down at his knees, and then squinted at the woman. "Huh? Wha?"

The woman stuck her hands on her hips and gave him an exaggerated look of disbelief.

"Eddie, it's me—Bobbi, your sister-in-law," she said. She held up her left hand and wiggled the digits. There was a gold wedding band on her ring finger. "I'm your brother Henry's wife—we got hitched last spring." She feigned a nasally, upper-class accent, "It was the *most* superb ceremony. The warden let me bring shrimp cocktail, at least on my side of the glass." She laughed again.

"Henry mentioned he was recently married," Eddie said, more to himself than to her.

"Of course he did, hon." She tilted her head and batted her long black eyelashes. "I'm probably all he ever talks about."

"Uhhh…"

She laughed. "Kidding you, Eddie—all your big brother talks about is chess. And, of course, he wants to know where I've gone recently that I can describe for him. He says you're real good at that, too."

Eddie nodded, taking it in, trying to understand what she was doing here. "Yes. Sure."

She stood on tiptoes and peeked over his shoulder into the house. "Isn't this about the time you should invite me in? We are *family*, after all."

Chapter 9

The woman who said her name was Bobbi Anderson Nichols Bourque didn't drink coffee. But if coffee was all Eddie had—he checked the cabinets, it was all that he had—she would like it mixed fifty-fifty with milk, and eight sugars. To Eddie, the concoction was a sin against nature, but he counted out the sweetener and fixed it the way she wanted.

Bobbi didn't need the caffeine. Seated at Eddie's kitchen table, she launched into a breathless story about a man she saw on the bus from New York. "He had on that kinda hat, you know the kind, with the floppy brim and the fish hooks coming outta the sides," she said, creating the hat in pantomime above her head.

"Uh, a fishing hat?"

She squealed, "Yeah, yeah! Let me get to that part!"

Eddie, feeling self-conscious, put on khaki slacks as she shouted the story from the kitchen. The point of the story, near as Eddie could figure over the next fifteen minutes, seemed to be that the man had worn a fishing hat on the bus.

The General watched the diversion from the morning routine from under the coffee table.

Eddie was patient during the man in the hat story, and he gleaned some useful information from her digressions. He learned that Bobbi was a divorcee living three miles from Henry Bourque's federal prison in upstate New York. She answered the phones at an advertising agency by day, and tended bar at night.

She had met Henry through the mail, somehow, became his pen pal, and then quickly his wife.

When her story was finally over, Eddie interjected, "Did you come all the way to Lowell just to see me?"

She gave a devilish grin and lifted one eyebrow. "Now you *are* a treat, Edward, but I'm here for my own benefit—and my husband's, of course."

"I don't understand."

"Your brother asked me a long time ago to look up your byline every day."

"He did?"

"When I saw your story on that medical examiner who lynched himself, I knew I had to come."

"Dr. Crane?"

"That's the one." She shifted at the table and leaned closer. Her makeup was meticulous, like it had been applied by Michelangelo. "I read on the Internet that you found him swinging in the breeze." She caught herself. "That's an expression, I don't mean to sound cruel, though I am furious at that so-called doctor."

Eddie looked into his coffee mug. "It wasn't breezy where I found him."

She put her hand on his. Her nails were painted pink. "It's terrible, I'm sure. Suicide always is." She patted his hand. "It *was* suicide, wasn't it?"

Eddie shrugged, distracted by the memory. "That's what it looked like to me, though I got a cop friend who suspects otherwise."

She put her hand to her lips. "Oh…why would the police suspect *that?*"

Eddie bristled. Had he said too much? He barely knew this woman. She didn't *feel* like his sister-in-law any more than Henry Bourque had felt like a brother. "I dunno," he said, trying to shift the subject. "What about Crane's death made you come here?"

Bobbi tensed her shoulders and tapped her fists on the table. "He killed himself over his mistakes in that kidnapping case, the one with that man from the bank," she said.

"Roger Lime."

"Yes! Did you realize this doctor was also the state's lead witness against your brother?" Her voice cracked.

"I did, but—"

"And it was Crane's testimony that got Henry convicted!"

"—that was more than thirty years ago."

She leaned back and looked into space, eyes glassy and roaming. For a moment, Eddie thought she might cry, but she collected herself and explained softly, "I didn't expect to get married a third time, and certainly not to a convict with a life sentence." She smiled. "Stupid me, huh?"

Eddie smiled back, gently.

She looked him in the eye. "I've known in my heart since I set eyes on Henry Bourque that he is an innocent man."

Eddie's stomach tightened. He had briefly entertained the same fantasy.

"You saw him in prison—he told me all about it," she said. "Did you see it too? The innocence? The golden heart under that shaved skull and that big ol' scar?"

Eddie stammered. "I can't…well… " He slumped. "Henry and I had a weird conversation."

She laughed. "That boy's mind does tend to skip around," she said, brightly. "I thought he was crazy before I figured out he was just an ordinary genius."

Her laugh was catchy. Eddie chuckled. It seemed that he wasn't the only one unnerved by conversation with Henry. At least Bobbi had gotten used to it.

"He's very proud of you," she said.

"Huh? How? Proud of what?"

"Your career as a newsman. When you worked in Vermont, Henry subscribed to your paper by mail. And when you came back to Lowell to work for—what was it? *The Daily Empire*?—he wrote your old newspaper to find out where you went."

Eddie was stunned. He put his hands to his head. "I had no idea."

"It's tough for him now because you're a freelancer and your work appears all over. Since I've known your brother, I've been searching the Internet every day for your stories, so I can print them out and mail them to him. I happened to see your story on the kidnapping case in my hometown newspaper. Henry was very interested in that piece."

"Yeah," Eddie said, distracted again and re-analyzing his conversation with Henry over the Roger Lime case. Another thought struck Eddie and he blurted, "Wait! You've never said why you came all the way out here."

She pressed her lips together and studied him for a moment. "Your brother," she said in a stern voice, "is a mule head."

"Excuse me?"

Bobbi wrinkled her nose. "Mister Mule, I call him—he's so obstinate. He drives me crazy. I've *told* him that this information coming out about Dr. Crane could overturn his conviction and get him out of that jail, so we can have a normal life."

"And he disagrees?"

"He doesn't think it will do any good. He says, 'What can *we* do about it?' Well, I've been studying the law. I told him we need a lawyer, a real shark, with a briefcase full of sharp teeth. And we need an investigator to collect some ammunition for the court brief." She threw up her hands. "But Henry won't hear of it."

"Is that why you came here?" Eddie said, still not following her reasoning.

"I got a few days off work and I came to Lowell to do some investigating of my own," she said. "And I thought you could point me to a place to start." She trailed off, then added: "But, most importantly, I thought you could help me convince your brother that it's worth a try. Maybe he'll listen to you, and together we can talk him into fighting for his freedom."

Eddie thought about what she was asking. What could *he* do? He didn't have a clue where she might start an investigation of a thirty-year-old double homicide. And he couldn't imagine why Henry would listen to the little brother he just met.

But if she was right? What if Henry was innocent?

He sighed.

She's on a fool's errand.

"I dunno, Bobbi—"

"Stop right there," she said. "I'm going to stop you before you say no, and we'll continue this conversation later, with no hard feelings. Okay?"

Eddie nodded. "Fair enough."

Bobbi grinned, then glanced to the pink duffle on the floor. "So," she said, "which room is mine?"

Eddie nearly gagged on his java. His eyes darted around the three-room cottage. "Ummm…"

She exploded into laughter. "Gullible," she howled. "So gullible, just like your brother—it's a precious quality in you Bourque boys." She laughed until Eddie was laughing, too, and then she said, "Maybe you can recommend me a good hotel?"

"I'll drive you downtown," he offered.

Seeing the Chevette's steering wheel on the kitchen counter, Eddie frowned, and then corrected himself, "I mean, I'll call you a cab."

◇ ◇ ◇

She waved at Eddie from the taxi.

Eddie waved back from the window.

Two weeks ago, he wasn't sure if Henry Bourque knew that Eddie had been born. And now? A sister-in-law from out-of-town just barged in unannounced, threw a sack of problems over Eddie's shoulders and bummed ten bucks off him for the cab.

Christ, she acted just like family.

He was still shocked that Henry had been watching him for years through his work. He couldn't help thinking of the possibility Bobbi had presented.

Eddie got his chess set from the closet and unfolded the black and white board on the coffee table. It was a cheap set; two bucks at a flea market. The wooden pieces—half black, half unpainted—were scratched and chipped. Some had bite marks from a previous owner's puppy, or maybe from a toddler. Eddie liked that the pieces were oversized; they barely fit in their squares.

Henry preferred the white pieces, because the white side moved first. Eddie spun the board so the white pieces were in front of him.

How would Henry open a game?

Aggressive? Like his in-your-face personality.

Or conservative? To lull Eddie into a trap.

Eddie leaned forward, elbows on his knees, chin on his fists, and studied the board.

Henry would be unconventional; Eddie had no doubt.

He grabbed a knight and jumped it over the picket line of pawns.

Eddie spun the board and looked over the black pieces. He imagined Henry sitting across from him, grinning, daring Eddie to match his opening move.

The phone rang.

Eddie lingered a moment at the board, and then answered the call. Springer from the Associated Press was on the line. "You working today?" he asked.

"I got transportation issues."

"That piece-of-shit Chevette in the shop?"

"In the funeral parlor."

"Oh, so then you *really* need the work."

Eddie laughed. He felt too distracted to report and write a news story, but Springer was right; Eddie needed the job. "Gimme something easy," he said.

"Roger Lime is back in pictures. The kidnappers have released another photo, apparently taken in the past couple days. The cops are offering the same deal as before—they share, we publish. You got the sources—your story was great last time."

"Where and when?"

"At the cop shop in one hour. Can you make it by then?"

The police station was a little better than a mile walk from Eddie's house. The sky had turned overcast and rain looked inevitable. He sighed. "Yeah, I'll make it."

Chapter 10

Roger Lime was back in another four-by-six snapshot. Oddly, Lime was pictured holding the current edition of *The Second Voice*—the edition that had carried the *first* photo of Lime. The kidnapped Roger Lime was holding up a published photo of his kidnapped self. Eddie wondered about the *next* edition of the paper. If the pictures kept coming, how long before Lew Cuhna's front page looked like two mirrors reflecting into each other?

Eddie recognized the rock wall in the background of the picture—same as in the last Lime photo. He recognized the five-sided table that Henry claimed he had built from scraps of poplar. Eddie squinted at the table leg and felt his face flush; he counted seven marks on the leg, like little frowns, maybe from a curved hatchet blade.

He made some notes for his story. Lime was wearing black sweat pants, a peach-colored dress shirt, un-tucked, and a black baseball cap.

He appeared no worse physically since the last photo, but something seemed different. Eddie leaned closer, studying every crease in Lime's face, then leaned back and stared at the photo from a distance.

The creases in his face.

That was what was different—his face had *different* creases last time.

His expression is wrong.

In the last photo, Lime's face showed anger, even arrogance, like he was running out of patience with an incompetent employee, and was about to fire him.

Not this photo—Lime's eyebrows were high on his forehead, his eyes huge and round, his cheeks drooped, and his mouth bent into a stiff frown.

He was terrified. Or at least he looked it. It all went into Eddie's notebook.

Eddie loitered for a moment after he had finished with the photo. Did he dare stop to visit Detective Orr? Would she still be upset that he had read Dr. Crane's suicide note?

Eddie thought of General VonKatz. The cat was never shy in telling Eddie exactly what he wanted—*Wake up! Food! More food!*—and he was never any worse off for speaking up. This time Eddie would ask Lucy for exactly what he needed for the story—the ransom note. What was the worse she could do? Throw him out of that tiny office? Eddie would step out before she could crawl over the desk.

He spun and marched off, walking straight into Lew Cuhna. The shorter man's nose smashed into Eddie's sternum.

"Ow," Eddie said, rubbing the spot on his chest.

Cuhna cupped his hand over his schnoz and cried, "Son of a bitch!"

"Shoot—sorry, Lew." Eddie stepped forward to try to help… somehow.

Cuhna waved him away. "It's fine, fine." He took a green pencil from behind his ear. "Not your fault, you didn't mean it."

Eddie watched him scribble *a-s-s-h-o-l-e* on his pad.

"Um, are you sure you're okay?"

Cuhna crossed out what he had written. He drew a giant exclamation point. "Lot on my mind, Bourque, okay? Got another paper to put out by myself again this week."

"News never stops," Eddie said, but Cuhna wasn't listening.

Cuhna drew a rainbow on his pad, or maybe a frown. "Don't need this, can't take another week of this," he said. He crossed out the frown, and then looked up hard at Eddie. "You're a good man, Bourque. A newsman. I trust a good newsman."

Were those tears in Cuhna's little green eyes? From hitting his nose, maybe? Cuhna just gazed up at Eddie, apparently waiting for some kind of answer.

Eddie nodded, unsure. "Okay, Lew."

Cuhna wrote *O-K* on his pad in heavy letters, and then headed off to do his job.

Eddie stared at the back of Cuhna's head for a moment, wondering what was going on inside it.

◇ ◇ ◇

"No way, Eddie. Not a chance in hell."

"Lucy, come on—you haven't even heard what I'm asking for yet."

Standing behind her desk, Detective Orr closed her eyes a moment and held up her hands like she was stopping traffic. "I don't need to know. Take this down in your notebook," she said, pausing a beat. "There is no way in hell that I could give up what you're about to ask for—no chance, no how, not in *this* lifetime, or the next one, and things are looking doubtful for the lifetime after that."

At least she's thinking about it.

The desk in Detective Orr's tiny office was strewn with manila folders and computer printouts. Eddie couldn't help himself; he glanced to the pile, just for a second—he couldn't read anything because the damn type was too light.

Don't they replace the toner around here?

Orr frowned, reached for a stack of printouts and flipped them over. "I got a lot of work to do," she said.

To most people that might have sounded like an invitation to scram; to Eddie it sounded like an opening. "I can help," he offered.

He smiled while his inner librarian ransacked his brain for any shred of logic that could explain how giving reporter Eddie Bourque some secret inside blab might aid the police investigation.

"I don't even want to ask."

"It's simple, really," Eddie said, stalling. His librarian was screaming and shoving over the bookcases. Eddie picked one word, almost at random. "Pressure."

Orr perked. "Huh?"

Eddie verbalized the brand-new thought as he was creating it: "You guys publicly released the kidnapper's photos of Roger Lime to turn up the pressure on whoever grabbed him, to educate the public into a tip generator. If they try to move Lime, he gets recognized and your phones light up."

She nodded slowly. "Right," she said, sounding suspicious, still searching for the trap.

Eddie turned an invisible valve in the air. "So crank up the pressure. Let me see the ransom note."

Detective Orr blanched, and Eddie talked faster: "When the kidnappers see their own note quoted word-for-word in a news story running in papers across the country, they'll feel heat. Maybe somebody will recognize the syntax and rat them out. You see what I'm saying? Is it handwritten? If it is, even better. Just leave it near a photocopier and turn your back." Eddie winked. "Presto—you can say you have no idea how that note got to the press, because you didn't see a thing."

Detective Orr looked at him and sighed. She pulled the vinyl-padded chair out from under her desk. The wheels screeched like an old shopping cart. She dropped hard on the seat.

Eddie pleaded, "Don't you want to catch the bastards?"

"I can't give you what I don't have," she said, suddenly sounding exhausted.

Delicately, Eddie prodded: "I know it's not exactly, precisely, particularly *your* case, but you have access—"

"There's no note," she interrupted.

She rubbed her eyes and then looked at her hands. "It's the most publicized case this department ever had, and we have no working leads," she said. "None whatsoever." Then she closed her eyes and massaged her temples. "And I can't get myself assigned to the case. I'm being shut out. The whole department is focused on finding Roger Lime, except me." She batted a stack of printouts with her hand. "I'm following the suicide of a medical examiner with a guilty conscience, or maybe with psychosis."

"So you think it was suicide?"

She looked at him. "Not for the record, at least not yet. Okay?"

Eddie hated taking tips off the record. He would never burn a source by printing something he had been told in confidence, so an off-the-record conversation sometimes made him feel like he was typing his story in handcuffs. But Lucy Orr was no ordinary source. She was the only friend Eddie had outside the newspaper business.

"Off the record," Eddie affirmed. "But I reserve the right to badger you into going on the record later."

She gave a sad smile. "We don't know what happened to Crane," she admitted. "The rope marks around his neck angle up toward his ears. Those abrasions—and the note, and the ladder—say suicide."

Eddie sensed a "but." He waited.

Orr continued, "But there's a bruise at the base of his skull we can't account for."

"I don't understand. A bruise?"

"Like maybe that's where a killer leveraged his hand when he choked Crane to unconsciousness, before he dangled him from the noose." She demonstrated, jamming her left palm into a make-believe neck, while her right hand jerked an invisible rope. "And then there's the noise you heard," she added. "You might have stumbled onto a murder minutes after it happened."

Eddie's imagination superimposed a life-sized image of the man in the ski mask, a noose in his hand, behind Detective Orr.

Eddie shut his eyes, willed the fantasy away. He looked at Orr. "Let's go with this a minute," he said. "The killer hears me calling for Dr. Crane and beats it. But he can't be sure I didn't spot him. So after your colleague, Detective Brill, releases my name to the headline whores from Boston TV, the killer follows me from home, lies in wait all afternoon and then offers me a body massage with his Goodyear radials."

Orr rubbed her palms together. "Could be, Eddie," she said. "But you've been in the news business a long time. We can't say how many people you might have pissed off over the years. It could have been an unhappy reader playing out an old grudge."

"There's no such thing as coincidence," Eddie said, stabbing his index finger on her desk for emphasis. His own words brought to mind Henry's tip about the disappearance of Roger Lime. He needed to find Henry's old partner, and Detective Orr could help.

"It's time I come clean with you about something I'm working on," Eddie said. He tapped his notebook. "Gimme half an hour to file this piece on the new picture, so the General and I can pay our rent."

◇ ◇ ◇

After Eddie filed an eighteen-inch story, he met again with Orr in her office.

She made a few notes in a handheld computer as Eddie described his brother's background, the letter Eddie had received from him and the strange tip Henry had offered during the prison visit.

When Eddie had finished, Orr tapped a stylus on her tiny computer and scrolled through her notes. She looked perplexed, as if in pain and trying to decide if badly hurt.

Finally, she said, "Are you thinking that Dr. Crane invented his testimony thirty years ago, to put your brother away?"

Eddie spread his hands. "I don't want to go that far—yet." The statement was one part lie, one part true. He was eager to believe his brother was not a killer, yet afraid to invest any hope in the long odds that Henry could ever establish his innocence. "I need to check out what Henry is telling me. I can't even be sure his old partner is still alive, or that he ever got out of prison."

Orr rubbed her chin. "Lots of those long-timers don't get out. Once they see how slow the time passes, they quit on life and pick up new charges—assaults mostly, occasionally attempted murder, or the successful kind."

Orr turned toward her desktop computer. "If this guy did get out, after all that time, he'll be on the probation rolls for the next thousand years."

She banged the keys.

Eddie laughed. "You type with two fingers—like me."

"I type at the speed I think," she said, pounding the poor plastic keys like they were the skulls of her enemies. "Any extra typing ability would only be wasted capacity."

Eddie smiled. Lucy Orr was practical to the point of being eccentric about it.

"Ah," she said, and stopped typing. "According to this, Mr. James J. Whistle is no longer a guest of the state. Wow—he got out early this year. He's on intensive probation, of course. The probation record is clean and complete, no unexplained absences or positive drug screens."

Eddie sunk to one knee behind her, and leaned in to read over her shoulder.

Orr shifted to block his view. "Sorry, Ed," she said. "These records are private. I can tell you that your man is out of state custody because that's public information, but there's a lot of personal info here that I can't release."

"I understand," Eddie said. He lowered his head in disappointment.

"Thanks."

She waited until Eddie began to stand, and then turned her attention to the spreadsheet on her computer.

As Eddie slowly rose, his chin lifted, as if pulled by a force outside his will. His eyes raked the computer screen, digesting the green block letters on Orr's ancient computer. A moment later he was standing, head bowed like a penitent.

Orr banged one key. The information vanished from her computer. She picked up her handheld organizer and tapped in some notes. "I'll put Mr. Whistle on my list of subjects to interview in connection with Dr. Crane's suicide," she promised. "I'll be interested if anything your brother told you gets a reaction from Whistle."

Eddie smacked a fist into his palm. "Lean on him," he said. "He's gotta know something."

Orr flipped her handheld computer onto a stack of papers. "I can't do that, Eddie," she said. "Your brother's crazy story…" She paused, clucked her tongue, stared at the wall a moment, and then gently started over: "With a perfect probation record, we have to assume that James Whistle is trying to start a new life. Until there's some evidence otherwise, I'm not going to do anything except ask a few simple questions, all right?"

Eddie couldn't stop nodding. He heard himself say, "Perfectly clear," as his brain worked out the shortest route to the address he had spied on her computer.

Chapter 11

Jimmy Whistle's apartment house was a tan triple-decker, with cream-colored trim and a brick foundation, in Centralville, a crowded neighborhood chopped up into maddening little streets that unexpectedly dead-ended, merged at odd angles or suddenly became one-way. This neighborhood, like Eddie's Pawtucketville, was north of the Merrimack, and west of where the money was in Lowell. It was hard to avoid a Jack Kerouac connection in any part of Centralville; his family lived all over it. Whistle's place was three blocks from Baulieu Street, where Kerouac's brother, Gerard, died of rheumatic fever in 1926, when Gerard was nine and Jack Kerouac was four. Thirty years later Kerouac wrote a book about Gerard. He never got over losing his brother.

Eddie tipped the cabbie heavy and sent him along. Then he surveyed the neighborhood.

There was a Brazilian restaurant across the street. A sign in the window said, *Closed for renovations*, which was code around here for "cash flow problems, need another loan." To the left of Whistle's place was another triple-decker, stripped of paint down to the bare gray wood, except the trim, which was pink. To the right was a square patch of yellow sand, weeds sprouting here and there. Whatever had stood there had been recently torn down.

There were no pedestrians in this part of the neighborhood, and no sidewalks. Just cars on their way to someplace more important.

Down the street, some of those cars turned into an upscale fitness club, a recent charge by the forces of gentrification.

Eddie climbed the steps and knocked. A window shade moved and a muffled voice yelled from inside the house, "Yeah?"

"Mr. Whistle?"

The shade fell back. "That shithead's around the side."

Around which side? Eddie walked toward the sand patch. The only door on that side was high above, at the second level, which led out into nothing. Maybe the person who built this place had figured on adding a deck. Or maybe he installed the door for his in-laws.

Eddie continued around the house. The backyard had not been mowed in a long time, if ever; the grass was waist-high and spitting seeds. Eddie could see an old-fashioned bicycle, single speed, with rust-spotted chrome fenders curved over the tires, on its side a few feet into the grass, at the end of a skinny track worn through the weeds.

Around the other side of the house, ten concrete steps led down to a white basement door.

Where else could he be?

Eddie stepped down three steps and then caught himself. What cover story would he use? That he was writing about ex-cons? That he wanted Whistle's comments for a retrospective on Greater Lowell's most mysterious double homicides? That Eddie was selling subscriptions to *Grit?*

I'm here for the truth…I won't lie to get it.

The door had a round window, like a porthole, shrouded by newspaper hung from the inside.

He knocked three times.

Eddie could hear somebody moving around inside, though nobody answered.

He pounded harder.

A man growled from behind the door, "Fuck you, bastards! I paid for two months on the first, and you won't get another cent from me until the end of next month. Goddam bloodsucker."

Eddie felt his eyebrows levitate. "Mr. Whistle?"

"Did you hear me, bastards?"

"I'm not the landlord, Mr. Whistle. I don't want money. I just want to talk to you."

The apartment was silent a moment. Then the door opened twelve inches and a head peeked around. "Talk to me?" He sounded curious, not angry. "Who the hell wants to talk to me?" Eddie got a whiff of Skin Bracer aftershave, the original scent that smelled like a barbershop.

Jimmy Whistle was older than Eddie had expected, late sixties, probably. He was Eddie's height, a little better than six feet. He had a reddish complexion, a big swollen nose and wore black-rimmed rectangular glasses, which magnified his deep brown eyes. The muscles at the corners of his lips were unnaturally tight, locking his mouth in a grimace; it gave him the look of a man forever agonizing over a tough decision. Whistle's voice was deep and clear, and Eddie guessed he probably was a good singer.

The head in the doorway looked Eddie over. "Do I know you," Whistle said, "because I think I know you."

"You don't. I'm a reporter, and I have a couple questions."

Whistle looked into his apartment, and then back at Eddie. "It's a mess in here."

"Two minutes, Mr. Whistle."

Whistle turned away, muttering, but he left the door open. Eddie followed him into a dank living room transported from the 1970s. Butter yellow plastic tile covered the walls, under a drop ceiling painted mold-green. The room was furnished with two ancient upholstered chairs that the Salvation Army wouldn't have accepted if you stuffed the cushions with money. The room smelled faintly of cigarette smoke and General Gao's chicken. Takeout food containers, a pizza box and about thirty orange Moxie cans littered the coffee table.

Whistle wore maroon penny loafers, no socks, tan slacks and a loose blue pullover, like something a hospital patient would wear. He looked around the apartment and spread his hands. "A shithole, like I said."

He didn't look like a killer. He looked like a lonely old man, as if he had recently become a widower and was struggling to care for himself after a lifetime of depending on a woman to buy his clothes, make his meals, clean his mess and find the TV clicker when it slid under the sofa. Prison had been James J. Whistle's wife. They had been married thirty years.

Looking him over, Eddie listened for the screams of James J. Whistle's victims—not just the armored car guards, shot or stabbed and buried somewhere in a shallow grave that nobody had ever found, but for all the people he had victimized early in his career. What had Jimmy Whistle been as a young man? Gang leader? Street punk? Strong-arm robber? How many people did he maim before the men in the armored car? Eddie listened, but heard only the wheeze of an old man.

He took out his notebook and plunged into the interview. "I'm a freelance writer working on a story—"

"What's your name?" Whistle demanded, calm but firm. He lifted his head and peered at Eddie under his glasses.

Eddie tapped his pen on the pad, stalling. He had promised himself he wouldn't lie to get the truth. And maybe it would help if Whistle knew who he was. He said, "My name is Bourque. You knew my brother."

Whistle's eyes narrowed and he nodded slowly. "Now I see how I know you." He backed up toward an end table made from creamy white plastic. Keeping his eyes on Eddie, he reached down, opened the drawer and took out a gun.

Eddie's throat tightened. He stiffened in place.

Whistle laid the black pistol on the table and stood beside it. Quietly, he said, "What do you want, Bourque?"

Eddie tore his eyes from the gun, and looked at his brother's old partner. Whistle had not pointed the weapon at Eddie. The message was more of a warning than a threat. Eddie said, "Is it legal for an ex-con on probation to have a firearm?"

"Is it healthy to have a nine millimeter slug bore through an eye into your brain? What the fuck do you care about legality after that?"

Eddie tried to stand at-ease, resting his weight on one leg. *He just wants to scare me.*

"Tough point to argue from my position," Eddie said.

Whistle's mouth smiled, but his eyes weren't involved. "Funny man, like your brother. He was a comedian—yep, a homicidal comedian. Did you come here to even the score for him? Well, you can forget it. I said what I had to on the witness stand." He glanced to the gun, then back at Eddie. "Don't forget that I went to prison, too. I did every goddam minute of the time I got. Henry can do the same. It's been more than thirty years. The statute of limitations has expired on his revenge."

Eddie suddenly realized that Jimmy Whistle wasn't trying to scare him, he was scared *of* him. Still, Eddie needed to tread lightly. He had covered enough murder trials to know that fear can reach critical mass and ignite anger, and that guns have a mysterious knack for going off when somebody in the room is angry.

"I'm not here to get back at you for testifying against my brother," Eddie said in a calm voice. He shrugged. "I wasn't even born then."

"Then what's your question?" he said, sounding impatient.

"Was my brother into woodworking?"

Whistle's mouth drooped open. "You hunt me down in my home, after thirty years…" He batted the air in Eddie's direction to show his disgust.

"Henry said he made a table before he got arrested."

"I don't remember."

"Light-colored wood," Eddie said. "Made it by hand, he told me. A five-sided table. I need to know if he's telling the truth. So if you don't remember a specific project he did, can you at least remember if he ever worked with wood?"

Whistle smacked his lips, grabbed his chin and looked to the floor. After a few moments he said, "The kid mentioned he wanted a workshop, I think."

"You *think?*"

Whistle's eyes flickered up at Eddie's hard tone, but that was all. He continued, "We were gonna split the score down the middle." He closed his eyes and laughed softly. "I was heading to Amsterdam, first class, with my dough."

"Amsterdam?"

"It was like Oz to the younger version of myself. Booze and hookers, no rules if you don't hurt nobody, and I figured that with my share of the money I could afford not to hurt anyone ever again." He gazed off and seemed to lose himself in an old regret.

"And Henry?" Eddie prompted.

"He wanted a big house right here in Lowell, the best part of Upper Belvedere." He snapped at Eddie, as if a thought had suddenly occurred to him: "Do *you* live up that way?"

"At the moment I couldn't afford a refrigerator crate in Belvedere."

Jimmy Whistle smiled, pleased by the answer. "Your brother had a place picked out—don't ask me where after all these years. Said it had land where he could build himself a workshop, someplace to put his tools."

Eddie jumped in, "He used tools? Woodworking tools?"

Whistle nodded. "I think he did. You know, I remember him whittling now and then, too—not really making anything, just shaving away a stick. But he seemed to enjoy it. So, yeah, I suppose he might have been a woodworker—I can't say I knew the kid too personally."

Eddie wiped his sweaty hands on his pants. Whistle's recollections seemed as close to confirmation as Eddie was going to get. The first part of Henry's story checked out, sort of—he *could* have made the five-sided table. But the second part—what Henry had done with his creation—would be harder to confirm.

I gave away the table I made to my partner's old lady.

How to bring up the subject? Eddie stalled, strolling toward a dusty window, high on the wall, which looked out to the weeds in the backyard. He had a hundred questions about Henry for Jimmy Whistle. "What was my brother like?"

Whistle snorted. "You really don't know, do you?"

"I've met him once."

"It was like that kid was made of electricity," Whistle said. "Nothing but nerve—raw nerves twisted together and stretched tight, like those power lines that are so fucking dangerous they put them on towers a hundred feet tall. He was all nerve, and no brain. He didn't understand there could be a downside to risk." Whistle paused, looked at Eddie. "Henry Bourque was a beast."

Eddie felt a sting in his throat, like he had been punched in the Adam's apple. He tried to swallow the feeling, but it wouldn't go away. "There's a lot I don't understand about the robbery," he said. "How'd Henry get involved? How'd you guys ever plan it? How did you get control of the truck?"

"Too long ago," Whistle said. "Who can remember?"

"Can we at least start with how you got the truck *open*?"

Whistle shifted, uncomfortably. "Like I said at the trial, I didn't deal with the details." He looked at his wristwatch. "I got things to *do*, Bourque. We're almost finished, right?"

Eddie didn't believe him. He couldn't imagine Jimmy Whistle had anything to *do* but drink soda and watch the calendar from this little basement prison cell he had created for himself. And Eddie didn't believe that Whistle had forgotten the details of the heist. Whistle had paid his debt to society in prison, so why wouldn't he talk about the robbery? After all these years, what was there to hide?

Eddie stepped to a faded color picture in a plain black frame, hung eye-high on a wall. A redheaded little boy in the picture, probably five years old, had his right arm cocked back, holding a softball. The ball looked huge in his hand. His face was determined; he was going to make a good throw.

Eddie turned. Jimmy Whistle was watching him watch the picture.

"My kid," Whistle said. "Jimmy junior." His lip quivered.

"Jimmy junior," Eddie repeated, marveling at the revelation that Whistle was a father. He studied the picture again. Maybe there was a resemblance, around the chin. The boy in the photo didn't fit Eddie's image of James J. Whistle. He had pegged

Whistle as a former street thug, nothing more. He reached a hand toward the picture, to take it off the wall for a closer look.

Whistle thundered, "Leave him ALONE!"

Eddie's hand jerked back as if scalded. "I was just—"

"Just NOTHING! You wanna talk to me? I'm over here."

Eddie felt the interview crumbling. He grasped for better footing. "What's your boy like now?"

Whistle rubbed a knuckle beneath his nose and grumbled, "How would I fucking know? I took that picture the month I got pinched. Last time I saw my kid, I was in the back of a squad car. He was crying and I think he pissed his pants." He laughed, sad and ironic. "I think we had both pissed ourselves. Five years of fathering was all that boy ever got. I hope it was enough. I saw to it that he was taken care of, protected—but you can't be a father through a wall."

It was the opening Eddie needed. He made a seamless transition to the question he needed to ask.

"What about his mother?"

Whistle bristled. He grew belligerent again. "What of her?"

"Who was she? What happened to her?" He hesitated. "Did she know my brother, too?"

"Hah! I wouldn't have let Henry Bourque within a mile of her, or anybody else I cared about."

Jimmy Whistle seemed to gather himself, as if preparing for a great leap. He said bitterly: "Not that it's any of your goddam business, but what *happened* to her? What happens every day to women like her? The trusting types—the one's who get conned by bad men? You need to know what happened to her? She wrote me in the county jail every day before my trial. She said she knew I'd never hurt nobody—and that's gotta make you laugh, because back then I hurt *everybody*. She couldn't wait for my trial because she knew no jury could ever convict me."

His eyes glistened. He ranted, within reach of the gun: "So then I pled out—took the thirty years. And still she don't believe who I am." He mocked a woman's voice: " 'Why'd you take the rap, Jimmy? Who are you protecting, Jimmy?'

"Uhhhh," he groaned. "She didn't get it. She came to the joint every week to see me. Said she'd wait, which was stupid on it's face, wasn't it?" He whipped off his glasses and shook them at Eddie, as if expecting an answer.

"Stupid? I dunno…"

"Oh, the hell you don't. To promise yourself to a man who can't touch you until he's too old to want to?" He slid his glasses back on. "I should have let her go, but I didn't. I *wanted* her to wait. To be locked behind that door, and know she was outside…" He suddenly dropped his head and was quiet.

Eddie put the gun out of his mind. He forgot about news stories and deadlines, about what he might write tomorrow. James Whistle had ranted his way to the edge of the truth. In a voice firm and gentle, Eddie pushed him over the edge.

"Tell me what happened, Mr. Whistle."

Whistle gave a little shrug. He said, "Her letters stopped coming so often, and she'd miss a visit now and then—always for something important, it seemed. But ten months into a thirty-year sentence, I had to ask if there was somebody else. She couldn't get the words out, but she didn't have to. We were never married, so there was no paperwork. A small thing in the big scheme, I guess, but I appreciated it at the time.

"She kept coming to see me, regardless, out of guilt maybe. A man in prison—with nothing to do and all day to do it—gets to be a good observer. I noticed the strain on her, and then I noticed the bruises. Her boyfriend was slapping her around. She denied it, protected him, told me she had fallen on ice or fell off her bike."

"You didn't believe her?"

"She lied like shit—never learned to do it right, even after being with me. If you've never been locked up you can't understand the frustrations of a powerless man. Imagination is a potent evil. I could imagine her, falling under a *fist*, with Jimmy junior hiding in a closet. Well, one day she showed up with makeup smeared over a black eye. I went back to my cell, tore the metal frame off my mirror and ground it all night against the concrete, until it was sharp enough to cut the last page of Revelations from my Bible.

"I could have been a killer that night," he said. "If I could have reached this cocksucker who was hitting her, I would have gouged out his heart and pissed down the hole. But the only person I could punish for hurting her...was me." He turned his palms up and showed Eddie the faded scars, from biceps to wrists, like he had tried to unzip his arms and dump the life out. "Well, she heard about what I had done and couldn't handle it. She was getting engaged, she told me, and moving to New Hampshire."

Whistle flushed with anger. "I begged her not to go. I demanded." His voice cracked, and he screamed, "I *threatened* her!"

He looked at Eddie, his face twisted in smoldering rage.

Eddie felt a stab of guilt at dragging Jimmy Whistle backward in time over the jagged parts of his life. But he needed to find this woman, to see if Henry had given her what he had made from wood. The table might lead to Roger Lime, but more importantly for Eddie, it would be evidence that Henry had been telling the truth, that maybe he wasn't as crazy as he seemed. Eddie needed this woman's name. Married name, maiden name—anything he could use to find her. He sensed that Jimmy Whistle was about to throw him out. He had one more question.

"Did she marry him, Jimmy?"

The answer came from someplace deep in Whistle's belly. It roared out in a spray of spit, "That night," he thundered, "*he fucking killed her!*"

Chapter 12

Eddie slumped in the back of the cab.

She was dead? Dead thirty years?

He massaged his temples.

…my partner's old lady.

Jimmy Whistle had seemed sure that Henry had never known this woman. Could Henry have known her behind Jimmy's back?

Perhaps, but what about the five-sided table? Eddie muttered out loud, "It's a table, not a piece of jewelry. You don't give a *table* to a secret lover."

The cabbie checked out Eddie in the mirror. "You all right, man?" He was maybe thirty-five, fair skinned and boyish. Eddie saw his profile for a moment as he turned to glance over his shoulder. His nose was long and pointed, with a bump just below the bridge. The back of his head was a thatch of brown cowlicks.

"I don't give up easy," Eddie said. "But I can't imagine what to do next." He stared out the window, feeling no need to explain.

"Gotcha—no specifics," the cabbie said. "Who needs 'em? I drove the night shift seven years, picking up people after last call, so I've heard every problem any guy could have. Lemme give you my standard advice package, no charge." He smiled at Eddie in the mirror. "If it's a woman, say you're sorry. If it's a man, bust him in the jaw. If it's a bottle or a needle, be tough enough to get some help. If it's your boss, tell him to screw—pardon my English—and then walk outta there with your pride. If it's family, well, then you've got real problems. Just bite on a piece of leather and think happy thoughts until the throbbing in your head goes away." He laughed.

Eddie chuckled. "Are these seats leather?"

"From high-tech synthetic cows."

"I'm low-tech," Eddie admitted. "My razor only has two blades." His cell phone buzzed in his pocket. "Excuse me," he told the driver. He checked the caller-ID and saw his own home number.

My number? What the hell?

Eddie had once tried to teach General VonKatz to turn on the VCR whenever the cat wanted to watch his bird tapes, but the General never got it; he would just fall asleep on the clicker. Had he figured out the phone? *Ed? It's the cat. On your way home, pick up a salmon.*

Eddie answered, "Bourque, here. Who's this?"

The phone squealed, "Hey little brother, it's Bobbi."

"Bobbi? What are you doing there? How'd you get in my house?"

"Oh, come on—your security is a joke, Eddie. It's like breaking into kindergarten."

"I don't know what that's supposed to mean…."

She cut him off with a laugh, and then said urgently: "Remember the pasta salad in the pink Tupperware? That wouldn't be spoiled, would it?"

She had lost him. No wonder Bobbi and Henry got along so well—neither believed in smooth transitions between ideas. Eddie struggled to understand. *Pasta salad?*

"In your fridge," she added. "In the crisper drawer."

"Oh! From the land of forgotten leftovers? Sheesh, I wouldn't eat that. It's still there because the landfill won't take hazardous materials." He laughed.

She paused. "But I already ate it."

Eddie slapped his palm against his head. "Oh, well, it's probably all right." The cabbie was smiling at Eddie in the mirror.

Eddie shrugged and gave him a look: *see what I mean?* "I'm on my way home now," he said. "Maybe we can have dinner, or something."

Penicillin, maybe?

"No time," she said. "Busy, busy, busy. I'll be gone by the time you get here, but I'll see you in the morning."

"Gone? Then why did you break *in?*"

"I needed a telephone, silly. You Bourque boys!" She laughed. "I'll see you at seven tomorrow, so be ready to go."

Eddie had lost his will to argue, and nearly his will to live. He held his head and said in a small voice, "Where are we going?"

"To see Sandra Lime, the so-called widow Lime."

"Roger Lime's wife?"

"Who knows Roger Lime better? Maybe we can learn something the police overlooked that could help us find him. Rescuing Lime would prove that Dr. Crane was a fraud, and then Henry can get a new trial. If nothing else, we have to persuade your block-headed big brother that it's worth hiring the best lawyer to fight for his freedom."

Eddie admired her certainty. Envied it, too. "I'm amazed you were able to get us an appointment with Sandra Lime."

"Eh," she said, like it was no big deal. "I told her secretary that you were Roger Lime's off-shore bookie, and you had dog track winnings to present to Sandra."

"What!" Eddie bolted up. He banged his head on the roof and crumpled in a heap on the back seat.

Bobbi snickered. "My gawd!" she said. "You Bourque brothers are *gullible*. I told Mrs. Lime that you were a writer working on her husband's biography, and you needed her help to write the ending."

"But that's not true, either," Eddie complained, unsure if she was kidding again.

"It's closer to true."

"Bobbi," Eddie said, pausing to calm down before he flung himself from the cab, "I'm a journalist. I can't lie to sources when I'm working on a story."

"You didn't—I did." She giggled. "See you at seven. Gotta go, I think that pasta salad is repeating on me."

"But…"

"Don't forget to have some cash on hand tomorrow to pay for our cab! Ta-ta!"

She hung up, leaving Eddie sputtering into his telephone.

◇ ◇ ◇

General VonKatz woke Eddie twice in the morning.

The first time was shortly after daybreak, when the General trampolined off Eddie's chest on a running jump to the window. Eddie gasped awake, then groaned. The cat whined at whatever was outside. In a half-dreamy state, Eddie thought of the man in the ski mask, and then snapped awake. He listened. A gentle rustling outside quickly grew distant and disappeared. The General got bored and hopped down.

Eddie grumbled, "Noisy damn raccoons." He drifted toward sleep, close to where the subconscious takes over, when stupid ideas make perfect sense. He thought about how easy it would be to catch raccoons with a giant pit trap in the front yard…

Maybe an hour later, General VonKatz stampeded Eddie and woke him again, when Bobbi slammed open the screen door at two past six.

She pounded the door. "Hoo! Hoo! Hoo! Little brother!"

Eddie squinted at the clock, failed to grasp the significance of the numerals, collapsed on the pillow and mumbled, "Too early."

"Oh Eddie!"

Giant pit trap…

Sharply Bobbi yelled, "Eddie! We gotta go!"

Her voice ripped Eddie from the happy warm palace of sleep and dumped him, cranky and fuzzyheaded, onto the dark tundra of consciousness, an unfriendly place at this time of day, before he had adjusted his perspective with caffeine.

"I'm up," Eddie yelled. He threw off the sheet and walked heavy-footed in his boxers to the front door. As he reached to unlock it, the door popped open. Bobbi stepped in, an American Express card in her hand. She wore white slacks, a floral print top with matching sheer scarf, and an oversized fabric pin in her hair, shaped like a dragonfly. She had an armful of loose newspaper.

"Some jerk threw your paper all over the lawn," she said.

"Bobbi, *please* don't force my door with a credit card," Eddie scolded.

She gave him a wide-eyed innocent look. "I was just letting myself in to save you the trip. What's wrong with that?"

Eddie knew there *had* to be something wrong with it, but he couldn't think of exactly what. He frowned. "Never mind," he said. "Just come in while I make some coffee."

"You going to put some pants on?"

"No," he said as he walked away. "I thought I'd try my luck with Mrs. Sandy Lime by showing up in my underwear. I hear she's loaded."

Bobbi laughed. "Somebody's bitchy in the morning."

"It's still *night*."

Eddie chose a potent bean from Zimbabwe for his morning quart of joe. While it dripped, he slid into his one good outfit: gray worsted wool trousers, white dress shirt, blue Brooks Brothers blazer with gold buttons. After debating a moment, he chose his lucky necktie, a beige silk dotted with tiny blue circles, each with a red letter "B," the emblem of the Boston Red Sox.

The General bounced onto the piano keys and played a dark chord as he bounded to the top of the instrument.

"Your cat needs another piano lesson," Bobbi said.

"He plays better than I do."

Eddie poured coffee into a heavy crystal wine glass and gulped it black. Instantly, he felt his mood brighten. It was all in his head; there was no way the caffeine could enter his bloodstream that quickly. But what did it matter *how* it worked, so long as it did? He put the glass down with a hearty, "Ahhh!"

Bobbi picked up the bag of coffee beans and read the label. "From Zimbabwe? Is this a joke?"

"Everybody thinks the best java is South American," Eddie said. "But the African coffees can compete with the best from anywhere."

She dropped the bag on the counter. "Give me sweet tea and I'm fine." She opened Eddie's freezer and looked over the bags of beans. "Where do you get all these weird coffees?"

Eddie sipped his second cup. "The Internet—I buy everything on-line."

"Aren't you afraid of identity theft?"

"My identity they can have, it's my money I can't afford to lose." The caffeine was starting to thaw Eddie's brain. "I thought you were going to be here at seven."

She closed the freezer and opened the refrigerator. "No, we have to be *there* at seven. I'm here early to make sure you're awake for our cab. Are these sweet pickles?"

"I'm sick of cabs," Eddie said. "I'm going to call a buddy of mine for some transportation on loan, while I look for a car I can afford."

Bobbi opened the pickle jar and sniffed. She frowned. "Sour dills," she said, and put the jar back.

"Our strategy today should be simple," Eddie offered. "I lay out the truth for Mrs. Lime and then ask for her help. No con job, no lies."

Bobbi rolled her eyes. "That is soooo boring," she said. "And what will she think if we admit we're interested in her husband's abduction because it might overturn Henry's murder conviction? Won't she be insulted?"

"We don't have to say that part," Eddie said. Bobbi's eyes twinkled, and Eddie realized he had already nibbled away at his own his plan to tell Mrs. Lime the truth. He felt an uncomfortable heaviness in his stomach. "Now hold on a second—"

The telephone rang.

"Hold that thought," he said to Bobbi, and then answered the phone. "Hello, this is Bourque."

"Eddie?" said a nasally voice. "It's Lew Cuhna."

"Lew?" Eddie was surprised. Cuhna had never called him before. He looked to Bobbi, shrugged, and then held up one finger, to ask for one minute of patience. She nodded and busied herself organizing Eddie's *Washington Post* on the breakfast table.

Eddie said, "How are you, Lew? Your paper has looked good the last couple weeks."

"Forget all that," Cuhna said. "I've left you messages just in case, but I can't take it anymore. We gotta talk, Ed."

"I haven't gotten any messages. Do you mean my cell phone?"

"No, no—it doesn't matter. I need to see you right away."

"I'm on my way out. How about this afternoon?"

"Fine, fine. At my office, two o'clock?"

Eddie grabbed a pencil and looked around for paper. There was none. He scribbled a note to himself on the countertop. "Your place at two. What's this about, Lew?"

"See you there." He hung up.

Eddie put the phone down.

"Sounds to me like you have a friend in trouble," Bobbi said.

Eddie rubbed the stubble on his chin. "Not exactly a friend."

A car pulled up outside, tires crunching on the sand at the side of the road.

Bobbi stood and looked out the window. "Our cab is early," she said. "Let's help your brother before you help anybody else."

As she walked past the piano, a little gray arm shot out and plucked the dragonfly from her hair. Bobbi grabbed her head. "He stole my pin!"

The General jumped down from the piano with his prey in his jaws. Eddie lunged for him, but the cat was ridiculously quick when he wanted to be. The General changed directions like a jackrabbit, flashed between Eddie's legs, and vanished into the bedroom. Eddie stumbled into the coffee table, knocked over his chess set and cracked his shin. The coffee table tipped on two legs, then slowly turned over and crashed to the floor. Eddie staggered over the up-turned table, lost his balance, tucked into a partially controlled somersault, and came to rest on his back, staring at the ceiling.

He didn't move.

"Are you hurt?" Bobbi asked.

He pointed. "I'm noticing some cobwebs up there."

◇ ◇ ◇

Sandra Lime lived in a low, sprawling modern home, behind a chest-high stone wall of such meticulous construction that there wasn't a crack between the stones big enough to stick your thumb in. Two white concrete lions guarded the driveway. Behind the walls, the yard was landscaped minimally with dogwoods, white pine, and clumps of fern. There was a kidney-shaped putting green in front of the house with six practice holes marked with flagsticks.

Eddie pounded the knocker three times. After a few moments, the chain and deadbolt began to rattle from within, and Eddie whispered to Bobbi, "I do the talking, and we tell the truth."

Her eyebrows shot up.

"Most of the truth," Eddie corrected himself.

The gigantic doorman looked like a professional football player moonlighting for extra cash in the off-season.

They followed him to a sunroom, where Sandra Lime was waiting. She was short and petite, maybe five foot four, with a pointy chin and thin, colorless lips. Her skin was smooth and perfect, her eyes a striking deep brown. Her hair was speckled with gray, and cut as short as Eddie's. The style might have looked too boyish on a less attractive woman, but on her, it worked. She wore a tailored grey pants suit, over a white blouse and a simple string of pearls.

"You're the writer," Sandra Lime said to Eddie. Her voice was ragged, too old for the rest of her.

Eddie nodded. "Yes, ma'am."

"Ma'am is for old ladies," she said. "Call me ma'am again and I'll sic Vincent, my doorman, after you." She didn't smile.

Was that a joke?

"And you're the assistant," Sandra Lime said to Bobbi.

"I am," she said. "But you must be Sandra's *daughter*. Is your mother available?" She smiled sweetly.

"You I like," Mrs. Lime said in the same sharp tone. "Follow me. We'll talk in the den." She spun and marched off.

Bobbi turned to Eddie, flashed a smile full of teeth and followed Sandra Lime. Eddie came last, taking his time, peeking into a room with greenhouse-style windows, a library with rows of built-in bookcases and a bathroom that smelled like strawberries. The den was a pine-paneled room crammed with burgundy leather furniture, a liquid plasma television hung like a painting, and a six-sided poker table covered with red felt. Original watercolors of yachts and seashores decorated the walls.

It had the feel of a hunting lodge, comfortable but not over-the-top. Eddie recalled Roger Lime's biography—he had grown up a street hockey player in the middle-class Lowell Highlands neighborhood; his wealth was earned, not bred into him. And despite his reputation as a hard businessman, many people who knew Lime insisted that the bank president didn't take himself too seriously.

"I want a chamomile," Sandra Lime announced. She put her hands on her hips.

Eddie couldn't decide if she was offering a round of tea.

"Milk and three sugars in mine," Bobbi ventured.

"Nothing here," Eddie said.

Sandra left without another word. When Eddie was confident she was out of earshot, he leaned to Bobbi and said, "This is strange."

"She's a little strict, maybe, but I wouldn't say strange."

"No, I mean look at this place—obviously her husband's game room, yet there are no pictures of him anywhere."

Bobbi glanced around. "I hadn't noticed."

"There were no pictures of Roger Lime in the hall, or any of the other rooms we passed, either."

"Maybe she put them away because they were too painful to look at."

Eddie was about to argue the point, but stopped when Sandra Lime returned with a tall chrome teapot on a silver tray, and two clear glass mugs.

"Fix it how you want it," she told Bobbi.

They reclined on leather. Sandra Lime sipped clear tea, and then got to the point. "I don't know what you're writing about my husband, Mr. Bourque, and I don't care. I would only caution you that the final chapter has *not* been written, and if you publish a piece prematurely, you are sure to be embarrassed."

Eddie took out his notebook. "How do you mean?"

She stared through him. "I mean that Roger has jerked me around with one childish prank after another for more than twenty years of marriage and I'm *sick* of it."

Eddie fought the urge to give Bobbi the I-told-you-so glance. He focused on Sandra Lime. Her forehead was tight, her left hand balled into a little fist, her right gripping the mug tightly.

Bobbi interjected, "So your husband was a joker?"

Sandra wet her lips with her tongue. "His immaturity was charming at first, when I was young. Back then he seemed childlike, not child*ish*. For an overeducated girl raised by nuns in parochial school, Roger was…" She looked away in thought; had a sip of tea, "…he was liberating."

She paused. Eddie thought about prodding her with a question, but decided to wait. Silence can be a great inquisitor; it inspires people to explain.

Bobbi interrupted the quiet: "But he went too far, right?"

Sandra frowned at the question. Eddie ground his teeth. *Don't blow it, Bobbi!*

She didn't. Sandra Lime started a story:

"Five years ago, Roger was out sailing, alone, off the coast of Hull, when he ran up onto a sandbar—I think he was drunk, but I've never proven it. He left the boat at low tide and waded to shore, ran into an old fraternity friend, and went off to drink port wine and play darts, or some such thing. The Coast Guard found his boat, abandoned, saw some fish blood on the deck, and concluded that Roger must have hit his head and dropped overboard."

Sandra Lime paused to warm her tea with a splash from the teapot.

"The report of his *accident* made the radio," she said. "Roger thought it was the most hilarious joke. He could have called in and reported himself safe, but instead he had his friend drive him home so he could watch me mourn for him." She stared out the window with narrow eyes. "I should have thrown a party. That would have shown him. I swore that I'd leave the very day he ever pulled a stunt like that again.

"The whole matter was a terrible embarrassment when it made the paper around here, and the Coast Guard sent a bill for ten thousand dollars in reimbursement for the time they spent searching for him." She sighed, angrily. "Roger paid them in nickels—he thought it was funny."

"I don't remember seeing that story," Eddie said.

"You were working in Vermont," Bobbi reminded him.

"So last spring," Sandra continued, "when the police said he was abducted, I was unable to be afraid. When they told me he was dead, I was unable to mourn. When I opened his will and saw that he wanted his ashes buried in a *green* coffin…" She trailed off and looked into her tea.

Bobbi was sitting forward, like she was about to spring at Sandra Lime.

She'll get there, Bobbi…take it easy!

Sandra whimpered, then quickly caught herself and said flatly, "When will that man stop tormenting me? I picture his funeral in my head and I wonder if he was there, in a disguise, counting the tears on every face to see who missed him most. I just want to know that he's alive, so I can get out of this purgatory, between widow and wife. I just want to slap his face and file for divorce."

She thinks it's a joke.

Mrs. Lime thought her husband had arranged his own kidnapping. There was certain logic to the theory—it would be easier to hide a man who *wanted* to be hidden. He could vanish for a few months, maybe with a mistress in the Bahamas, and then return in pictures as if by magic—or by miracle. But Sandra was overlooking something.

"What about the bones?" Eddie asked. "In the car. Those were *somebody's* bones, if not your husband's."

She looked at Eddie, wide-eyed at what the question implied. "Roger is sick," she said, suddenly defending him. "But he wouldn't have *killed* someone over a prank." She looked at Bobbi, who nodded with gentle reassurance.

Bobbi said to her, "Your husband could have paid somebody to steal a skeleton from an old family graveyard—not that it's *right* to do that."

"A crime," Sandra agreed, "but not murder."

Both women looked to Eddie, as if waiting for him to validate what they both believed for their own reasons—that Roger Lime had faked his own abduction. "I don't know," Eddie said, softly, though he wanted to believe as badly as they did.

Chapter 13

The cab left Eddie and Bobbi on Merrimack Street, in downtown Lowell, in front of the Dunkin Donuts. It was a short walk for Bobbi back to her hotel, and an even shorter walk for Eddie to get another coffee. It was getting close to noon, and Eddie remembered that they hadn't eaten.

"Do you want a hot chocolate or a slice of pizza?" he offered. "There's a good place around the corner."

"Too much to do, too much to think about," Bobbi said. "I'm going to try to call Henry, if he has any phone time left." She stared at him. "Your brother is one stubborn son of a bitch, but I'm going to try my best to convince him it's worth fighting for his freedom."

Eddie knew what she was saying. She wanted him to talk to Henry. He looked to the gum-stained sidewalk. "You're his wife," he said. "I barely know him."

She laughed softly.

Eddie couldn't see the joke. "What?"

"You barely know him?" she said, tears in her eyes. "Ed, you *are* him. Jesus—the two of you are like little clones."

"Huh? Because we're both gullible?"

"Yes, that's one thing. There's about a million others." She reached for him, stroked his neck tenderly one time. "I talk to you and I hear Henry. Like him or not, he's your family. And I promise that if you got to know him, you'd like him."

Eddie sighed heavily. "For my whole life, Henry has been my dark secret," he said. "My closest friends in this city think I'm an only child."

She stepped back and looked at him intensely.

"I see it now," she said. "The shame—a lifetime of it—weighing you down. You're afraid to let it go. How come?"

She waited. Eddie wouldn't answer. She answered for him: "Your shame is some kind of badge of honor for you. 'Look at me,' you can say, 'I'm so *good*, not like that nasty person in jail.'"

She had struck close to the truth, but hadn't reached deep enough. "That's not exactly right," Eddie said, surveying inside himself for the answer. He couldn't see it; it was hiding from him.

Bobbi let out a deep breath and then slumped a little. "Enough berating on my part," she said. "For now." She playfully punched Eddie's shoulder. "Just think about it. You have nothing to lose and a brother to gain. I'll bet he'd give you a battle across a chessboard."

Eddie smiled. "Are you sure you don't want lunch?"

She nodded and hurried off. "I'll be in touch. Thanks, little brother-in-law."

It wasn't like Bobbi to turn down free food, but Eddie didn't complain. He had a meeting with Lew Cuhna in just over two hours, and he had to solve his transportation problems.

But first, more coffee. He bought a hazelnut with cream, and then used his cell phone to dial Durkin at *The Daily Empire*.

After four rings came the answer, "Yo."

"Durk, it's Eddie Bourque looking for another favor."

Durkin chuckled. "The ink truck doesn't come again for two weeks, skinny boy," he teased. "Can you fit in my duffle bag?"

"Different kind of favor—not newspaper files."

"Wanna see if you can fit in the bag anyway?"

Eddie smiled. "That's it, old man," he said. "I will beat you with your own crutches if you don't shut your friggin' pie hole and *listen* for two seconds."

Durkin laughed like a revving chainsaw: "Ha-ha-ha-HAAAAA! HAA!"

"I need transportation," Eddie said, "and I know you're something of a gear head. Can you save me from blowing any more beer money on cab fare?"

"Mmmm," Durkin said. Eddie could picture him stroking his stiff beard. "Possible, Bourque. What's your criteria? Fast? Roomy? Off-road capability?"

"Cheap."

"Ha! Cheap we can do. A buddy I served with in Vietnam just croaked—God rest his soul." Durkin quietly blessed himself, "…name of the Father, Son and Holy Ghost." He continued, "So my buddy's widow gave me his wheels, which I can't use because my left leg is stuck in a cypress tree about nine thousand miles from here, and I haven't had time to modify the vehicle. You can take it as a loaner, until we can track down something you might want to pay for."

"I need it now," Eddie said.

"Of course you do, you demanding little bastard. You know Tony's place?"

"The Italian restaurant?"

"Naw, the other Tony. The auto-garage."

"I thought the cops shut him down for making book."

"He's open again. Got acquitted after a witness refused to testify—he got cold feet."

"Better than cement feet, I guess," Eddie said.

"Meet me at Tony's in twenty minutes and I'll hook you up with a new ride." Durkin chuckled in a way that put a lump in Eddie's throat.

◇ ◇ ◇

Tony's place was a one-story white clapboard garage that sagged in the middle. There were two rusted double-gravity gas pumps outside that probably hadn't moved fuel since Henry Ford stopped here for a fill-up. The side lot was dirt and weeds, with dark oil spots and a row of junked cars—old Buicks, first-generation mini-vans, an ancient green Packard with what looked like bullet holes in the door and—Eddie gasped!—a Chevy Chevette, with four flat tires and patchwork body of Bondo and primer.

I'm in love.

Tony was a stocky guy in his late forties, with rough curly hair, a short black beard, and a limp. He was reading a *Phantom* comic book when Eddie arrived.

Durkin showed up in his black Corvette two minutes after Eddie. He climbed out of the car on his crutches, nodded to Eddie, and then flipped Tony his middle finger.

"I'll snap that thing off and pick my teeth with it," Tony warned.

"How's your foot?" Durkin asked.

Tony shrugged. "Screws are pressing against the skin," he said. "I'm going back next month to get the plate taken out."

"Or I could just countersink the screws into the bone for you," Durkin offered. "Lend me a drill."

They both laughed, and Durkin explained to Eddie, "Biker humor. Everybody gets mangled eventually."

Eddie pointed to the Chevette. "How much?"

Tony looked it over, and then squinted toward heaven, looking like he was performing some complicated calculus in his head. "For that piece of shit, three hundred."

"Sold!" Eddie said.

"And an extra three hundred if you want us to put the engine back in, add some respectable pre-owned tires, and sneak it past the inspector."

Eddie frowned. *Love hurts.* "How about five hundred?"

Tony smiled. "Gimme a week."

"In the meantime," Durkin said, "I'm lending him Chuckie's old ride. Can you bring it around?"

Tony nodded. "If it fucking starts, sure."

Eddie watched him limp around the garage, and then said to Durkin, "I really owe you this time, man."

Durkin patted Eddie's shoulder. "Wait till you see it!"

From behind the garage came a deafening bark, like the sound of battle between two Gatling guns. Tony came riding around the building on the most decrepit motorcycle Eddie had ever seen. Durkin beamed. Tony drove a circle around them, and then killed the engine.

Eddie stared at it, open-mouthed. He said, "What the hell…is *that?*"

"My buddy's old rat bike," Durkin answered.

The motorcycle was painted flat black. It had old-fashioned spoke wheels, a tractor-style seat in the shape of an ass, and black leather saddlebags with brass rivets and leather fringe on the flaps. A greasy black drive chain stretched to the rear wheel. There was no chrome or plastic anywhere on the bike, and every square inch of machine was caked with dusty black grime.

"It looks like what the barbarians rode to chase Mad Max after the apocalypse," Eddie said.

"Mm-hm," Tony said, proudly. "Hardtail frame wrapped around a Harley shovelhead engine."

"Forward controls," Durkin added. He patted the handlebars. "Ever ride a bike with ape hangers like this? They get your hands in the air so the wind can yank out your armpit hair."

Durkin and Tony laughed.

Eddie's mouth went dry.

"Is it leaking?" Eddie asked.

"Aw, shit, Bourque, that ain't nothing," Durkin said. "Don't park it in your living room if you're afraid of a little oil."

"Better the bike leaking than the rider," Tony added. He climbed off, then brushed his hand over the gas tank, which was scuffed and dented. "Had a little road rash when Durk brought it in. I hammered out the worst of it."

Eddie took a closer look. The bike's previous owner had wrapped rosary beads around the handlebar cables, and had glued a two-inch crucifix to the tank, next to a small metal heart. Eddie looked even closer. "A Purple Heart," he said.

Durkin explained, "Yeah, Chuckie got his medal in Vietnam the same day I got mine. We met in the hospital." He looked over the bike, smiling like a proud father. "Sweet machine, huh Bourque?"

Eddie looked to the ground. He kicked a pebble, embarrassed. "Uh, I've never ridden a motorcycle before."

"Never? Not one time?"

"Does renting a motor scooter on the Vineyard count?"

"Not one bit."

"Then never."

Tony shrugged and offered: "It's a fuckin rat bike, just ride it like you stole it."

"He probably needs some more specific instruction," Durkin said.

Tony frowned, thought it over and explained, "Down here on the right-hand side, you flip out this kick-start pedal, pull out the choke, and stomp here to fire it up—assuming it starts."

"Assuming," Durkin agreed.

"Then ease the choke back a bit. This handlebar lever, here on the left, is the clutch. With your left foot, you have your gearshift. First gear is down and the next three are up."

"It's why I can't ride it," Durkin said, wistfully. "Can't shift the gears."

Tony continued, "Your right foot works the rear brake, right hand works the front brake."

Eddie's stomach was tightening. "Should I not use the front brake?" he said. "I don't want to fly over the handlebars."

Tony slapped his own forehead and cried, "That's a negative! This isn't the ten-speed you pedaled to school, boy! Most of your braking power is in the front. An old lump of scar tissue like *me* could ride all day on just the rear brake, but a virgin like *you* would depart this life with a mouthful of road salt. But don't forget to *use* your rear brake, too, and don't lock it up, but if you do lock it up, keep it locked up until you stop. If you let that rear wheel grab traction again in a skid, you'll do a high-sider."

Eddie didn't ask for a definition of high-sider—his brain was swimming with Tony's instructions. It was enough to know that a high-sider probably included the wail of an ambulance and six months of physical therapy.

"If something's in your way," Tony continued, "don't look at it. You'll get target fixation and bore right into the obstacle. Look for your opening instead, and you'll steer right into it. Okay? Any questions?"

The movie in Eddie's head was a full-color loop tape of his battered body turning cartwheels down Route 495 at seventy miles per hour.

"Is this even legal?" Eddie wondered.

Tony shrugged. "The bike's muffled enough to not be a cop magnet, and the tires have just enough tread to pass. It's registered and inspected—though I think the sticker might be stolen. Whatever. Just ride like you're not afraid to be pulled over and you probably won't be."

"Don't I need a special license?"

He gave a backhand wave. "Eh, who knows? I've never had one."

Eddie thought about why he shouldn't take the bike—there were about a hundred reasons. But he couldn't keep taking cabs everywhere.

"I dunno, guys," Eddie said.

Durkin slapped Eddie on the back and sent him staggering two steps. "C'mon Bourque! Who wants to live forever?"

"Well, not forever, necessarily, but I was looking forward to the weekend."

Tony grinned. "I got what you need." He limped to the garage, reached inside the door and came back with a small can.

Durkin smiled. "Industrial degreaser," he explained.

Eddie didn't trust their smirks. "Am I suppose to use it on the bike?"

Tony flipped open a saddlebag and dropped the can inside, into a mess that looked like Eddie's junk drawer at home.

"This is a courtesy for the Department of Public Works," Tony said, "to help them scrub your grease spot off the road the next time this bike lays down in a curve." He slapped Durkin high-five and they both laughed.

Durkin traced the Sign of the Cross again. "Like good ol' Chuckie."

Eddie looked over the fresh scuff marks on the fuel tank, and frowned. "Durkin," he said, "exactly how did good ol' Chuckie die?"

Chapter 14

The black "shorty" helmet on Eddie's head fit like an upturned mixing bowl, barely covering the tops of his ears. Durkin had also given Eddie a pair of round aviator goggles so he wouldn't lose an eye to a stray pebble or an unlucky bumblebee.

The bike handled better than it looked, though it had taken Eddie a dozen harrowing laps around Tony's garage to understand that steering a motorcycle was a little counter-intuitive. He also had to train his foot to shift gears, and he had almost run over Durkin in verifying Tony's warning about "target fixation." Eddie's hands shook on the handlebars every time he thought about Durkin's friend, the late Chuckie, who had died on this bike—under it, actually.

But as he cruised the city's byways toward Lew Cuhna's newspaper office in South Lowell, Eddie enjoyed the warm wind on his face. He enjoyed the odd looks he got from motorists and pedestrians, who seemed to view him as something between nuisance and criminal. He could even learn to overlook the high-velocity grease splatter the bike's chain spit on his pants.

The Second Voice newspaper was in a former laundromat, with apartments on the second floor, overlooking a busy intersection on the outskirts of a commercial zone of big-box department stores. Not the best place for a news office—it was often a slow crawl through traffic to downtown Lowell, the center of city government and the arts community. Cuhna's building was painted light peach with white trim. The paper's name was stenciled in white letters in giant headline font on a picture window that looked into the office. The fluorescent ceiling lights were on inside, but Eddie didn't see anyone at work as he drove up. The digital clock at the bank across the street said that Eddie was three minutes early.

He threaded The Late Chuckie's rat bike down the alley between Cuhna's building and a wallpaper store, and then killed the engine next to a Dumpster. He left his goggles and helmet on the seat and walked to the front door. He was about to knock when he noticed that Lew Cuhna had taped an index card inside the window. It said:

Side door. Wait til nobody's looking!

An arrow pointed to the left side of the building.

Cuhna's cloak and dagger personality was getting annoying.

Eddie walked down a concrete wheelchair ramp and around the side. The door there was glass, formerly the entrance to a diner.

Eddie looked around, made sure nobody was looking, grimaced at his own silliness in going along with Cuhna's note, and then went inside.

The old diner's breakfast counter was still in place, though the stools had been removed. There were no booths, either, just skinny L-shaped spots on the Linoleum, where the booths used to be.

The place was noisy. A radio on the counter was broadcasting the local afternoon talk show—guys yakking and laughing. Eddie heard a low whistling from another room, and, from deeper in the office, some clunky machinery.

"Hey Lew?" he yelled.

Nothing.

Eddie looked around again. The breakfast counter had been turned into a distribution center. Bundles of newspapers, bound by yellow plastic bands, were stacked chin-high. Two gray cabinets stood like sentries on either side of the door. Their drawers were open; a few manila folders were on the floor. Lew Cuhna was either messy, or had tried to find something in a hurry. The walls were covered with calendars given out free by local restaurants and insurance agents, cork bulletin boards papered with take-out menus and scribbles torn from notebooks, and a street map of Lowell, with circuitous distribution routes marked in pink, yellow and green highlighter.

Eddie turned off the radio.

He followed the whistling noise around the breakfast counter, through swinging double doors, and into a kitchen. The kitchen probably hadn't changed much since the building had been a restaurant; it was crowded with gleaming stainless steel appliances and countertops.

The whistle was coming from a round teapot on the stove. Eddie took it off the heat and turned off the flame. He noticed that Lew Cuhna had placed two ceramic mugs on the counter, a bag of chai spice tea in each.

Is he making me tea?

The teapot was nearly empty; most of the water had steamed out.

A side door led to a full bathroom, with sink and tub, a paper towel dispenser, no shower curtain and no mirror. The current edition of *The Daily Empire* was on the floor. The paper had come out in the early afternoon, so somebody had read it in here recently.

Eddie left the kitchen the way he had come in, walked around the counter again, and then into the main newsroom, a former laundromat. Eddie had to agree with what Cuhna had told him—the place had an overpowering smell of lemon detergent.

Nobody was there.

The room was a clutter of former laundry-folding tables, now piled over in documents, files, ancient telephone books, and newsprint. Most of the laundry equipment had been taken out, though there was still an oversized avocado-colored washer pushed against the wall, next to a whirling commercial clothes dryer with a digital countdown timer and a little glass porthole in the door. It was at work drying what sounded like a load of coconuts.

A row of steeply slanted tables against one wall drew Eddie's attention. They were old paste-up stations—the finest in 1980s-era newspaper technology, still in use at *The Second Voice*. Under this production system, a special printer spit news copy in paper strips, the width of a newspaper column. A paste-up artist—at this rinky-dink operation, probably Lew Cuhna himself—would cut the strips of type with a razor knife to the proper lengths to fit on a newspaper page. Using hot wax as glue, the artist arranged the columns of type on cardboard sheets, leaving spaces for the photos to be added later. The completed sheets then went to the camera room. Modern technology had done away with the whole setup; the job could be done more quickly on a computer screen.

A phone rang.

Eddie jumped. He slapped a hand over his heart in relief, feeling a tingle as a squirt of adrenaline upped his blood pressure. He had been invited to come here—there was even a note on the door telling him to come in—but he still felt like an industrial spy who had broken into a competitor's laboratory.

The ringing phone was on a receptionist's desk, near the front door. He considered whether he should answer. Cuhna obviously had ducked out in a hurry, not even bothering to shut off the stove. Maybe he was calling to explain. Would he have expected Eddie to answer the telephone in a foreign newsroom?

Eddie answered. "Hello?"

"*Second Voice?*" said a woman in a clipped tone.

"Yes it's the right number, but—"

"You people owe my bridge club a terrific apology!"

Eddie said, "Ma'am, I'm not the person you want to speak with."

But the caller didn't want to hear any excuses from Eddie Bourque. She berated him: "We were expecting a photographer for our Pawtucketville tournament yesterday, and nobody from your arrogant little paper showed up."

Eddie grabbed a pen. "Uh-huh, uh-huh," he said, taking down the complaint. "I'll pass this message to the editor when he gets back."

"That's it?" she shrieked. "Our tournament is ruined, and you'll make it up to us by *passing a note?*"

Eddie had fielded a hundred angry calls like this one during his journalism career. He had learned that it's not worth thirty minutes to explain why a paper with a tiny staff and ludicrous deadlines can't cover every neighborhood bridge tournament. But calls such as this allowed Eddie to exercise his God-given talent for sounding deathly serious whenever he wanted to, an ironic gift for a joker.

"Oh, I'll pass the note along," Eddie said gravely, "and when Mr. Cuhna gets the message, I expect he'll *fire* the photographer immediately. This newspaper doesn't tolerate mistakes like that. She's outta here."

A pause, then she repeated: "He'll fire her?"

"Neglect of duty is inexcusable, single mother or not."

"She has children?"

Eddie lowered his voice, like he was sharing gossip: "Ever since her husband passed away, she's made one screw up after another. I'm sure that *this* will be the last one."

Her anger now in perspective, the woman decided she wasn't so unhappy after all, and tried to talk Eddie out of giving the note to Mr. Cuhna. Eddie hedged, let her beg for a minute, then promised to throw away the note, and hung up.

He was pleased with himself for getting rid of a complaint and saving Lew Cuhna a headache, when he realized he didn't know what to do—should he leave? Or put the tea back on the stove and wait?

Waiting didn't make much sense. If Cuhna had ducked out for just a moment, he would have been back already. And if some emergency had come up, he would have called, or at least left a note.

Eddie sat at the receptionist's desk to pen his own note, telling Cuhna to call to reschedule. He added his cell phone number at the bottom, and then looked around for some tape.

Bzzzzzzz!

Eddie jumped again.

The commercial clothes dryer was buzzing as its time had expired. Eddie watched the laundry inside spin over.

The note fluttered from his hand.

The dryer load spun once more and Lew Cuhna's face thumped against the glass.

Chapter 15

"*This* one ain't a suicide, that's for damn sure," Detective Orr said dryly. "Wounds around the neck clearly indicate strangulation."

Eddie didn't look at her. He sat on the front steps of *The Second Voice* and watched traffic, as he had for the past two hours.

He said, "The telephone cord was still around his neck when I found him." He stared at a small stone in the parking lot, relaxed his eyes and let his vision blur. "I unwrapped the cord, tried to get him out of there…"

"There was nothing you could have done, Ed."

"The body was hot to the touch. He felt bruised all over. He was fucking *cooking* in that thing."

"He was dead before he went into the dryer, Ed."

"Then why put him in there?"

"Because some people are sick," she snapped. She pulled out her notebook and flipped a few pages. "But more likely, to heat the body to make it impossible to determine when the crime took place. In this case, the medical examiner can't estimate the time of death based on body-heat loss."

"He must have died early this afternoon," Eddie said. "Our appointment was for two. He had water boiling for tea."

"Two mugs," she said. "But you don't drink tea."

Eddie shrugged. "How would he know?" He stiffened as the black-suited men from the funeral home wheeled the black bag on a stretcher to a waiting hearse.

"Are you sure you have no idea what he wanted to see you about?" Orr asked.

"I've been thinking about that. Lew was a strange guy. Last time I saw him, he said he trusted me—or something like that—I thought he was under too much deadline stress. What did he want to tell me? Could have been anything." Eddie put his head in his hands. "I hope it wasn't what got him killed."

"We have to go over the basics, Ed. Can you do it now?"

"Let's get it over with."

Eddie described for Detective Orr the call he had received from Cuhna, and then everything he had done—and everything he had touched—after he had arrived at the news office. She took it all down in shorthand.

"You two didn't have any disagreements, did you?" she asked. "Nothing I'm going to find out about later, right?"

"Lucy!"

She raised a finger and scolded, "You ask tough questions in *your* job, and I don't get offended."

She was right. She was doing her job; it would have been irresponsible for her not to ask. He shrugged. "I barely knew the guy. We met for the first time at the cop shop the day Roger Lime's photo first appeared."

"What was Cuhna's reputation in the news business?" she asked. "Was he aggressive? Could he have been doing an investigative story on some criminal element? Maybe he made some enemies that way."

"Oh, please," Eddie said. Realizing he had sounded dismissive, he explained: "Lew was the editor of the paper and the only writer on staff—all those other bylines were fakes. He had no time for in-depth investigation. That's not even the kind of journalism *The Second Voice* does. They do art reviews, doughnut shop openings, the police blotter, and the school lunch menus, when they're not chasing the daily news a week behind the daily papers."

"I don't like this coincidence," she said. "Kidnappers show Roger Lime holding Mr. Cuhna's newspaper, and then somebody kills Mr. Cuhna."

They watched the hearse drive off, its wheels scuffing over some sand on the parking lot.

"I had an old editor in Vermont," Eddie said, "who said that everything we write is all part of the same story."

Orr thought that over. "I had an old sergeant who used to say pretty much the same thing. That's why I had hoped the tip from your brother would pan out, but no luck. I tracked down your brother's old partner, Mr. Whistle."

Uh-oh. Eddie's stomach flash-froze. He had forgotten that Orr planned to talk to Whistle. If Jimmy told her that Eddie had visited him, too, Orr would suspect that Eddie lifted the old con's address from her office.

He waited for the toothy fake smile that Orr used when she was about to grill him. But the smile didn't come.

"Mr. Whistle was responsive to questioning," she said, slipping into copspeak, "but could not provide any information useful to the investigation."

How about that! Eddie marveled at the irony—Jimmy Whistle testified against Eddie's brother thirty years ago, but he hadn't ratted on Eddie.

"Did he remember anything about Henry?" Eddie asked, probing as his gut thawed.

"He could not provide any information useful to the investigation," she repeated. She gave him the piano key smile, and Eddie knew to drop the subject.

He took a deep breath to reboot his RAM, and focused on Lew Cuhna. "I suppose there will be a funeral," he said.

Detective Orr was busy with her notes.

"Did Lew have a family?" Eddie asked.

"Huh?"

"Next-of-kin, in copspeak," he said. He gave a sad smile.

Orr frowned. "No family that we know of." She flipped to the first page of her notebook. Eddie liked that—her first questions had been whether the dead man had family. "I spoke to the advertising manager at this newspaper. He told me that Mr. Cuhna's parents had passed away. Cuhna had no siblings, no spouse, no ex-spouse. No steady girlfriend. No boyfriend either, as far as anyone knows." She closed the book. "There's nobody."

Eddie imagined Lew Cuhna's funeral—an open casket in front of two dozen empty folding chairs.

If a priest gives a eulogy and nobody hears it...did it matter that the person died?

It was easy for Eddie to picture his own body in the casket. If he had burned up in the Chevette, who would have come to the funeral? The widowed aunts who had raised him, some reporter friends left over from his work at *The Daily Empire*.

Is there nobody else?

"No family," Eddie said, thinking aloud. "No one to mourn him."

"At least there's nobody to be devastated by his death," Orr said.

Eddie thought that over a moment. "I can't decide if that's a relief, or the saddest thing I've ever heard."

◇ ◇ ◇

The bike rumbled under Eddie on a meandering route toward downtown, past the Lowell Cemetery. For a moment he thought about turning into the graveyard and winding the bike along the curlicue streets, but the bright blanket of lilies and impatiens at the gates turned him away; he found the flowers too full of hope and he wanted to plow the bike through them. Lew Cuhna's murder had left Eddie angry and choked with frustration. What had Lew wanted to tell him?

Eddie needed a place to sort his thoughts.

He gave The Late Chuckie's rat bike the gas, and felt it lurch toward the Grotto. Jack Kerouac and his mother used to pray there. Eddie found it a good place to think.

He could pray, too, he told himself as he drove there, but knew he wouldn't. Eddie was an odd variety of spiritual person—he dropped often to his knees in thankfulness when times were good, but he preferred to meet crisis alone. It never seemed right to ask God to alter His world for Eddie Bourque.

He also refused to pray when he was drunk, but that was just good manners.

The Grotto was across the river from Eddie's neighborhood of Pawtucketville, not far from the brick funeral home where Jack Kerouac was waked after his death in 1969. The Grotto was a shrine to the Virgin, modeled after one of Catholicism's holiest spots: the rocks and natural spring near Lourdes, France, where Saint Bernadette claimed in 1858 to have witnessed visions of Mary.

The Lowell shrine was concealed behind a grand old Victorian mansion of red brick and slate, formerly the Franco-American Orphanage. A person could live decades in Lowell and never know the shrine existed. Eddie had discovered the Grotto in Jack Kerouac's novel *Doctor Sax*, and had been thrilled to learn that a piece of Kerouac's youth had remained essentially unchanged.

Eddie slowed the bike at the Grotto's entrance, a curving paved road between a parking lot and playground. Down the right-hand side of the road were a dozen small shrines, each like a little wood and glass church, on pillars of smooth stones and concrete. Red lights in each box illuminated taffy-pink figurines representing the characters in the Stations of the Cross.

The shrine was built by a Canadian religious order; the Stations are labeled in French.

Jesus est condamné a mort.

At the end of the road is a man-made mound of rock and concrete, a little urban mountain the size of a house, blanketed by ivy, topped with a few small fir trees and a life-sized crucifix. From a notch in the mound, a statue of the Virgin gazes to Heaven.

Eddie swung his leg off the bike.

Sometimes the Grotto was crowded with elderly people praying the rosary, or uniformed parochial school boys punching each other when the nuns weren't looking, but not today.

Eddie was alone.

A shallow cave in the side of the mound contained a stone table, which was covered with two dozen white candles in clear glass jars, about half of them lit. Eddie wondered who had lit them. Faithful people, probably. Or people in trouble and desperate for faith. There was a little wooden bench in the cave, too, and a few prayer books on the table.

Eddie could hear traffic from behind the red brick mansion, but otherwise the shrine seemed to radiate silence.

Kerouac had written of the Grotto: "Everything there was to remind of Death, and nothing in praise of life."

For Eddie, the shrine was not about death; it was proof that literature is immortal.

He walked to the far side of the stone hill and climbed the stairs that rose like a spine on its back. At the top, Eddie could see the Merrimack River, fat and lazy, through the green screen of a willow. He leaned against the iron cross and watched a wind surfer on the river pulling against a bulging blue triangle of sail.

He wondered what Henry was doing at that moment.

Perhaps he was staring through an inch of safety glass, out the one skinny window in his 11-by-7 cell. Eddie tried to imagine what Henry's view would look like. Razor wire. Trees in the distance. Cars whizzing along the street, going places no prison lifer would ever see.

Eddie had grown up in competition with Henry, though Eddie had never won as many trophies nor done as well in the classroom. That competition had driven Eddie; it had molded his personality. But even when he fell short of what Henry had accomplished, Eddie always knew that he had beaten his brother. Henry was a murderer and Eddie would never be—and that score eclipsed every road race Henry had won, and every test he had aced in algebra.

So why did Eddie still compete?

Through his life, Eddie had come to think of Henry as a different species. They shared parents, but so what? Eddie had gotten DNA from his folks, and not much else. He never felt a blood connection to his brother, and had been curious about him only from a distance, the way an anthropologist is curious about a backward and primitive tribe in the deepest recess of a distant land.

Shame had always kept Eddie from acting on that curiosity.

Eddie's parents never would have had a second child had Henry not been jailed for murder. Reduced to the barest and most brutal mathematics, Eddie owed his existence to Henry's double homicide.

He heard the inner echo of something Henry had said through the glass.

If you went back in time to save me, you'd destroy yourself.

Eddie pressed his palm on the metal cross, felt the heat it had collected from the sun. A secret truth suddenly revealed itself.

That's why I'm so goddam competitive.

He had not been chasing Henry's grades nor his high school track records. Not really.

Henry had killed and Eddie was born. Other lives had been traded for Eddie's. Not directly, of course, but that didn't seem to matter. For more than thirty years, Eddie had been competing with the universe to justify the trade.

He thought about the possibility that Henry was innocent.

Why had Eddie been so reluctant to believe that his brother could have been wrongly convicted? What if Henry could prove his innocence? How would that change the calculus of Eddie's life?

Eddie chuckled to himself, imagining Thanksgiving dinner at Bobbi's house every year. She'd probably make Eddie bring the turkey, and cook it, too.

But would it change me?

He looked up at the feet of the figure on the crucifix, just above his head. They reminded him of Dr. Crane's feet, suspended above his garage floor. Eddie realized that in almost every important way, Henry Bourque had been dead for thirty years. Bobbi was convinced that Eddie was the one who could bring his brother back from the death of a life sentence.

This really was a resurrection story, he thought.

Eddie breathed deep and looked down to where the shadow of the cross lay over his feet. The Grotto had been built for *those who believe in what they cannot know.* So had the Catholic Church, for that matter—so had all the churches.

Eddie pulled out his cell phone and dialed Bobbi's hotel.

She answered on the third ring after the call was transferred, sounding distant and unsure, "Um...hello?"

"I'll do it."

"Eddie?"

"I'll talk to Henry."

She paused. Eddie heard her sniffle. "Oh, little brother," she said softly. "I just knew."

"When?"

"I'll see when he's allowed another call."

"I can't promise I can persuade him of anything."

She sounded confident. "You'll do it."

They hung up.

The Late Chuckie's rat bike needed a dozen kicks before it started. Eddie didn't mind. He was moving on autopilot, barely paying attention to the labor of stomping on the starter. The bike finally agreed to do its job.

He roared toward home, feeling new confidence in his skills with the motorcycle, and a nervous chill over the possibility that Henry could win his freedom.

With the state's star witness against Henry hopelessly impugned, a motion for a new trial might have real legs. If the physical evidence against Henry still existed, the defense could argue to make it available for DNA testing that wasn't around when Henry had been convicted. If the evidence was no longer in police storage somewhere, the case file could still overflow with reasonable doubt—with the right lawyer pushing the right buttons.

Eddie parked the bike outside his house and bounded up the stairs. He should make some notes of the argument he would present to Henry.

Inside, the house was dark.

He closed the door, looked around.

Why were the shades drawn? He didn't remember—

A hand from behind seized Eddie by the collar and the open-mouthed kiss of a gun froze the tender skin below his ear.

Chapter 16

The gun against his neck pushed Eddie roughly into the room. Eddie's knees went weak and he stumbled. The man holding the gun grunted, the hand on Eddie's shirt pushed him to his knees, and then bent his torso backward, the way Eddie imagined the mob would hold a guy before they whacked him. The gun knocked against Eddie's skull.

The room smelled like Skin Bracer.

"Where's my cat, Jimmy?" Eddie said. He was surprised at the level calmness in his own voice.

Jimmy Whistle whispered close to Eddie's ear, "Locked in the bathroom, and he's gonna starve in there while you're dead on this floor, unless I get some fucking answers."

Eddie flinched at Jimmy Whistle's wet breath. But he felt relief.

This is an interrogation, not an execution.

If Eddie stayed calm, he could get out of this. He looked around the room for a weapon, just in case. His chess set was splayed over the coffee table. The piano bench was tucked neatly under the upright. His lumpy sofa bed with no back support could not be used to injure anybody, unless Eddie could get Jimmy to sleep on it. His eyes fixed on the brass pole lamp beside the sofa. It was five feet tall with a corrugated lampshade like the cap from a giant tube of toothpaste. The lamp was Eddie's best option, though hardly a handy weapon to wield.

"You had me fooled earlier," Jimmy said. "I was buying what you were saying at my place, but I should have known better. I've been double-crossed by a Bourque before."

"I didn't double-cross anybody."

Jimmy tightened his grip on Eddie's collar. "Then who put that lady cop on me, eh?" he growled. "She came right after you did, asking what I know about this guy Lime, the kidnapped bank president. The thing is, I'm a good actor. You know how many shakedowns I saw in the joint? James J. Whistle, prisoner number zero-five-three-nine-two, is smart enough to play stupid."

Jimmy had played stupid with Detective Orr so he could take out his anger on Eddie. "I was just looking for information," Eddie said.

"Bullshit!" The gun pressed painfully into the flesh at the base of Eddie's skull. "What are you and your brother trying to pull?"

"Pull? We're not—"

"You and Henry are pulling something," Jimmy insisted. He paused. "You're chasing the money, aren't you?"

Eddie said nothing. Jimmy shook him and roared, "AREN'T YOU?"

Chasing what money? Eddie wanted to say. But he didn't want to aggravate Jimmy Whistle, who seemed to be slipping into desperation. Desperate people are capable of anything, especially pulling a trigger. He wished he could see Whistle's face, so he could read how close Jimmy was to going over the edge. Eddie thought about it. *Chasing the money?* The money from the robbery Jimmy and Henry had pulled off?

That cash was never found, but that was more than thirty years ago. Would bills that old even be passable?

"You stole it," Eddie said. "Why don't you chase it?"

Jimmy banged the butt of the gun across Eddie's spine. The startling pain sent Eddie wrenching against Jimmy's grip, but the cold barrel went right back against the hairless spot behind Eddie's right ear.

General VonKatz called for Eddie through the bathroom door.

Jimmy Whistle leaned close behind the barrel and informed Eddie, "That's *my* fucking money."

Eddie said nothing.

"I rotted in the joint, kept my mouth shut and told myself every day that I didn't care about the gold." He panted noisily. "When I got out I thought I didn't need it, but things have changed. If you're going after it, I want my share."

"The papers never said anything about gold," Eddie said. "It was cash. A banking transaction."

"The paper's were full of shit," Jimmy whispered. "They print what the cops tell them, and the cops didn't want anybody to know they were looking for gold bullion, untraceable if it's melted down and recast."

Eddie was doubtful. "Why would the cops lie?"

"Maybe they didn't want to start a treasure hunt, or maybe they didn't want to explain why they couldn't find a thousand pounds of fucking gold."

A thousand pounds?

Jimmy Whistle seemed to read his mind. "That's right, Bourque. One thousand seventy-one pounds of gold bar. Worth six hundred grand back then, which was a fine haul." He twisted Eddie's shirt collar, pinching Eddie's throat. "I checked the metal markets today and then did the math. That gold is now worth six point six million."

Jimmy let the number sink in a few moments, then ground the gun against Eddie's skull. "Half of that gold is mine," he said. "Your brother took it from me thirty years ago, *and I want it.*"

"Took it from you? You took it together."

Jimmy Whistle gave a hoarse growl, stepping in front of Eddie.

Eddie looked up from his knees. He felt sizzling dread at seeing Jimmy's purple cheeks and wet, red-rimmed eyes. He looked like a man with nothing to lose. He imagined a ski mask over Jimmy's face. Could he have been the one who tried to burn him?

Eddie wanted to tell him to calm down, but when he tried to speak Jimmy Whistle grimaced in rage and jammed the gun into Eddie's mouth. The steel cracked Eddie's top front tooth. Pain rocked Eddie's jaw and made his eyes water, as if he had been stabbed through the roof of the mouth with an icicle.

"Henry double-crossed us and took all the money!" Whistle thundered.

He pushed the gun deeper, until Eddie gagged.

Whistle's cheeks quivered as he spoke, seething: "I threatened to kill your brother, the son-of-a-bitch, but that animal just laughed. He said it was his insurance, to make sure he was treated on the up-and-up. Well, fuck him!"

Eddie clamped both hands around Whistle's wrist and stared up at him. He heard the General scratching at the bathroom door.

Jimmy Whistle yanked the gun from Eddie's mouth and pulled Eddie roughly to his feet. Both men lost their balance. Eddie steadied himself against the sofa. The brass lamp was at his elbow. Eddie felt something sharp in his mouth—a triangular shard of tooth that Jimmy's pistol had sheared off. Eddie rolled his tongue around the fragment; the shard was like a tiny razor.

Jimmy stepped toward Eddie, his face inches away, the gun between them, in Eddie's ribs. Eddie could count the pink veins squiggling across the whites of Jimmy's eyes.

Then his empty black pupils got bigger.

He's going to kill me.

Eddie tipped up his chin and in a sudden puff of breath blasted out the bone shard.

Jimmy slapped his free hand over his left eye. "You fucker!" he screamed in shock.

Eddie grabbed the lamp and swung it like an ax. Its base was heavy and came sluggishly through its arc, but it struck solidly across Jimmy's wrist and knocked the pistol flying. Jimmy squealed in pain and reached for Eddie. "Bastard!"

Eddie grit his teeth and drove a palm into Jimmy's sternum. The older man recoiled and Eddie scrambled for the gun.

The pistol was L-shaped and black, its handle wet and warm. Eddie was surprised at how heavy it was, how its vampiric touch seemed to bleed away his soul.

He leveled the gun at Jimmy Whistle.

Whistle's left eyeball was stained with a crimson dot where the tooth had cut him. Though ugly, it looked superficial. Whistle touched his wound and then inspected the blood on his finger. "It's all fun and games," he said dryly, "until somebody loses an eye." He nodded to the gun. "What the hell do you expect to do with that thing?"

Eddie looked at the pistol. What the hell *did* he expect to do with this thing? Shoot Jimmy Whistle? Of course not. If Jimmy rushed him, Eddie might smack him with the gun, but Eddie knew he would never pull the trigger.

Jimmy knew it, too.

"You lack your brother's killer instinct," Whistle said. "If he was where you are, I'd be dead three times already." He laughed, pointing to the pistol. "The safety is on." He was calm now, and bitterly sarcastic. "You oughta know how to work your own gun—and it *is* yours, now that your fingerprints are all over it.

"I'm *shocked* that you pulled that gun on me," Jimmy said, "to threaten me for information, after you invited me here to talk about your brother—and that's my story." He gave an exaggerated smile. "I guess violence runs in your family. Don't forget to flick off the safety when you want to kill me."

Goddam him, he was right. The gun was black market treasure, bought off a street corner, no doubt, with no paper trail connecting it to Jimmy Whistle. Detective Orr would never believe that Eddie had pulled a gun, but some other cop might. Who could say? Eddie decided that the authorities would not hear about his scuffle with Jimmy Whistle.

He looked Jimmy over again, seeing him in more detail now that he was disarmed. Whistle wore red tennis shoes, black socks, and blue polyester suit pants that were too short because they were hiked too high on his belly. His baby blue polo shirt squeezed him. His rough red face sagged around the jowls. He looked pitiful, like an unemployed clown who could no longer afford his makeup.

Had he really been about to kill Eddie?

Jimmy had admitted he was a good actor—he must have been to fool Detective Orr. Eddie rubbed his tongue against his chipped tooth. The hole felt like a canyon. Adrenaline that had dulled the pain was wearing off, and his jaw throbbed.

"Who killed those guards thirty years ago after the armored car robbery?" Eddie demanded. It was a prosecutor's question. If Henry hadn't killed the guards, Jimmy Whistle might have.

Whistle shrugged. "Henry, I assume."

He assumed? What Jimmy *assumed* was not evidence against Henry, only what he saw. "Did you *see* Henry do it?"

"Didn't have to." He hiked his pants even higher. "I know Henry Bourque. There's something sinister in that boy. I saw it the day my ma hired him on her farm, the Lord rest her soul." Jimmy made the Sign of the Cross, which seemed an odd gesture coming from him.

Eddie lowered the gun. He had never imagined Henry working a job, like a real person. But of course he would have had to work. It wasn't hard to picture his muscled brother on a farm, a hay bale over each shoulder.

"So that's how you met him?" Eddie asked.

"I saw him work—the boy was *strong*—so when I needed muscle I knew where to go," Jimmy said. He bit his bottom lip. "But Henry was a fuckin' wacko. Should've trusted my instincts, but I didn't." He held out his arms so Eddie could see the whole of him, the husk left over after three decades of life had been wrung away in federal prison. "Look what it got me."

"I'm not after the gold," Eddie said.

"Whatever you say—you got the gun."

"I want to help Henry prove he didn't kill those guards."

Whistle laughed bitterly. "Like I said, the truth is in your hand."

"Maybe *you* killed them."

"Open your eyes," Whistle said. His thumb and forefinger spread the lids of his wounded eye, and he gazed spitefully at Eddie with the little pupil of blood. "Henry killed them, Henry hid the bodies and Henry stole the money. There's no other possibility." He let go of his eye and rubbed the spot on his chest where Eddie had shoved him.

"I need the money, Bourque," Whistle said. "Not all of it, not half, not even a third. I just need *enough*." He jabbed a finger at Eddie. "Yeah, I got secrets—a few good ones, lots of bad ones. But I didn't whack those guards."

Eddie didn't necessarily believe him, but he left the option open. "Well," Eddie said, "maybe nobody killed them."

Jimmy squinted at him, an ironic smile over his face.

"A thousand pounds of gold would buy two blue-collar guards a nice life in the Cayman Islands," Eddie said. "You said you never saw them murdered."

Jimmy sounded doubtful. "They had families."

"Maybe girlfriends, too."

"They were tied up with rope." He hiked his pants again. "I thought maybe we could sell them for ransom."

"I read the news reports," Eddie said. "One of the three guards escaped. If one could, they all could. So maybe two of them—"

"Dumas and Forte."

"—those two escaped with the gold. Henry was charged with their murders and wrongly convicted so nobody ever looked for them. They could be the elders in some tropical village by now."

Jimmy chuckled softly. "I'm done telling you what to believe, Bourque." He rubbed his hands together as if to clean them of something. "I'll be leaving now so I can pedal home before dark—unless you're going to kill me in your living room."

"No, I just vacuumed."

Jimmy Whistle let himself out. He looked back to Eddie from the front steps. "I don't need much of the money, Bourque. You'll never miss it."

Eddie didn't bother to argue. He locked the bolt behind Jimmy Whistle, and then inched the sofa against the door.

The gun felt like an alien life form in his hand. He wanted to get rid of it. Down the storm drain? Off University Bridge into the Merrimack? Or something less public. Eddie sealed the gun in a plastic zipper bag and brought it into the bathroom. The General was cautiously trying to sip from the dripping spout in the tub. The cat drank daintily, like a well-bred old lady.

Eddie removed the toilet tank cover. He dropped the gun in the tank and watched it sink, listened to the *thunk* when it landed. He replaced the cover thinking of what Jimmy had said. Then Eddie heard Henry's voice in his head.

I gave away the table I made to my partner's old lady.

Henry Bourque had worked for Jimmy's mother.

His partner's old lady.

Chapter 17

The night was long, sleepless and frustrating. In the morning—Sunday morning—Eddie brewed an organic Mexican Arabica and guzzled it black. It was weak, and he realized in disappointment that he had been too damn sleepy to make the coffee right.

Eddie's *Washington Post* was intact for the first time in days, but he was too distracted to read it. General VonKatz sat on the kitchen table and pawed at the paper in its little plastic bag, trying to coax it to life, so he could chase it and slay it. As an indoor cat, the General didn't have many opportunities to hunt. Eddie had long considered importing a few live mice from the pet store, but he couldn't overcome his moral resistance to what amounted to throwing slaves to the lion, even if the mice had originally been bred as snake food.

Eddie scratched the cat behind the ears.

Outside, a few sprinkles fell from a grim sky. Low clouds pushed down on the neighborhood, crushing Pawtucketville like a claustrophobic's nightmare.

Eddie tuned his TV to one of the Sunday political talk shows, just for the background noise, and then wandered to his bedroom and booted up his computer.

A few students had emailed their mid-term papers. Eddie opened Margaret's. His eyebrows lifted; she had covered a Zoning Board meeting. That was a difficult board for a novice in municipal government; zoning can get technical. Eddie printed a paper copy and read Margaret's opening:

> Mr. Brown said that the setback requirement couldn't be applied because the applicant cannot be building on a "optioned lot" though Mrs. Curry thought it was fine since the "purchase and sales" is pending, so why couldn't the board, with the advice and consent of the assistant solicitor, recommend a "temporary" easement to allow for the vehicular traffic to Lexington Garage, which had earlier, through an attorney from out-of-state, raised the point that traffic cannot "go around the bend" because Allen Street is one way, and would it be better to seek an opinion from the city planner? "You really can't approve this without site plan review," said a man named Paul, who addressed the board but didn't give a last name because they knew who he was.

Oh God! Eddie grabbed a red pen to recommend some edits, but couldn't imagine where to begin. What was the building project? What was the outcome of the hearing? Who the hell were the people being quoted? This story didn't need editing, it needed to be burned, the ashes stuffed into a space capsule and blasted into the sun.

I'm the worst teacher alive.

He gave up and printed another paper, from Gerard, who had decided to cover a School Committee meeting. Fine choice; that's where most of the tax money was spent in municipalities. He read:

> With the poignant memories of chalk dust and the clap, clap, clapping of erasers echoing in my mind, and, alas, the empty recollections of lost schoolboy love, I descended the creaky steps into the bowels of the concrete beast known as the School Administration Building. It was here that I found them, seated

upon a stage as if actors in a real-life educational drama—the School Committee. What decisions awaited me and my pen of blue? My empty pad thirsted for knowledge, for quotes, for statistics.

Eddie gently put the paper down. Gerard had made the story about himself. This article was a sin against community journalism. It needed to be executed in a public square.

I'm the worst teacher who ever lived.

He wandered back to the living room and checked the clock. Ten-fifty in the morning.

This was going to be a long day.

Assuming that the farm Jimmy Whistle's mother had owned was in the greater Lowell region, the Registry of Deeds would have land records on it. The registry was closed on Sunday. It would open in the morning. Whistle's old lady was dead; her farm probably had been diced into housing lots by now, but Eddie wanted to know where the farm had been. It was his only lead.

His cell phone rang.

"Hello?"

"Knock, knock, little brother."

"Hey, Bobbi."

"You sound exhausted, boy."

"Didn't sleep," Eddie said. He glanced into his empty mug. "Made weak coffee this morning, too. Listen, did Henry ever mention a farm job he had as a teenager, before he went to prison?"

She was quiet a moment, and then said: "Your brother doesn't talk much about the past. I can barely get him to talk about our future. He's stuck in *right now.* I think that's part of the reason he has trouble getting excited to fight for his freedom." She was quiet a little more, and then asked brightly, "Why are you asking? Have you found something?"

Eddie considered telling her about Jimmy Whistle, about Jimmy's old lady and the gun in the toilet tank, but he couldn't. He didn't want to raise her hopes before he had something solid that Henry could use to persuade a jury—and which Eddie could use to persuade Henry. And he didn't want Bobbi interfering with his research, demanding to be taken along. He brushed her off with, "I don't know what I've got, probably nothing. I'll know better tomorrow."

She sputtered, prying for more.

Eddie steered the conversation away, asking: "How did you meet my brother?"

She cooed, "Oooo, I've always loved men in barbed wire." She laughed. "Actually, I got sick of cheaters. Married two of them, dated about a hundred. I call them 'excuses guys.' Always got a good excuse for why they're late, why they didn't call, why they can't drop by the restaurant and meet my friends. I told this one guy: if you're really working all that overtime, why do you drive such a piece of shit?"

"You should have been a detective."

"Naw, not that I have any great brain for it. I've just heard every excuse ever written, so none of them work on me anymore."

"Anybody ever use the grandparent's funeral excuse on you?"

She snorted. "I was dumb and love-struck, but I'm no idiot," she said. "Nobody ever had the stones to pull that one on me, at least not without an obituary in the paper as proof."

Eddie thumped the empty coffee mug against his forehead. No more grandma exemptions in class.

Bobbi said, "When I was sick of scrubbing other women's body odors out of my man's undershirts, I swore that I wouldn't settle down until I had somebody I could trust."

"You can bet Henry won't be cruising the bars tonight."

"No, he'll be trying to keep from getting knifed," she said, suddenly shading toward serious. "I was looking for a man with golden character. I didn't expect to find him in the federal pen. A friend of mine came across this Web site that matches prisoners with pen pals around the country. It's run by an ex-con who learned computer programming in the joint. This guy posts letters from inmates on the Internet, so people like me can read them and decide if they want to write to one particular inmate or another. I noticed a bunch of letters from men in the prison in my town."

"Tough way to date," Eddie cracked. "The closest you can get to sex is to both screw the same postman."

"It's not all about romance," she corrected. "It's about men desperate for some human contact outside those walls."

Something in her tone suggested that Eddie was being shallow with his wisecracks. Or maybe the suggestion had come from inside Eddie. Either way, he was embarrassed. He tossed the empty mug onto the couch, sat on the piano bench and rubbed his eyes. "You're right, of course," he said, chastened. "So why did you decide to write to Henry?"

"His letter was different than the others."

"I'll bet."

"I could see that he was smart, though he didn't stick it in your face," she said. "He didn't use a lot of two-dollar words. Just made his point in clear language that I thought was pretty. He wanted somebody who traveled a lot, who could describe things for him, so he could travel, too. I'm surprised he even wrote me back. I mean—where do I ever go?"

"Why do you think he wrote you back?"

She laughed. "I smelled good."

"You told him so?"

"He liked the way my letter smelled. I didn't drench it in perfume or nothing—like I said, this wasn't about romance in the beginning—but whatever scent I was wearing on my wrist must have gotten on the note. Henry wrote me back to say it was…hmmm…how did he put it? The first time in nearly thirty years he had enjoyed a direct sensation of unchained humanity." She giggled. "For you and me it's such a little thing. A dab of perfume. Who cares? Henry Bourque *cared*. I knew that he wouldn't take one minute for granted if I gave him a little of my time. So we exchanged a couple notes, and then I invited myself for a visit. The question, 'My place or yours?' never came up." She giggled again.

Bobbi sounded happily drunk with the memory. Eddie pictured her beaming and twirling a finger in a lock of hair.

She whispered, "I try to remember if I loved him before I knew he was innocent, or did I start loving him after I figured it out."

"Might have happened at the same time."

"As good a theory as any."

"When did Henry tell you that he didn't do it?"

"He never told me."

Eddie sprang to his feet. "Never?" he asked.

She was calm. "He didn't do it."

"Right, sure, I know—but he never *told* you that he didn't?"

Bobbi, still calm, spoke slowly. "Your brother did not kill those people."

Eddie sat down. He heard Bobbi's breath. The enormity of her faith in Henry struck Eddie as he listened to her. She was the *living* proof that Henry was not a monster, for a monster cannot be loved. He smiled, marveling at this logic. Then Eddie's thoughts turned inward. If there was no monster, then Eddie Bourque could not share any monster's blood.

They finished with small talk about downtown restaurants and the forecast for sticky weather the rest of the week. Eddie promised to call as soon as he knew whether he had discovered a worthwhile lead. They hung up.

The General paced restlessly, sniffing table legs and chairs—things a million times sniffed.

Eddie scooped up the cat. "You bored, too? How about a movie?" He set the General on the coffee table, and then flipped through his video collection. "I got *Casablanca* and I got one of your tapes, *MouseHouse, Part Two*. Which one do you want?"

The General waited quietly on the table.

"You're right," Eddie said. "We've seen *Casablanca* a hundred times." Eddie pushed a tape into the machine, then refilled his coffee and reclined on the sofa.

On the screen, white mice zipped around, burrowing under cedar chips, squeaking, sniffing, rolling around on top of each other. They hid part-way in paper towel tubes so that just their fat little butts and wavering tails stuck out, then they disappeared into the tubes entirely, and tender pink twitchy noses appeared at the other end.

General VonKatz was enthralled. He shrank into a compact mass of muscle on a hair trigger. Occasionally he quivered and chattered at the on-screen villains. "What's the *plot?*" Eddie asked. "This is the problem with sequels—I missed the original *MouseHouse*, so now part two doesn't make any sense."

He checked the clock and sighed. Around twenty-two hours before the deed registry opened for business.

Chapter 18

Colonial-era fieldstone walls, speckled with dry moss, marked the property line of the old Whistle farm in both directions, broken only for the driveway. Eddie checked the plot map he had copied from the deed registry. Yeah, this was the place. He had spent most of the day chasing paper on the farm. It had once belonged to Jimmy's parents, Ivan and Beatrice—that much had been easy to figure out, and Eddie had been shocked to learn that the forty-acre property still existed intact.

Its history over the past thirty years was muddled in divorce, three lawsuits, a probate fight over a disputed will, and two bankruptcies. The owner-of-record was a real estate holding company in Indiana, which bought the place at tax sale ten years ago, and had since undergone two reorganizations.

As far as Eddie could tell from the public record, the place had been vacant and untouched for a decade.

To find it, Eddie had driven deep into tiny Dunstable, Mass., north of Lowell near the New Hampshire line. The area was still rural, and the potholed street that led to the farm cut through woods thick with hundreds of sugar maples that bore the black scars from where they had been tapped for their sap. The floor of the forest was clogged with underbrush, dry leaves and downed trees, the softened wood rotting into soil to begin again the journey back into a living tree.

Eddie looked down the farm's long driveway—two parallel tracks of packed gray stonedust, a swathe of knee-high weeds between them. The entrance had been blocked long ago with three great sloping boulders, each now wearing a skirt of tall grass. The boulders would stop a tank, but not a motorcycle. Eddie eased The Late Chuckie's rat bike between the stones. He saw a shallow gully to his left, and steered the bike into it. From the road, the bike would be hidden and would not invite an investigation by any police patrol with nothing to do on a summer evening in the country.

Eddie hesitated a moment before he killed the bike's engine. If he had to leave in a hurry, would the bike cooperate? It never cooperated. Well, he couldn't just leave it idling. He shut down the machine.

The forest instantly tried to swallow him in silence.

He walked slowly down the driveway. The sound of his shoes crunching on the gravel seemed big enough to fill the whole farm. He caught a sweet whiff of Concord grapes, and paused. The grape vines were hugging a dying red oak. Eddie ran his hand along the vine, a stiff, ruddy-colored rope that shed papery little slivers. He tugged on it and startled a crow that cursed and fluttered off.

The driveway bent steadily to the left, then broadened into a teardrop-shaped hayfield cut from the woods. Golden wheat lay flat against the land. Three ramshackle buildings slouched in a line at the far end of the field. They had long ago been painted white, though the paint was now flaking off, exposing the weathered gray clapboard. The small building to the far left was a one-car garage, with a single swinging double-door, and a rusted weathervane on the roof. It sagged more dangerously than the other buildings, and looked like one hard shove would knock it over.

The building in the center was the farmhouse—a two-story cube with a fieldstone foundation, a wraparound porch and a dozen broken windows. A tattered yellow curtain on the second floor waved lazily in the breeze.

To the right was a monstrous barn of wide wooden planks, in better shape than the house and the garage. Newer maybe?

The barn was two and a half stories tall, with a massive sliding door on the ground level and an opening on the second floor for loading by winch. Two swallows sailed into the opening, and immediately three sailed out.

There were no signs that anyone had been here in years. No tire tracks, no footprints. How long would footprints last in the packed stonedust? Not long; his own were barely visible. Eddie pictured Henry striding across the wheat field, shining with sweat after an afternoon of pitching hay bales onto a flatbed truck.

"Henry? Now that the hay's in, these logs gotta be split to quarter rails, but I can't tell you where I put my husband's ax."

"Maybe he took it when he ran off, Mrs. Whistle."

"If that's the case, I don't want you finding that son-of-a-bitch and bringing him back here."

"No ma'am, I won't look too hard."

Eddie shook off the daydream. He had three buildings to search in only two hours of daylight. For a moment, he considered turning around. He could come back in the morning—with Detective Orr and a dozen of her well-armed friends. No, he decided, what happened here thirty years ago couldn't hurt him now.

Eddie started with the garage. Striding toward it, he came upon a ring of fieldstones, ten feet across, like the fire barrier around a big campfire. The stones marked the opening of a deep-water well. The shaft was smooth cobblestones. It sunk ten feet before it hit the waterline, and then kept going for at least another ten. The water was still and clear.

Stepping carefully away from the well, Eddie kicked something in the tall grass with a bang and startled himself. He searched the grass and found an old bucket of galvanized steel, on a long rusted chain. Had somebody been fetching water? *Am I not alone?*

Eddie whirled and looked into every window of the old farmhouse. He saw nobody. He spun in a circle and scanned the woods. His instincts insisted someone would be there, watching him, and Eddie was surprised to see no one. The wind cooled his brow like the touch of an old ghost. Eddie rubbed his arms.

This is stupid. There's nobody here.

He walked to the garage. The windows were coated with dust on the inside. Through the dust, Eddie could make out a tractor-sized vehicle under a canvas tarp. A padlock seized with rust fastened the door. There was no way into the garage short of cutting off the lock.

Eddie moved to the house. The mortar between the basement stones was disintegrating into coarse gray crumbs. Dry rot infested the clapboard. Squirrels had packed dried leaves in a hole in the eves. Eddie stepped onto the porch, heard the crack of rotted wood, and decided to check the barn.

The sliding barn door had rusted shut, but Eddie slipped easily into an opening in a wall where a plank was missing. The barn was strewn with antique hand tools: shovels, rakes, a pick, a wedged maul for splitting logs, a two-man saw with two-inch teeth. On a workbench Eddie found a kerosene lantern. It was an old-fashioned design, but seemed in good shape, the little mesh mantle intact within the glass. He shook it gently, heard fuel sloshing inside. He unlocked the lantern's fuel pump with a twist, and withdrew the short brass rod to be pushed in and out to pressurize the fuel. The pump was well oiled and slid easily. The rusted hand tools in the barn could have been untouched for thirty years. But not the lantern; it had been used recently. How recently? Eddie couldn't tell.

He put the lantern back, left the barn and explored the house.

The rotted porch was like a poorly camouflaged pit trap, but the floors inside the house seemed sound. The wind blew through the building like living breath, and the whole place creaked and moaned like an old man getting up in the morning.

The house held an abandoned collection of junk left to slowly disintegrate in the elements. Eddie searched the place, trying to picture the house as Henry would have seen it thirty years ago. Eddie imagined rooms full of Shaker style furniture, shelves lined with knick-knacks, milk cans stuffed with cut sunflowers, the smell of hot cardamom bread.

"Henry?"

"Yes, Mrs. Whistle?"

"I put chipped ice in the pitcher for you, little sugar in there with it. Take it outside and draw some water from the well for yourself."

"I'll get to it, ma'am."

"Don't you ma'am me. You need to drink if you expect to finish splittin' those rails in this heat."

"Amen to that, ma'am."

Eddie tugged open a door and discovered stairs leading down to a black hole. He didn't want to go down there, but the basement was the last place he hadn't looked. He couldn't go down there without light.

Hmmmm…

Eddie hustled from the house, back to The Late Chuckie's rat bike. Rummaging through the saddlebags he found a book of matches—from the "Rump and Grind" gentlemen's club.

Chuckie, you horny dog.

He trotted to the barn and grabbed the lantern. With a glance to the setting sun melting over the treetops, he ducked back into the house, to the basement stairs. Kneeling with the lantern, Eddie pressurized the fuel with a dozen pumps. He struck a match and put the flame to the mantel. It lit with a gasp and then hissed steadily. The bright white light hurt to look at, and just a moment's glance at the flame left floating green spots before Eddie's eyes.

The wooden stairs groaned in surprise under Eddie's weight. Downstairs, the basement floor was made of poured concrete. The walls were fieldstone, like those in the pictures of Roger Lime that the kidnappers had taken.

Eddie lifted the lantern to one of the walls.

This could be the one from the picture.

Any of them could have been.

The old house creaked above him. Eddie held the lantern at arm's length and followed it around the basement. He felt its heat and listened to its hiss; it seemed like a living thing and it made Eddie feel less alone.

The basement seemed to be a rectangle, with a plank-and-beam ceiling about six feet high. Eddie had to duck his head as he explored. There were scattered cobwebs between the ceiling posts. A fine white dust covered the floor. Eddie lowered the lantern. He saw footprints in the dust—the knobby pattern of a workboot, and another pair with no tread at all, from a sock maybe? Eddie's face flushed. He compared the footprints with his own. His fresh footprints were sharper.

These are old prints.

Relieved, he looked around some more. He discovered that the basement was not a rectangle as he had first thought—it was L-shaped, with a wing off the far side. Eddie walked the lantern around the corner, into the wing, inspecting the stone walls closely. He wasn't sure what he was looking for. A secret door? A message written in blood?

On the floor, near the base of the wall, he noticed a small dark spot, a perfect square, about two inches across. He knelt with the lantern. The square was a faint impression in the dust, nothing more. He noticed another nearby, and another.

Five in all.

Eddie stood back and connected the spots in his mind.

They made a pentagon.

Eddie's imagination superimposed an image of Henry's five-sided table over the marks in the dust. It seemed right—he imagined the table legs leaving the squares, like the marks pressed into a carpet by a heavy piece of furniture.

"Split logs all day and spend all night in the workshop? What kind of life you living, Henry?"

"It doesn't look like much now, but it's gonna be a table."

"Hush up! It's wonderful. I wish my boy Jimmy had a talent with wood like that."

"Maybe when it's done you can keep it here, Mrs. Whistle."

By the marks on the floor, it seemed *possible* that Henry's table had been left in this basement long ago, and then taken away more recently, but the evidence was hardly conclusive. Eddie needed more. He crouched with the lantern and swept the light inches from the floor, studying the dust that filled the little cracks in the concrete.

He duckwalked with the light, looking for…what the hell *was* he looking for?

He had gone only a few steps when he noticed a patch of concrete that seemed different from the floor around it—it was a slightly lighter shade of gray and a little bumpier, though Eddie would never had noticed had he not been looking so intently. The patch was roughly oval, maybe six by three feet. He stomped on it, listened to the thud, then stomped next to the patch, to compare the sounds.

Was it his imagination that the patch sounded thinner? Hollow, maybe?

Options…options…

He could get Detective Orr, bring her back here tomorrow. Or he could come back alone in the morning, look around some more, maybe search the woods around the property for a telling clue.

It was a stupid argument because he knew what he was going to do.

Eddie hefted the lantern, felt the fuel swirling around—there was plenty, plenty of light left in it.

He ran for the stairs.

Outside, the sun was gone except for the fading pink underbelly of a distant cloud. As Eddie hurried to the barn he was surprised to feel the call of a big news story. How long had it been since he had uncovered a real scoop? He couldn't remember, but he was too excited to care. Eddie lifted the lantern to illuminate a jumble of old tools.

He grabbed a ten-pound pick.

◇ ◇ ◇

The first blow seemed loud enough to shake down the house, but it barely dented the concrete. The low ceiling made it impossible for Eddie to swing the pick over his head. He widened his stance, bent his knees and gripped the pick at the end of its handle to increase his leverage. He swung again. A satisfying clump of concrete dust sprayed over the floor.

Wham. Wham. Wham.

Eddie's ears were ringing. He was breathing hard and sweat gathered on his back. He pulled off his shirt, threw it on the floor near the lantern, wiped his brow on the back of his hand, and then attacked the concrete again.

He wasn't sure what he hoped to find. There might not be anything under there. But Eddie was sure that the floor had been patched at least once before, some time after the original floor had been poured. He was certain he was not the first person to chip away at the concrete at this spot. He wondered if the last person to dig here had used the same pick.

Yellow sparks and chunks of concrete the size of ice cubes shot out from under the point of the pick. Eddie's arms burned. He stopped, leaned on the pick and panted. The old house creaked again, three times, as if some heavy spirit was walking across the floor above. He shuddered and listened, but heard only the angry hiss of the lantern.

No wonder people go mad living alone in big old houses.

The handle was damp with his sweat. He swung the pick again. Concrete splashed.

Wham. Wham. Wham.

Eddie couldn't help thinking that he was digging a tunnel for a prison break.

He wanted to write a news story that cleared his brother's name. As he worked the pick against the floor, he allowed his imagination to explore the future. A writer freeing his own brother would be a story itself. *The Daily Empire* would want to write about it. If the new management at the *Empire* was smart, they'd have one of Eddie's old colleagues call him for the interview.

To free a brother after thirty years would be a nationwide story. *Time* and *Newsweek* would scratch each other's eyes out over who got the first interview with Eddie Bourque. Eddie smiled over the daydream. It was an excellent fantasy, but not the one he wanted the most. He imagined Henry visiting Eddie's shack in Pawtucketville for the first time. He could see Henry reaching down, snapping his fingers to coax General VonKatz to come over. The brothers would split a six-pack of Rolling Rock, and then Eddie would set up the chessboard. Henry would play the white pieces—Eddie would know without asking what side Henry liked to play. It was the kind of detail brothers knew about each other.

Wham! The pick broke through the concrete and buried itself to the handle.

Eddie wiggled it out and inspected the blade. It was covered with dirt.

He looked around for the first time in a long while. Night had fallen outside. No light bled into the basement from the stairwell. The lantern glowed steadily in the center of a white circle that faded to blackness all around it, as if even light was afraid to venture into the basement's dark corners.

His arms were beat and the pick felt like lead, but Eddie assaulted the floor around the hole he had punched, widening the opening with a series of hard blows.

Soon the opening was large enough to reach his hand into. He felt hard soil underneath the floor. It was obvious the hole would have to be a lot larger for Eddie to investigate what was down there. He chopped to widen it. The concrete had weakened under the relentless pounding, and large chunks started breaking off. Eddie pulled out the chunks by hand and tossed them aside. Soon, he had removed nearly the entire concrete patch, uncovering black earth, the blackest dirt he had ever seen, like a deposit of designer potting soil. Sweat dripped from his nose into the hole.

Above him, the old house squealed, as if suddenly startled.

Eddie shook his fist at the house for trying to scare him, and then smiled to himself.

Nothing but soft earth to dig.

He swung the pick three times, loosened some soil, and then reached into the hole with cupped hands and scooped out the dirt. Then he swung the pick three more times. He soon lost himself in the rhythmic monotony of the task, until the hole was knee-deep and he was standing in it.

How deep should he go? Waist deep? Eye-level? For the first time since he had started to dig, Eddie felt a sliver of doubt. What if there was nothing under there?

I'll dig until the lantern burns out, he promised himself. He moved the lamp to the edge of the hole. The very next stroke of the pick uncovered something metallic in the dirt.

Eddie tugged it gently.

A key.

Terribly rusted, the key was attached to a plastic yellow key chain in the shape of an "S." He wiped a soiled thumb over the key chain and read a set of raised letters:

Solomon Secure Transport Co.

Eddie felt a cold chill, as if sleet was suddenly falling against his bare skin. The key had been here thirty years, since Henry Bourque and Jimmy Whistle had heisted the armored car.

He looked at the keychain and then into the hole.

The gold?

Eddie dropped the keychain and hefted the pick. He slammed the tool into the dirt, raked the soil.

Henry and Jimmy must have used this farm as a base when they hijacked the armored car. Jimmy's mother was already dead, the ownership of her farm was tied up in probate, and the place had been shuttered. This was where they had kept the three guards hostage, before one of them managed to escape.

If Eddie's suspicions were correct, then Roger Lime was held captive in the Whistle farm basement until recently—which meant that Jimmy probably was in on the crime. Eddie pictured Jimmy Whistle as he dug. Jimmy seemed too pathetic to handle Lime alone, even with a gun. He must have had a partner.

The pick slammed deep into the earth and then didn't want to budge. Eddie levered it back and forth and saw that the pick had pierced a round white rock a little smaller than volleyball.

Eddie dug with his hands around the rock and then pried it up with the pick. It came up surprisingly easy for such a large stone, impaled on the end of the pick.

Eddie wiped the stone, found it oddly smooth.

Then turned it and saw teeth—human teeth.

"Oh! Jesus!" he screamed.

The pick had entered a human skull through an eye socket. Eddie panted hard, fighting the urge to throw the pick and run.

Long dead…can't hurt you…

Eddie bit his bottom lip and wiggled the skull off the pick. He held it to the light. There was no bottom jaw. Black dust packed the brain cavity. The dust trickled from the spinal opening.

Eddie set the skull down gently. He kicked through the dirt in the hole and found a rib, definitely a rib. Then another long white bone, maybe from the forearm? And the edge of a buried pelvis. There were many more bones he could not identify.

Roger Lime?

Seemed doubtful—these dry bones were long dead and Lime was alive in the kidnapper's photos just days before.

No, this skull had been dead for thirty years. Eddie looked at it. "Which one of the missing guards are you?" Eddie asked under his breath. "Mr. Dumas? Or Mr. Forte?"

Not that it mattered. There seemed to be enough bone in the hole to make two skeletons. There was probably another skull in there somewhere, too.

From the corner of his eye, Eddie spotted a ghost in the shadows. It was coming silently toward him.

Rational thought abandoned Eddie for a moment.

He saw that the ghost had a noose of brown rope in one hand. Eddie had time to blink once. Time to recognize the figure in a ski mask.

And then the man was on him.

Chapter 19

Eddie dived aside with a grunt as the attacker's weight glanced off his shoulder and the noose of rough rope brushed Eddie's face.

Eddie grabbed the pick, swung it awkwardly at the man, but the attacker was too quick. He ducked. A fist shot like a missile into Eddie's jaw. Eddie didn't feel a thing, but he heard the thud of the blow and the clack of his teeth slamming together. He tumbled backward out of the hole and onto the floor. He heard glass shatter and saw the world go black and knew he had landed on the lantern.

The pain all arrived at the same instant, a supernova in his head, stinging cuts on his back. His eyes watered and he wanted to scream, but managed no sound at all. He clutched his head and rolled over in silent agony.

The man in the ski mask was fumbling around, feeling for Eddie in the dark.

"Son'bitch!" the man growled. "Come over here!"

The taste of his own blood woke Eddie to reality. He felt a hand on his foot. The man said, "Ha!" Eddie kicked in the dark, felt air and kicked feebly again. The invisible attacker grabbed Eddie by the belt. An unseen hand found Eddie's throat, and squeezed.

Eddie drove his forearm into the man's bulk, but the attacker's chest was thick and powerful. A thumb pressed into Eddie's windpipe. Eddie twisted fiercely away. He gasped one noisy breath. A fist glanced off Eddie's ear. It stung, but did no real damage. He felt a fist swing past his cheek, then the hand found his throat again and the attacker settled his weight on Eddie's hips. Eddie felt the rope scrape over his temple.

The man was trying to get the noose around Eddie's neck. Eddie bucked and kicked, but could not break free.

This motherfucker's too strong!

Eddie's arms thrashed; his hand brushed on something hard on the floor.

The skull. Eddie jammed two fingers and a thumb in the eye sockets, as if gripping a bowling ball. He guessed where in the dark the man's head would be, and swung with all his strength.

Bone cracked against bone. The skull bounced from Eddie's hand. The man screamed in pain and shock, the grip loosened and Eddie wormed free.

Where to go?

Eddie crawled blindly away in the dark, wheezing quietly for breath. He heard the attacker muttering. Eddie headed away from the sound. His jaw ached; his mouth wouldn't open all the way. The punch had rattled him, filled his mouth with blood. His thinking had begun to clear and he realized he could not take another straight shot to the chin. With clear thinking came the understanding that the attacker was too powerful for Eddie to beat in a fair fight. For the first time in his life, Eddie wished his big brother were around—like the man in the ski mask, Henry was built like a cement truck.

The attacker was stumbling, searching for Eddie in the absolute blackness of the basement.

Eddie's crawled until his shoulder brushed a wall. He silently drooled spit and blood to the floor, and then crawled along the wall, until he reached a corner. There he huddled and considered his options.

If he continued to crawl along the walls, he would eventually bump into the staircase. The problem was that Eddie had become disoriented in the moments after he was hit on the chin, and he didn't know what direction he had crawled to get away. He pictured the L-shaped basement in his mind. The room had five corners—five places where walls came together. He could have been huddled at any one of them.

The attacker was coming Eddie's way.

Eddie heard the man's shoes scuffing the floor, and the man's hands on the wall. He was feeling his way slowly around the room, as Eddie had done.

Run? Or fight?

Eddie considered taking a free swing at his unsuspecting enemy. What were Eddie's chances of knocking the man down with one blind punch in the dark?

Not good, he decided. The man's head was an invisible, moving target. Eddie had no weapon. And Eddie's arms were exhausted from an afternoon of heavy digging; even super-charged with adrenaline, he lacked his full strength.

Eddie rolled quietly away from the wall and waited, breathing silently through his mouth. Sweat ran into his eyes and stung. His heart pounded inside his chest like a runaway piston and Eddie feared the crazy beat would give him away.

The shoes shuffled past his ear by inches.

The man felt his way into the corner and took a left turn, down the next wall. Eddie rolled silently to his feet, put a hand to the wall and listened. He heard the man stub his shoe on another wall, then stumble and catch himself.

He's at another corner.

The man took several more steps and then knocked into another obstacle, making a hollow thud.

The stairs!

Eddie instantly placed himself on a mental map of the basement, at the lower left-hand corner of the L.

He sneaked along the wall, trailing his attacker, keeping a hand out to feel for the next corner. When he reached it, he turned left and slowly made for the stairs. More blood pooled in his mouth. He drooled it into his palm and then wiped the hand on his pants.

Reaching a hand low in front of him he felt the bottom stair.

The old wooden staircase would be too noisy to slink up. Once he stepped on it, the man would be coming after him. Eddie took a deep breath, rocked back on his heels and then exploded up the stairs on all fours. At the top, he ducked his head and plowed his shoulder into the door. It popped open and Eddie rolled onto the floor.

Footsteps thundered up the stairs behind him.

Eddie bounced to his feet. The house was dark, but not black like the basement; dim moonlight filtered through the broken windows. Eddie tore through the kitchen, searching for the way out. He ran to the next room, then the next, saw the door and whipped through it.

Outside, a crescent moon was tangled in the treetops. Far from any city lights, the stars were brilliant on this cloudless night. As he sprinted alongside the house, Eddie listened for the man's footsteps behind him on the porch, but heard nothing.

Could I have lost him?

Ahead, a black shape crashed suddenly out a first floor window, rolled over in Eddie's path, bounded up and ducked into a linebacker's crouch.

There was no time to be nimble. Eddie lowered his shoulder and plowed into the attacker. Both men groaned and rolled to the ground. Eddie was first to his feet. He took one step, heard the man growl and felt a hand grab for his shoe. Eddie tumbled again, rolled over, staggered to his feet and dashed off, the attacker right on him.

Eddie felt the man at his left shoulder, then jigged right and headed across the hayfield for the woods. The Late Chuckie's rat bike was in the other direction, but Eddie had no choice—if he couldn't lose this guy, the bike would be renamed for The Late Eddie.

Running through the tall grass was like running through water. Eddie was a speedster on pavement, but the terrain favored the more powerful attacker. Eddie could hear him panting almost in his ear as their strides landed step-for-step. The man grunted, clubbed Eddie on the shoulder and put Eddie down.

Eddie rolled to his knees and tried to scramble away, but the rope flashed over his head. He grabbed for the rope with his right hand, felt it hit his palm, just under his chin, before the man yanked it back. The rope pinned Eddie's hand against his throat as the attacker wrenched the rope tighter and wrestled Eddie to the ground like a roped calf.

The man growled, "Die now, little bastard."

He straddled Eddie, buried his elbows into Eddie's back for leverage and pulled on the rope.

Eddie's knees pushed into the cool, damp soil. His left hand grasped a fistful of grass. His right hand pulled against the rope around his neck, allowing him only the tiniest gasps of air. His vision blurred and he felt lightheaded.

Eddie saw mountains ahead, dark and hazy. That made no sense to him. There were no mountains here. He stared at the mountains' rounded backs and pulled against the rope.

"Just give up," the man told him, a strain in his voice, "and it'll be over in two minutes."

Two minutes. Five minutes? Eternity? What's the difference?

Eddie pulled forward, fell to his elbow and got half a breath of air before the rope clamped down again.

The man kneed Eddie's ribs.

Eddie felt nothing at all. He reached his left hand out and walked forward two steps on his knees. The man walked with him, pulling against the rope, riding Eddie the way he might break a stubborn burrow.

The man demanded, "Why can't you just *fucking quit?*"

Even if Eddie could have spoken, he would not have known how to answer. He pulled forward again against the rope that was slowly killing him. His left hand tore out grass by the roots. The strange mountains looked close enough to touch. He imagined how Lew Cuhna spent his last few moments, no doubt choking beneath this same powerful assassin. Did Lew fight? Eddie hoped so. The grass tickled Eddie's cheek.

Eddie blinked hard. Fantasy lifted from reality.

Those are not mountains. Those are stones.

He recognized the stone ring around the open well.

A new determination ignited in Eddie for one last desperate pull. He thrashed against the rope with a violence that startled the attacker. Eddie caught another half breath and willed his burning legs three steps forward on his knees. His left hand grabbed for a stone at the edge of the well. The attacker walked with Eddie, keeping the tension on the rope. He seemed to realize what Eddie was trying to do, and dug his heels into the soft earth and leaned back against the noose. His left leg pressed against Eddie's cheek.

In a life or death struggle, there is no sportsmanship. Only survival. Eddie jerked his head around and sunk his teeth into the man's thigh just above the knee.

The attacker shrieked in pain and slapped an open hand over Eddie head. Eddie clamped his teeth deeper into the flesh and shook his head like a pit bull in a dogfight.

The man howled and the rope went slack. The assailant pounded his fist frantically into Eddie's head, as he tried to lift his leg and hop away.

On his knees and lower to the ground, Eddie had an advantage in leverage over his more powerful attacker. He shot a hand under the man's groin and clutched the back of his waistband. He pulled the man toward the open well as he released his bite.

As the attacker fell, he grabbed a fistful of Eddie's hair, and both men tumbled over the edge of the deep well in a tangle of arms, legs and rope.

Chapter 20

Eddie got one deep breath before he plunged underwater and sank. He spun slowly over and saw a circle of night sky through a liquid lens. The stars blurred and it seemed they might wash away. The water grew colder as he sank. He could sink to the bottom, if he wanted to…he needed to decide what he wanted. In the water above, the attacker was thrashing like ten cats in a bag.

I can't beat him…

The bottom of the well seemed a fine place to hide. Eddie had enough of the beating, the choking, and the fighting with a man far stronger than he. Eddie was tired. He was despondent that his last chance to trap the man in the well had failed, because Eddie's trap had swallowed him, too.

The attacker was kicking to the surface. The muffled commotion sounded like it was miles away, as if Eddie were in a sound-resistant bubble traveling to the bottom of the well.

There was no way for Eddie to overpower the man, and no way out of the well even if he *could* beat him, so why not hide at the bottom? Down where the water was cold, and even the attacker in the ski mask was afraid to come. As he slowly sank, Eddie watched the silhouette above him paddling its legs, treading water.

You can't get me down here.

Eddie's lungs were starving; his chest felt like a coal fire. It was the opposite of a real fire; a real fire died when you cut the oxygen—this fire burned hotter by the second. I'll just stay down here, Eddie decided, and wait for the fire to burn out.

Just give up and it'll be over in two minutes.

What the man had said was true, and Eddie hated him for being right. He had never felt such loathing; he was drowning in it. Eddie felt pleasant warmth around his midsection and realized his bladder had released. Another reason to hate him.

That's not him you hate, it's yourself—for giving up.

Yeah, maybe, Eddie thought. But he didn't see how it mattered. The man would just drown Eddie, or choke him, or beat him to death.

Then make him do it.

What would be the point?

It would piss him off.

Yes...

The moment before he kills you, don't forget to give him the finger.

Eddie's face bent into a smile. That was reason to live, even for just one minute longer. The new purpose cleared his fuzzy head. He righted himself in the water, kicked his legs and swept his arms over his head, as if clearing a path. Two strokes...three. He broke the surface with a giant, scratchy breath of air that doused the coal fire in his chest.

The cylindrical well was about seven feet in diameter, which left little room for maneuvering and no place to run except back down. Eddie steadied himself with a palm against the wall, kicked his feet to stay afloat and noisily gulped air.

"Goddam you," the man grumbled. He had a low, purring voice, like that of a mature man, at least a decade or two older than Eddie. "Why do you make this so fucking difficult?" Eddie had pissed him off already—it had been worth coming up.

Eddie had accepted that he would never get out of the well alive, so he wasn't afraid for his life. But now with enough oxygen to think effectively, Eddie was horrified at himself for nearly giving up without a fight.

The man's ski mask was soaked and glistening. He swam at Eddie. Fighting in water was nothing like fighting on land, or even on ice. It was like fighting in zero gravity. There was no leverage, and strength was less of an advantage.

Eddie landed a sharp right hand to the attacker's cheek. The man grunted but otherwise showed no effect. He tried to push Eddie to the side of the well, but Eddie shoved his foot against the wall and pushed back to the center. There they fought. From above, the two men might have looked like a single growling, splashing beast that had risen from the bottom of the well.

Eddie was soon exhausted and it became more difficult to slip repeatedly out of the man's grasp.

He has to be tired, too.

What could Eddie do? Swim until the other guy grew weary and drowned?

The man suddenly changed tactics and disappeared below the surface.

Eddie spun, treading water, looking for his adversary. The water was still.

Suddenly, the man's shoulder hit Eddie in the ribs from below and drove him into the side of the well.

Stunned for a moment, Eddie flailed meekly. The man grabbed under Eddie's chin and knocked Eddie's head back against the stone. The pain was blinding and it drained whatever fight had remained in him.

"Goodbye, Bourque," the man said, "I should have finished this a long time ago."

He pushed Eddie's head beneath the water.

Eddie's scream came out in a gurgle. He struggled up, grabbed a breath, and was forced back under.

He looked up to the rim of the well. Ten feet from freedom. Ten goddam feet.

Wait!

That was the way out, he thought. The walls that trapped them could save Eddie Bourque.

He thrashed his head above water again, coughed, and wheezed his lungs full of air. "When I'm dead," Eddie cried before the man could dunk him again, "so are you!"

Ploosh! Eddie went under again. He was limp. He was done fighting. Either his plan was going to work, or else…

Eddie's head broke the surface, and he could breathe. The attacker held Eddie's neck just above the Adam's apple. Eddie coughed, spit water and then enjoyed delicious air and its damp, mildew smell. He panted, coughed.

The man in the water was just a big square head. Eddie could see the outline of the ski mask, where its eyeholes were, but at this angle it was too dark to recognize the eyes.

The man asked calmly, "What the fuck did you say to me?" His thick breath seemed to fill the well with swamp gas.

Eddie inhaled deep, coughed out a mouthful of water and croaked: "Look at them sheer walls." He took three deep breaths without coughing. "Unless you're Spiderman, there's no way you're climbing out of this well once I'm dead."

The head tilted up, swiveled side to side.

He's thinking about it.

Eddie breathed deep a few more moments, and then pushed the point. "This water's cold, no more than sixty degrees," he said. "We've been splashing around, keeping warm, but look at us now that we're still—my teeth are chattering and I expect yours are, too. You might not survive the night. Water this cold can kill as fast as five or six hours."

"I'm not cold," the man growled. He tightened his grip on Eddie's throat, but not enough to choke him. It seemed he had decided to hear Eddie out.

"Maybe you can survive until the sun warms you in the morning," Eddie said. "But how long do you think you can tread water before you drown?"

"Huh?"

"How long can you stay afloat? The world record is thirty hours," Eddie said. He had picked the number out of the air. He had no clue about the world water-treading record, but who did? Not this guy, for sure.

"Thirty hours?" The man's grip slacked as he looked away and seemed to be doing the math.

"That's thirty hours for an expert swimmer who's *fresh*—not somebody who's been running around all night expending energy trying to kill a guy."

The man grunted and dug his fingernails into Eddie's skin; he hadn't liked Eddie's sarcasm. But the man was boxed in and Eddie was right—neither of them could get out of the well alone.

"The nearest house is a mile away," Eddie said, still breathing heavy. "Nobody will hear you scream. And even if somebody did, would you want them to find you here with my dead body?"

Eddie gave the man a moment to consider his argument.

"No matter how you figure it," Eddie continued, "you're dead by tomorrow evening, if not sooner, either frozen or drowned."

The man clutched Eddie's throat and looked around the well some more. Eddie guessed his thoughts. "Go ahead and try to get out," Eddie offered. "I'll wait here."

The man sounded suspicious. "I'm not leaving you alone."

"Alone?" Eddie chuckled. "Do you think I'm going to run away?" The man said nothing and Eddie guessed his thinking again: "I'm not going to cold-cock you when your back is turned. Then I'd be the one alone in here, drowned or frozen by tomorrow."

That seemed to make sense to the man. He let go of Eddie's throat and swam across the well. He felt along the wall for handholds.

Eddie rested his back against the side of the well and kicked his feet lazily to keep afloat. He needed time to recover, to slow his racing heart and get his breathing back to normal. He took a mental inventory of his injuries. His throat was sore and his windpipe felt bruised, but not dangerously so. There was a lump on the back of his head. Eddie touched it, felt warm blood. He pressed it, grimaced at the shallow pain, and decided it was a serious *scalp* injury, which was way better than a *skull* injury. He could not taste blood in his mouth anymore, though his jaw was still stiff and it hurt to open his mouth. It reminded him of the time he took a baseball to the chin off a bad hop—in two weeks he was fine. There were numerous other superficial welts, scrapes and pulled muscles in his back, neck and arms that would hurt tomorrow, if he lived that long. Those problems were of no concern at the moment. Overall, Eddie was pleased. He had come close to death without a debilitating injury that would make escape impossible.

The cold water was a minor concern—he had been truthful that sixty-degree water could kill them before sun-up. But Eddie was confident he could stand the cold for another hour or two. By that time, he'd either be free or murdered.

The man scraped his feet on the wall in a useless attempt to scale the stone.

"We're kinda fucked, aren't we?" Eddie said. He used the word "we" deliberately, to reinforce the idea that they were trapped together, and that the killer needed Eddie to escape.

"Shut up," the man ordered. He felt his way along the curve.

Eddie was quiet for a minute. His breathing slowed to normal. When the man wasn't actively trying to kill him, Eddie found the masked assailant fascinating. What would drive a man so far beyond the reach of his own conscience? Eddie couldn't help himself from beginning an interview: "Why did you try to run me down in your van?"

The man kept his attention to the wall. "To kill you."

His matter-of-fact manner sent a shiver through Eddie. He had grown used to his lack of fear when all seemed lost and he had nothing to lose. Since then, fresh air and a hope for escape had replenished Eddie's will to live—now he had something he was afraid to lose. He forced a laugh. "Okay, dumb question," he said. "*Why* do you want to kill me?"

"You peons make trouble for me, Bourque." The man tried to exploit a tiny crack between two bricks as a finger hold. His fingers slipped when he tried to pull himself up and he growled in anger.

The man thought of Eddie as a peon—a pawn, the lowest ranking soldier on the chessboard. How did he view himself? As the king, no doubt. And nobody sacrifices a king to destroy one pawn. The assailant was desperate to kill Eddie, but he wouldn't trade his own life to complete the job. It had to be obvious to the man that even the best rock climber in the world would drown if left alone in this smooth-sided well.

Watching the man's clumsy attempts to climb gave Eddie confidence—the assassin would soon be forced to agree that he needed a living Eddie Bourque to help him.

"You know," Eddie said, not caring if he sounded like a know-it-all, "the more energy you waste on futile escape attempts, the less you'll have for a realistic effort."

The man's head whirled around at Eddie, but he said nothing and quickly returned to searching the wall. Eddie splashed one stroke across the well to allow the man to search the area where Eddie had been resting.

Eddie waited, bobbing gently in the water, growing ever colder and trying to be patient. He thought about what the man had told him.

You peons make trouble for me.

"I don't understand how *I* make trouble for *you*," Eddie said. "You're the one who tried to run me down, you're the one who burned up my beloved car. I had to pay a cash deposit on a new Chevette, and I'm getting porked on the price."

"You should've charged it," the man offered. "It's not a bill you'll have to pay."

Eddie chuckled, though at an octave higher than he would have liked. Still, he was pleased to engage the man in conversation. They would need to be on speaking terms if Eddie was going to get out of the well.

"Had I only known," Eddie said, "I would have leased a Porsche."

"You should shut up now."

"You haven't answered my question. How is it that I make trouble for you? Do I know you? Is that why you wear a ski mask in the summer?"

The man completed his survey of the well. "Get over here," he commanded, "and boost me up."

Eddie laughed. "Two problems with that," he said. "There's no chance I'm doing it, and it wouldn't work anyway."

One stroke, no splash, and the man was on him—a bruising grip on Eddie shoulder, a sharp, cracking chop across Eddie's nose. Eddie's head snapped back and his sinuses burned. Blood ran from his nose, over his lip.

"Boost me," the man ordered. Eddie could see him smiling.

Eddie coughed, blinked to clear his eyes. He gasped, "No—my way, or nothing."

The man unleashed his frustration on Eddie Bourque, clubbing a fist over his head, knocking Eddie from reality and parking him in the ether. Eddie was vaguely aware of the man climbing onto his shoulders, trying to use him as a springboard. Eddie's head slipped under. He inhaled liquid and tasted blood.

There's blood in the water.

He thought he saw a shark before reality blurred and went black.

◇ ◇ ◇

"Puke it up, asshole."

A hand thumped three times between Eddie's shoulder blades.

"Puke it up."

Eddie coughed violently. He gasped for air, and then coughed so hard he thought he would pop a vein in his head.

The assassin floated next to Eddie. He had one arm under Eddie's ribcage, holding him up. The killer's other hand pounded Eddie's back, ejecting water from Eddie's windpipe. Eddie wheezed. His feet began kicking by instinct and he realized that the man had pulled him up as Eddie was drowning.

"I'm pushing you back under if you need mouth-to-mouth," the man promised.

Eddie nodded, coughed, gagged, spat, and then agreed in a whisper, "Please do."

The man held Eddie in silence for a few minutes, until Eddie was able to float on his own. The cold had burrowed deep inside him. There was little time left to get out. He knew that the next time he went under would be the last.

The killer's eyes gleamed in the moonlight. Not eyes Eddie recognized. But not eyes he would ever forget.

"What's your way?" the man asked.

"Huh?"

"Your way! Your way *out of here.*"

"Real simple," Eddie said. "We climb up back-to-back, feet on opposite walls, until we reach the top."

The man looked to the top of the well but said nothing.

Eddie guessed his thoughts again. "It'll work—this stone should provide plenty of friction against our feet, and so long as we move in unison, keeping even pressure against each other, the opposing force will allow us to stay elevated."

The killer seemed to think about the plan for a long while. Then he said suddenly, "I had a rope."

Eddie rubbed the bruise around his neck. "I remember."

"It's gone. Must have sunk. Dive down and get it off the bottom."

Eddie shook a finger at him. "So you can tie yourself to me?" he scolded. "And then kill me when we reach the top? No fucking way."

The man reared up in the water and came down with finger clamps around Eddie's throat. "Get down there and get my rope!" His eyes raked over Eddie's face. His mouth bent into a mirthless grin.

Eddie croaked, "This…is…your…grave."

The man's eyes seemed ready to ignite. He roared, heaved Eddie to the middle of the well and then slammed his fist on the water.

Eddie rubbed his sore neck, and then smiled behind his hand.

I'm gonna beat you.

Eddie said, "I'm glad we settled that without anybody getting killed." He was sarcastic and cheerful sounding. "When we both get to the top, we'll each grab the side of the well closest to us. If you're on your feet quicker than me, you can run around the well and kick me back in."

The man snorted.

"Yeah—I thought you'd like that part. But if I'm out quicker, I'll kick *you* back in."

It was a lie, a carefully placed suggestion.

"You don't got it in you," scoffed the assassin.

"To kill? Maybe not. But I can tell the cops where to look for you. They'll want to see how pretty you are under that mask. I can't wait to hear you *splash*."

The killer went *grunt, grunt*. "I should have finished you, Bourque. After you got out of the car I should have come back and finished you."

"Why didn't you?"

"Against my better judgment." He spun a half-turn around. "Get your back against mine."

Eddie swam to him and pressed his back against the killer's. Both men placed their feet against the sides of the well and pushed. They rose to the level of the water, lost balance and slipped back in.

The man spit a spray of water. "It's not working!"

"It'll work," Eddie assured him. "We both need to take a wider stance with our feet. Keep the pressure *even*. You can't try to race me outta here."

Back to back, they pushed against each other and slowly spidered out of the water, a few inches at a time, and then hovered in air. For balance, they clasped hands. The attacker's fingers were like sausage casings packed with hard clay.

"I'm stepping my left foot," Eddie announced. "Now you step your right." Pressed together they climbed, left, right, left. Eddie's thighs heated under the strain. He was aware of the thick muscles overlaying the killer's broad back.

"If not today," whispered the assassin, "I'll get you someday, Bourque."

"Left foot," Eddie answered. "Good, now the right. Keep the pressure."

"You'll turn the key and I'll be behind the door."

"How lovely," Eddie said. He panted from the physical strain of climbing the well. "Now the left foot again—good."

"When you lie down to sleep—"

"We're more than halfway there."

"—I'll be under the bed."

"Bring coffee," Eddie said. "Keep your stance wide."

The assassin also breathed heavy from the labor. He said, "Use up all your jokes, because the moment you feel safe, that's when I'll appear."

They neared the top of the well.

"We'll need to reach for the rim at the same moment," Eddie said, "or we'll both fall back in. I'll reach for the right, you reach for the left and we'll maintain the opposing force to the last instant. No sudden moves until we have a grip on the wall."

"Got it."

"And then I'll run around and kick you back down," Eddie reminded him.

The killer chortled.

The men slowly unclasped their hands.

Eddie reached his right arm for the top of the stone rim. He barely had a hand on it when the killer lunged for the opposite wall. Eddie had anticipated the double-cross and he slapped his hand accurately on the rim as his body swung into the wall. Hanging by one hand, his cheek against the stone, Eddie heard the killer clambering up the opposite side of the well. Eddie reached his other hand up, found a solid grip and heaved himself in an overhand pull-up. In adrenaline frenzy, Eddie wormed the bottom of his ribcage over the lip of the well, smacked his right elbow down for leverage and swung his left leg over the lip. He rolled over the stone ring, popped up and looked for the killer.

The man was still struggling to climb up. Eddie ran around the well toward him.

The killer spotted him, growled and rolled awkwardly over the lip. He scurried away from the well on all fours, so Eddie could not kick him back down. But Eddie never had any intention of taking that chance. He had planted the suggestion simply to buy a few seconds' head start.

Eddie exploded in a sprint down the driveway.

"Chicken shit bastard!" the attacker screamed.

Eddie heard footsteps pounding behind him. He careened into the woods. Small branches, invisible in the night, scratched his face and bare chest. Eddie ran with abandon among the trees, leaping stones and downed branches, plowing over maple saplings. He listened to the crashing footsteps behind him, falling ever more distant as Eddie pulled away. Ducking limbs, dashing around tree trunks—it seemed more like slalom skiing than running. Eddie settled into what runners called a groove, the place where speed met efficiency. He felt like he could run for hours.

The footsteps behind him disappeared. The man had lost him, or had given up.

Eddie ran through the woods, lost, growing ever further from The Late Chuckie's rat bike, but generally heading in a straight line by keeping the moon over his left shoulder. He guessed he had bushwhacked about two miles when he came to a small rise covered with evergreens, on which he stopped to listen.

Nothing.

He had gotten away. Eddie had beaten the assassin and he was giddy.

The man's words repeated in Eddie's memory.

The moment you feel safe, that's when I'll appear.

Eddie stared into the forest.

Not tonight. Tonight I am alive.

He walked through the woods, listening to the sounds of an unseen race between the forest's hunters and their small prey. He learned not to jump at the sound of rustling leaves. His wet pants and shoes began to dry. He had walked an hour, maybe more, when he came to a road—dark, winding, poorly paved. He walked it for about half a mile, and then dived into the brush when headlights approached. He hid as the car cruised past him. What would the assassin be driving? Eddie couldn't say. He could trust no cars until morning.

Staying a few paces inside the woods, he followed the unlit road until the first grays of dawn, when fatigue clubbed him like a mugger and Eddie burrowed, near delirious, under dry leaves and pine needles for just a moment's rest, and thudded into a bottomless sleep.

Chapter 21

He woke to thundering drums. An electric guitar shrieked; Eddie recognized the riff—an old Ozzy tune. Then he heard tires on the pavement nearby, and a car blew past his hiding spot in the woods, taking the music with it down the road.

The sun was high overhead and the air summer-steamy.

Oh no, I slept all morning.

Eddie tried to sit up. Waves of dull pain in his back and neck pushed him back down. He rotated his jaw against a painful stiffness; his fingers explored the swelling under his chin, the left side of his neck, and the back of his head beneath hair matted with tacky blood glue. His hands were scratched and rubbed rough. Eddie swept the blanket of leaves from his chest and gasped. Two dozen scratches decorated his torso. He looked like he had been whipped with a hickory switch. He rolled on his side with a groan, gripped a white oak sapling and hauled himself up.

His pants and shoes were caked with crumbly dried mud. He took a few unsteady steps toward the road, patting himself to inventory his body parts. Everything was still where it was supposed to be. No bones broken. His throat ached, it hurt to swallow and he was sluggish from dehydration and caffeine withdrawal. He felt like a zombie who had misplaced its human soul during an extended tequila bender.

He stumbled onto the road, a country street too narrow to deserve the single yellow line painted down the middle. There were no houses, no sidewalks or utility poles. Just trees. Eddie had no clue where he was. He turned left down the road in the direction the passing car had been heading, on the theory that if people were driving that way, it must lead *somewhere*.

He made lists as he walked of everything he needed to do when he found civilization. First, he had to find a phone, to call Detective Orr. She needed to work out the jurisdictional issues and get to the old Whistle farm immediately.

Second, Eddie needed two liters of Columbian Supremo in an I.V. drip. Stat!

A big gray Buick swayed lazily around the corner, toward Eddie. He squinted at the driver—a woman, black hair in a short bob, no ski mask—and then waved both hands at the car. The car slowed a moment, drew closer, then suddenly roared off with a squeal, the driver staring Eddie down with an open-mouthed grimace.

What's her problem?

He walked some more.

Third on Eddie's list, go home and feed General VonKatz. The General was not accustomed to being left alone overnight, nor did the cat appreciate missing a meal. Eddie imagined the General would be expressing his unhappiness with claws today, maybe converting Eddie's suit trousers into Bermuda shorts.

Fourth, Eddie had to fix that goddam deadbolt on his front door so it couldn't be opened by MasterCard or Visa. He believed what the assassin had told him; Mr. Ski Mask would be back.

Three other cars passed Eddie over the next hour. Nobody would stop. He sat in the middle of the road, on a long straight-away, determined to force the next driver to help him, or run him down.

Time passed. The sun beat on Eddie. He sweated as he sat there.

I had to wander into the least traveled road in Massachusetts.

Another car finally approached.

Good holy heaven, a police cruiser!

Finally, some better luck!

Eddie struggled to his feet. The police car said "Nashua" on the side—that's in New Hampshire. Eddie had crossed the state line during the night. No matter—he waved the cruiser down. The car pulled over. A broad-shouldered cop climbed out slowly, with a hand over his gun.

"Easy, pal," he said in a gentle voice, the tone you'd use to approach a strange dog.

"Really need a telephone!" Eddie blurted. "I was digging this farmhouse basement and I found a skull and a bunch of bones from that old robbery and then this asshole in a ski mask who tried to kill me last week showed up and I spent half the night in a well and the other half in the woods…"

"Whoa!" the officer said. He signaled for a time-out. "You need to get in the back of the cruiser, and we're going to start this story over from the beginning."

Keeping an eye on Eddie, he unsnapped his holster guard.

As Eddie climbed in the back seat, he saw his likeness in the rear view mirror and shrieked, "Jesus and his barber!"

Who was that bare-chested, unshaven, wide-eyed mountain man in the mirror? The one wearing dust and dried blood like pancake makeup and rouge? Eddie scratched black-rimmed fingernails on a scab over his cheekbone. A purple bruise circled his throat. Fortunately his injuries were not as bad as they looked, or he'd have died three times.

"Do you have a towel, or something?" Eddie asked, as the officer slipped into the front seat.

"At the locker room at the station." He slipped the gearshift to "drive." The cruiser made a three-point turn and sped off.

Eddie picked bits of forest off his scalp. "And I could use a comb—I got enough dried twig in my hair to weave a sparrow's nest."

"Yessir, at the station."

"Maybe some coffee, too?"

"We got all kinds."

Is he making fun of me?

"Just call Lowell Police," Eddie said. "Tell Detective Lucy Orr that Eddie Bourque got mixed up in it again." He leaned back and closed his eyes. "She'll know what you mean."

◇ ◇ ◇

Detective Orr let Eddie do the talking during the ride from downtown Nashua to the Whistle farm in an unmarked Lowell police sedan.

Eddie explained as patiently as he could, but it drove him near insane that she kept to the twenty-five miles per hour speed limit. Weren't they in a rush to get to the farmhouse to investigate the shallow grave Eddie had uncovered?

"The perimeter of the farm is secure," Orr promised him. "Tell me the rest of the story."

Was she slowing down? Eddie took a deep breath. He looked human again in a borrowed blue police recreation league t-shirt, sweat pants and canvas sneakers. His pants and shoes were on the seat in a plastic bag. Ten minutes in the men's room had improved his face and hair, and three mugs of Arabica had overhauled his disposition. The two EMTs that had evaluated Eddie at the station had concluded that he was not seriously hurt, though after hearing snippets of his crazy story they had wondered aloud if he was a danger to himself.

Eddie explained to Orr: "So I had the skull in my hand for, like, two seconds when the son-of-a-bitch in the ski mask jumped me. He must have been waiting in the shadows until I found something incriminating."

"And the two of you got trapped in a grave?"

"No, a *well*...that comes later."

"And why were you digging in the first place?"

"Lucy—I told you, I thought it was the basement where the kidnappers had taken the photographs of Roger Lime."

She sighed. "And *you* did the digging?"

Eddie held up his hands. "Wanna see the blisters?"

"Can't you give a better description of this perpetrator than 'ski mask'?"

"It was dark."

"You were with him half the night," she said. "You must have noticed something else about him."

"This was attempted murder, not a fender bender," Eddie said, sharply. "We didn't exchange driver's licenses." They drove in silence a minute. "You don't believe me, do you?"

"It's quite a story, Ed."

Eddie turned his body toward her. *Ouch!* "Look at me—I didn't beat myself purple."

"Nobody doubts you were in a fight last night."

"Then what's the problem?"

"Finish the story," she told him.

Eddie did, describing his fight with the killer, his escape and how he had wandered the woods into New Hampshire.

The police radio cackled; it was unintelligible to Eddie, but Orr seemed to understand. She took the microphone, mumbled some codes into it, adding: "He's with me now. Ten minutes."

She looked straight ahead and said to Eddie, "There's nothing illegal about a person defending himself."

Eddie shrugged. "Of course not."

"Just so long as they tell the truth about it."

"I'm telling the *truth*," Eddie cried. He stopped, enforced calm on himself and began again. "I know it's a cracked-up story, but that's exactly how it happened."

◇ ◇ ◇

Police cars from Lowell, Nashua, Dunstable, and the Massachusetts state police were parked haphazardly along the country road outside the old Whistle farmhouse. A uniformed officer on traffic patrol waved Orr's car through. She parked beside the boulders blocking the driveway. Police had roped off the end of the driveway with yellow barrier tape.

Orr got out without a word and explained briefly who she was to a statie at the tape. He nodded and looked Eddie over.

Eddie got out with his bag of dirty clothes. "I parked over here yesterday," he said. "There—there's my bike."

The Late Chuckie's rat bike was where Eddie had left it. The police had penned it in with yellow tape. Eddie ducked under the tape and flipped open a saddlebag. The contents were a mess, the bag had obviously been searched. He didn't like the police going through his stuff, but he couldn't blame them; he had forgotten to mention that he had arrived on the bike. He stuffed the bag of clothing inside.

"I didn't know you had a motorcycle license," Orr said.

"Yeah, right…um…" Eddie pointed. "The well is down the driveway—let's take a look at it." He led her to it. In the daylight, the well was not a frightening liquid grave; it was a source of clear and harmless water.

"I found the digging tools over there, in the barn," Eddie said. He led Orr to the main house, warning her, "Watch the porch, the boards are rotten."

"You certainly know this place," she said.

"I *told* you that I was here most of the day yesterday."

Police were walking through the house, photographing stuff and making notes.

Eddie waved Orr along. "The basement door is in the kitchen. The stairs are narrow, but they're sturdier than they look." He stood aside to let two detectives in suits come up from the basement. They stared at Eddie's neck bruises as if they were gills.

"Looks worse than they feel," Eddie assured them. He led Orr down the stairs into a basement crowded with portable lights and cops. Flashbulbs were going off. Police were mumbling to each other. An officer dusted for fingerprints on the red lantern Eddie had used the night before.

A man called out, "Detective Orr?"

Eddie recognized the voice—Brill, the cop who had leaked his scoop about Dr. Crane's hanging. He mumbled to Orr, "Not that asshole again."

She shushed him.

"What does that guy have against reporters?"

"I said *shush!*"

Brill said, "The body's around the corner, there."

Orr looked to Eddie and then followed Brill.

"I told you," Eddie said, trailing behind them. "That's where I found the bones." Eddie walked around the corner and looked into the hole.

What he saw was not possible.

Somebody had dug the hole deeper, nearly waist-deep, and had piled the dirt nearby.

In the hole was the battered body of a man, lying face-up— not bones, a dead *body*, and it was wearing a ski mask.

"Choked to death," Brill said.

"Uh-huh," said Orr.

"I'm done here," said a police photographer.

"Take the mask off," Brill ordered.

A uniformed cop reached into the hole and peeled away the mask.

The body's skin was waxy and purpling. There were rope burns around the neck. The eyes were closed, the face relaxed, and blood had trickled from one nostril. The body in the hole was so far removed from the reality Eddie had expected, he pointed into the grave without thinking and shouted: "Holy shit! That's Jimmy Whistle!"

Chapter 22

Back in Detective Orr's sedan—Eddie in the back seat, Orr and Brill up front—Brill gave Eddie the squeeze:

"So you wanted to give Jimmy Whistle some payback for helping put your brother away all those years ago, is that it Bourque?" Brill said. "So you two decided to meet up here, to hash it out?"

Eddie stared at the dome light and tried to delete the mental image of Jimmy Whistle in the grave. He thought about Whistle's son, Jimmy junior, who didn't yet know that he had lost the father he barely remembered. It was another tree-falls-in-the-woods question. If he hadn't seen his father in thirty years, would his murder matter?

"What about it, Bourque?" Brill demanded.

Eddie had conducted enough adversarial interviews as a reporter to know that using logic against crazy scenarios was no way to win. "My statement from before stands," he said. "I found this place on my own. I dug the floor. Discovered a skull. Got jumped. Fought for my life. Called you guys as soon as I found help."

Brill looked away for a moment. As he turned, Eddie watched the bulging trapezoidal muscle at the base of his neck squirm under his shirt like a cobra getting comfortable. Brill turned back and came at Eddie with a new tactic. "Look Bourque, everyone knows Whistle was a punk," he said. "Nobody does thirty years in prison unless they deserve it. If a piece-of-shit like Jimmy Whistle came after me, I'd fight back hard. Who wouldn't?"

"Jimmy wasn't here with me last night."

Brill shrugged, too deliberately, like an actor in a high school drama. "Jimmy was wearing a ski mask."

"It wasn't him," Eddie insisted. "Whistle was a broken down old man. The guy in the mask last night was *strong*."

Brill got angry, leaned over the seat and shook a finger at Eddie. "Dr. Crane, Lew Cuhna and now Jimmy Whistle—there's three bodies in your tracks, Bourque."

Was that a question?

Eddie said nothing. Orr hadn't made a sound during the interrogation. Eddie couldn't remember even seeing her blink. Was this supposed to be good cop-bad cop? Or something else? Mute cop-asshole?

Brill asked, "Is your brother calling the shots here?"

"My brother is in the federal pen."

"Yeah, in upstate New York. You were there recently, according to their visitor logs."

He had already checked the logs?

"So what?" Eddie said. "I visited my brother in the can." *Don't you visit your mother in the whorehouse?* He almost said it, but caught himself in time.

"There's blood evidence in that basement," Brill said. "Maybe that's *your* blood down there."

No maybe about it, and no sense denying what a few simple tests would confirm. "I told you guys I fought for my life down there last night," Eddie said. "I probably dripped blood from here to New Hampshire."

"Stay with me here," Brill said. "You visited your brother in the can, and then the doctor who testified against him dies on a rope. Next, you lead us to the body of your brother's old partner—a street punk who testified against Henry Bourque at his trial. Not to mention that the body is in a shallow grave you admit you dug yourself."

Wow, when you put it all together like that...

Eddie sputtered, "But how would Lew Cuhna fit in?"

Brill frowned, grim. "Don't know, Ed. Why don't you tell us how Cuhna fits in?"

Goddam it!

Eddie had fallen for the trap of applying logic to Brill's crazy hypotheticals. "Like I told you guys," he repeated, "my statement stands. Obviously, somebody removed the bones during the night, then whacked Jimmy and dumped him here."

"Probably the guy in the ski mask," Brill offered, obviously patronizing him. "But not Jimmy—it's the *other guy* in a mask."

"I see why you made detective," Eddie answered, icily.

Brill smiled. He said, "No more trips to New York until we get to the bottom of this, Bourque." He got out of the car and slammed the door.

Orr got out, closed her door gently and had a hushed conversation with Brill.

Eddie struggled to hear what they were saying—no luck.

Orr got back into the car. "Are you in shape to ride that awful bike?" she asked "Or do you need a lift?"

"That's it? I'm not under arrest or anything?"

"Brill knows you didn't kill Jimmy," she said. "He was just trying to rattle you. I told him it was a waste of time."

"But…how?"

"A driver reported a madman fitting your description wandering some back road in New Hampshire this morning. She was pretty scared and called right away from her cell phone. That was more than four hours ago."

Eddie brightened. "I remember that woman!"

"The medical examiner says there's no rigor yet, and body-temperature loss has been minimal, even in that cool basement," she said. "He guesses that Whistle died less than three hours ago, though he can't pinpoint it any better than that. You also left an obvious track through the woods when you ran from here last night—blood smears, footprints in the mud, broken branches—so that part of your nutty story checks out."

"So why did Brill strap me to the rack?"

"Because he thinks you know more than you're telling, Eddie," she said. "And so do I."

"Lucy—"

"Stow it!" she interrupted. "I want to know why you're obsessed with the Roger Lime case, and what you thought you were going to find in that basement."

Eddie massaged the welt on his chin. "It's for Henry," he admitted with a sigh. "And my sister-in-law."

"Since when do you have in-laws?"

"Her name's Bobbi—Bobbi Bourque. She tracked me down in Lowell after Dr. Crane died. She's convinced that Henry is innocent of murdering those armored car guards, and she asked for my help to prove he didn't do it."

"That was thirty years ago."

Eddie shrugged. "You can't discourage this woman—I've tried. Look, Lucy, it was a circumstantial case against Henry." He looked down to his borrowed high-tops and wondered from where his sudden wave of mournfulness had come. "I think Bobbi's right. Henry was a screwed-up kid, mixed in a stupid holdup scheme, but he didn't kill those guards."

Eddie suddenly recognized he had lost an important opportunity in the basement of the old house. Frustration boiled up in a froth. "I had found real evidence, the bones!" he shouted. "And I let them slip away."

"The way you tell it, you didn't let anybody do anything—you fought."

Eddie wouldn't hear it. Tears were not far off. "I let that assassin in a ski mask take my brother from me."

◇ ◇ ◇

Eddie was barely capable on the motorcycle when healthy, and didn't dare ride it after getting choked, beaten up, and nearly drowned. By the time the flatbed tow truck reached Eddie's house in Lowell that evening, the neighborhood's barbeque grills had perfumed Pawtucketville with charcoal and roasted meat.

With the bike stowed in the driveway, the tow driver thanked and tipped a fiver, Eddie grabbed the dirty clothes from the saddlebag, picked an intact *Washington Post* off the lawn, and went inside.

"What the hell…?"

For a moment, he thought the place had been ransacked—a snowstorm of shredded paper covered everything: the carpet, the furniture, the windowsills. He was about to phone for help when into the mess strode General VonKatz, the ripped remnants of a cardboard paper towel tube in his jaws.

Eddie groaned, "I know you've missed a couple meals, but that was a brand-new roll!"

The cat dropped the tube, dug in the mess to gather shredded paper into a little pile, and then pounced on the pile and scattered the paper again.

Eddie muttered, "I gotta clean this place with a rake."

He fed the General a can of chicken hearts and liver, and then inched the sofa across the room and in front of the door. He skipped dinner, flopped onto his sofa barricade, and tried to sleep. He saw an image of Jimmy Whistle in his mind, in the grave, rubbed raw around the neck. Eddie turned over and ordered his brain to think about baseball. The players had rope burns around their throats.

The moment you feel safe, that's when I'll appear.

Eddie didn't feel safe. Did that mean the man was not coming? The question twirled in his mind as he fell into fitful sleep.

Chapter 23

Eddie felt pressure on his neck and woke with a start. He grabbed for his throat and felt fur. The General screeched in surprise and bolted from the sofa.

"Sorry!" Eddie called after the cat.

The clock read seven-thirty. Eddie had slept thirteen hours. He rolled sore off the sofa and peeked through the blinds. Bright sun. Kids choosing sides for a whiffleball game in the street. *Washington Post*, intact once again, on the lawn.

Eddie brewed hazelnut coffee, pushed the sofa out of the way, and got his newspaper.

The General sat at attention next to his empty food dish. The cat's message would not have been clearer if he had typed it in headline font. Eddie threw a handful of crunchy food in the bowl, which attracted one sniff and an incredulous *are you bloody kidding me?* meow.

"Okay," Eddie said. "No sense us both starving." He fed the cat a can of chopped chicken parts in savory gravy, which stank like a landfill. *Cripes!* What "parts" of the chicken did they grind up and pack in these cans?

General VonKatz seemed to like the bouquet. He nosed into the dish.

Eddie hadn't read the paper for three days, maybe the longest dry spell since he had entered the news business. His obsession with his brother's case had consumed him. He had lacked the processing power to digest a world's worth of news. But Eddie and the General had to eat, and Eddie needed another writing assignment.

He wiped shredded paper towel off the table and sat down with black coffee. He scanned the morning's mayhem on the front page and then flipped to the classified section.

The phone rang.

Eddie reached for it, and then hesitated.

What if it's HIM?

He shook off the thought as ridiculous and answered, "Bourque."

"It's Lucy," said Detective Orr.

Eddie laughed with relief. He said, "Are you just seeing if I'm all right?"

She was all business. "I've been doing some checking. How much do you know about this sister-in-law of yours?"

Checking? On Bobbi?

"I know she married Henry about six months ago," Eddie said. "I know she takes eight sugars in her coffee." What *else* did he know about her?

"The records show that her marriage to Henry Bourque was filed in Essex County, New York state last spring."

"Sounds right."

"That was the day after her divorce from her second husband."

"The next day?"

"Yup—after fifteen years of marriage she got a divorce and remarried the very next day."

Eddie thought it over. "Well, sure," he offered. "She was probably separated when she met Henry, and they had to wait until her divorce was official before they could get married."

"Have you heard from her today?"

Eddie double-checked his answering machine. No blinking light. "I have not." Should he have? He felt a flicker of worry. "Huh."

"I'm sure she's fine," Orr said. "The next time you hear from her, have her give me a call."

"Why? You don't think—"

"I don't think she did anything wrong," Orr interrupted. She lowered her voice: "But somebody is killing the people connected to you, to your brother, and the Roger Lime investigation. I need to know who your sister-in-law has been speaking to around Lowell. She could be in danger, or she could be unwittingly stirring up old secrets and putting other people into harm's way."

Orr wouldn't lie to Eddie, but Eddie didn't believe she was telling him the whole truth. What did Orr suspect Bobbi was up to?

"I'll tell her to call," he promised.

They chatted a few minutes about Eddie's recovery from his night in the well. Orr told him: "Keep your nose out of trouble."

"No problem there." Eddie had no leads, nowhere to go, nothing to do but wait for the police to catch the man in the ski mask, or for the man to catch Eddie.

They hung up.

Eddie gave a glance to the chessboard, the pieces frozen two moves into an imaginary game with Henry. He forced his eyes to the classifieds.

There has to be some work in here...

An advertisement halfway down the first column stopped Eddie hard:

```
Attention EDDIE B.
   Trouble for me. I trust only jour-
nalists. Left the key with the two
giants, you know the duo. Don't send
the cavalry; follow the Union rider
to General Lee's surrender. —LEW
```

Eddie read the item three more times.

Was this a message from Lew Cuhna? A message from the grave?

How was that possible?

The last two days of the *Washington Post* rested intact and unread on the table. Eddie tore them open, found the classified sections—the same odd advertisement was there, in both editions.

He rifled through the paper until he found the telephone number for the *Post*'s classified department, and then snatched up the telephone and dialed it. He negotiated the automatic answering system until he found the human he needed.

"Classified—accounts payable," answered a woman with southern flavor in her voice.

"Hi, my name is Lew Cuhna," Eddie said. "I'm afraid I have a paperwork problem. I placed a prepaid classified ad for my company recently, and I can't remember the dates it was to run, so I don't know when to renew it. My boss is on my case about it."

"Oh my!"

"Yeah, he's a stickler for record keeping."

"Just give me a second, Mr. Cuhna." She rapped a keyboard. "We don't want out customers in hot water with the boss."

"No ma'am."

"Oh, there it is," she said. "You're all set, prepaid for three more weeks."

"And you're sure the name on that ad is Lew Cuhna, of, um…" *Where the hell did Cuhna live?* "…of Massachusetts?"

"Yup—Chelmsford, Mass."

"Very good, thank you." He hung up.

Eddie thought back to the recent trouble with his morning delivery, when the paper was torn apart every day. He never did find those classified sections.

His paper started getting messed up after Eddie spoke to Cuhna. But the *Post* had arrived intact each day since Lew had been murdered.

Those weren't raccoons that were rifling through Eddie's paper every morning.

It was Lew.

Eddie slapped his palm on the table. Of course! Insurance!

Lew was in some kind of trouble and Eddie was his insurance. Cuhna knew that Eddie studied the *Post*'s classifieds every day—they had spoken about it at the cop shop. Cuhna placed a message in the paper that only Eddie would recognize, prepaid in case something happened to him. And each day Cuhna detoured through Pawtucketville on his way to his office, stopping early in the morning to swipe Eddie's classified section.

As long as Lew was healthy, Eddie would never see the message. It wasn't the sort of arrangement Cuhna could have expected to keep up for long—you can't steal a man's paper forever. He must have thought the danger would soon pass, whatever it was.

Eddie cursed himself for not reading the *Post* the first day he had found it intact. He had already lost two days. But at least he had found the message. He read it over again. Now what the heck did it mean?

Trouble for me.

That much was obvious.

Lew had placed the ad because he suspected someone might be after him, yet he did not go to the police. Why not? Perhaps Lew had gotten mixed up in something illegal. If he had been dabbling with the bookmakers or the heroin wholesalers, he would have been reluctant to ask the cops for help.

I trust only journalists.

Eddie tried to remember what Cuhna had said to him at the police station. Something about Eddie being a newsman, and that Lew trusted a good newsman. Maybe that was Cuhna's way of telling Eddie that he had chosen him to receive the message. Christ, Eddie thought, he could have been more specific about what he was entrusting to Eddie.

Left the key with the two giants, you know the duo.

Made no sense. They key to what? A lock? To the mystery of Cuhna's murder? Or the key to this riddle? Eddie couldn't think of any "giants" who formed a duo. He thought for a moment about the tallest people he knew. Two giants? Two big cops who were partners, maybe? Naw, this line had to be allegorical. Two giants…a duo…This message was so goddam cryptic! For all Eddie knew, Cuhna was talking about the duo of peanut butter and Fluff.

Don't send the cavalry; follow the Union rider to General Lee's surrender.

The cavalry could be the cops. Why wouldn't Lew want Eddie to call the cops? Especially if he knew the message would only be seen if he were abducted or killed? Eddie rubbed his eyes. No cops…hmmmm, could there be a leak in the Police Department? Eddie read the line again.

Was Cuhna afraid of a dirty cop?

The last part of the message seemed nonsense.

Union rider? General Lee?

Civil War General Robert E. Lee had surrendered to the Union at Appomattox. Eddie couldn't imagine that Lew Cuhna had meant for him to ride The Late Chuckie's rat bike to Virginia. It seemed to be another metaphor. But for what?

Dammit Lew. Why couldn't you have just spelled it out?

Eddie knew the answer—Cuhna had hidden something of great value and didn't want to lose it to the wrong people. So he had created a cipher he thought only Eddie could break.

Eddie drained a full pot of coffee while experimenting with Cuhna's words. He assigned numbers to the letters, jumbled the characters, read things backward, tried to decipher anagrams. No luck. Either Lew Cuhna had typed his classified ad with the Enigma machine, or this message was somehow simpler than it seemed.

The phone rang.

He glanced to the clock as he answered; he had been working on Lew Cuhna's code for two hours.

Bobbi was on the line.

"I was getting worried about you," Eddie said.

"Some worry lines would do you good," she said. "So you won't look young enough to be my baby."

"You don't need an under-employed kid in his thirties."

"I'd take one if I could," she said. She suddenly shifted the topic. "Have you seen the paper—this guy they found dead in Dunstable, James J. Whistle? He testified against Henry at his trial thirty years ago. Did you see that?"

Eddie frowned. "I didn't see the paper yet, but I, uh, heard about it."

"That guy could have helped us, but now it's too late."

"He may help us yet," Eddie said. He pulled a topic switch on her for once. "Have you and Henry ever talked about having a family?"

She laughed. "You mean kids? This just reminds me that I've never touched the man I married. Closest I've come is touching his letters, which I know he had in his hands—oh, gawd, look at the time!"

"Wha?"

"Forget all that because this is *important*. I'm hanging up now, but don't go anywhere—not even to the bathroom."

"Huh?"

Click.

Eddie shrugged and stared at the cordless phone. His sister-in-law was as puzzling as Lew Cuhna's message. She had called for something *important*, so she had to hang up? Maybe it was best that she and Henry couldn't have kids. *Oh, dammit!* Eddie had forgotten to tell her to call Detective Orr.

The phone rang in Eddie's hands.

He answered sharply, "What *now*?"

A man's voice asked, "Mr. Edward Bourque?"

"Oh! Sorry. Yes, this is he."

The man explained that he was a counselor in the federal penitentiary system, working at the facility holding Henry in New York.

Eddie felt a flash of terror. He was speechless. What had happened to Henry? *Stabbed. Hanged. Shot trying to escape.*

"You there, Mr. Bourque?" the man said into the silent telephone.

Eddie cleared his throat. "Yes, yes. What's the matter with Henry?"

"Nothing, sir—hold please."

Classical music came on the line while Eddie was holding.

Eddie felt relief. This was *strange*—it was odd to worry for his brother. He had rarely thought about Henry before his brother's letter had arrived. And now Eddie was getting heart palpitations over a phone call from the prison.

The line went quiet a moment and Eddie thought he was disconnected, then another man got on the line:

"It's not my voice you hear, of course, it's only an approximation."

"Henry?"

"My voice exists in the physical world as a disturbance among molecules of air. The telephone replicates the disturbance on your end."

"Sounds like a good copy, Henry."

"The real magic is in your mind," Henry said. "After the air molecules play a beat on your eardrum, the rhythm becomes electrical and goes to the brain. That's where the mind, the larger part of you, in between man and God but much more like the latter, interprets those electrical pulses and gives you the music of my voice. It's no different if there is no phone and we are speaking in person. It's still not my *voice* you hear, only the simulated echo of an idea that starts in my mind and ends in yours."

Henry's brain was like a rocket with no wings, twisting wildly in the stratosphere at a thousand miles an hour. If Eddie could only help him focus his thought…

"I think you ought to fight for your freedom," Eddie said, pulling a topic switch on Henry, too.

"Did you find my five-sided table?"

"I'm closing in on it," Eddie said. "I saw Jimmy Whistle."

A pause. "How is that son-of-bitch?"

"Fine when I saw him, but now he's dead—murdered."

"They know who did it?"

"Nope."

"And here I am, locked away without an alibi."

The words chilled Eddie, and he wasn't sure why—when it came to gallows humor, journalists were nearly as bad as cops. Henry seemed to sense Eddie's unease.

"I can't cry for Jimmy."

"I wouldn't expect…I mean—he testified against you."

"It's the damndest thing," Henry said, "but I can't cry at all. I used to cry every day after I got locked up. Most guys here, they wail into a towel to cover it up. But I said, what the fuck? I wanna cry, I'll cry."

"What happened?"

"There was this big motherfucker, nicknamed Monk because he barely ever said two words—as if he had taken vow of silence. He saw me cry one time. I'll never forget what he told me. 'Boy,' he said, 'I don't like your face like that.' This was the longest conversation Monk ever had in twenty years on the block. I pissed battery acid in those days, so I told him, 'You don't like my face, what you gonna do about it?' "

Henry laughed at the memory.

Eddie laughed, too. "So what did Monk do?"

"He didn't like my face, so he tried to cut it off."

Eddie jumped to his feet, slack jawed, screaming without sound. He pictured Henry's scar, the long, purple earthworm around his head.

"Since then, I can't cry," Henry explained. "He stole that from me, and I never forgave him. So you can forgive me if I don't show my compassion for Jimmy Whistle."

Eddie stammered, "Yeah, Henry…sure."

"My bride tells me you've been helping her out in Lowell," he said, cheerfully. "You're a good man, little brother. Smart. That's what I like. That's why I knew I could turn to you. I knew you could find the truth."

Eddie didn't understand. "Do you mean about Roger Lime?" he said, but the moment had passed and Henry was already into a new thought.

"We've only got a little time left," Henry said. "I'll think about what you told me, maybe call the public defender."

"You mean you might challenge your conviction in court?"

"It would be a leap of faith I haven't been able to make." The line beeped three times. "Uh-oh, we have, like, ten seconds to say goodbye."

Eddie had too many questions, about Henry, Roger Lime, the five-side table, Lew Cuhna's note from the grave. Henry may have been borderline crazy, but he was *brilliant.* Eddie blurted, "Where in Lowell do I find Lee's surrender?"

Henry laughed. "Have you tried the library?"

The line fell silent without even a click.

Chapter 24

Try the library?

Maybe Henry was more wiseass than genius.

I'm trying to solve a murder, not write a book report.

The phone rang again in Eddie's hands.

"Hello?"

"Did he call? Did you talk to him?" Bobbi sounded tense, crackling with nerves.

"Yeah, he called. And that reminds me, you need to call Detective Orr from Lowell police. Nothing to worry about—she's a friend of mine, a straight shooter."

She didn't seem to hear him. "What did he say, Ed? Will he do it? Will he fight for his freedom?"

"He's thinking about it."

"Uh!" she groaned. "Ed, we gotta do better than that. He's *thinking* about it? That's like when you ask your dad for a pony and he says, 'We'll see, lemme think about it.' It's the easiest way to say no." She sighed and moaned dramatically a few times. When Eddie said nothing, she sighed a few more times.

"I get the message—you're ticked," Eddie said.

"Henry told me that he wanted to hear what *you* thought about his chances, and that he'd do what you told him to do."

"Who said he won't?"

"I thought you'd get a commitment out of him." She was scolding Eddie, not harshly, but her disappointment was clear. "You're his *brother*."

"I barely know the guy."

"What would that have to do with it? It's family, Ed—you got leverage with family you need to use in tough scrapes like this. You got to lean on that frustrating, pigheaded man, make him see that he has a chance, that it's worth it to try to be free—that *I'm* worth it, goddamit!"

"How would you know what leverage I have with my family?"

"Because *everybody* has it," she said. "In every family! Jesus, Ed!"

Eddie heard her slap the phone on a table. She held it there a moment, then picked it up. She clucked her tongue, took a deep breath, gave a playful "grrrrrrrr" and a flighty chuckle. Sounding brighter, she said, "I need to remind myself that you don't know the first thing about siblings, do you?"

The question embarrassed Eddie. Why should he be embarrassed? He wasn't the one in prison the past thirty years. None of this mess was Eddie's fault—not Henry's incarceration, nor his parents' split, nor the way his folks had faded from his life. Yet he had trouble admitting aloud that his family was a disaster. He swiped his hand over the General's back as the cat strolled across the table. He had no answer for Bobbi.

She was tender to him. "Relationships between brothers are normally made when you're both little kids," she said. "You're doing it as an adult. It has to be hard—like learning Chinese."

"Chinese kids can speak it when they're four," Eddie said, completing her thought.

"So you'll do it the hard way," she said. "Big surprise—one of the Bourque boys is doing things the hard way. You are so much like your brother…" She trailed off, laughing.

Eddie smiled—couldn't help himself.

"We've found some circumstantial stuff that might help Hank's case," Bobbi said, businesslike all of a sudden, "but we need *more*."

Eddie looked over the notes he had made trying to crack Lew Cuhna's code, and frowned. "I think our best chance right now is to see what we can learn from Jimmy Whistle. I interviewed him recently and I know where he lived."

"Isn't he *dead?*"

"That's an inconvenience we'll have to work around," Eddie said. "They say you can't take it with you, so all Jimmy's stuff is still in his apartment. By now the police have searched the place, but I'd like to see what they found, and what they missed. You can learn a lot about a guy by what he keeps hidden in the back of the closet."

"Take me with you!"

"Not a good idea," Eddie said. "The cops might have the place roped off, or even guarded."

"Then you'll need *me* to pry open the lock. I got eleven credit cards, and I know how to use them."

Eddie had figured on finding an open window, slipping into Jimmy's place and poking around. He didn't have a backup plan if the place was locked down. Reluctantly, he gave in: "Your sister-in-law's credit cards—don't break into a home without them."

◇ ◇ ◇

Eddie waited a hundred yards down the street from Jimmy Whistle's place, in the parking lot of an upscale athletic club—the kind of place that played nothing but dance music, and where even the tanning beds were plated in chrome. European sedans shared the parking lot with a dozen gigantic SUVs that each could out-tow a battleship, though the ship would get better mileage. Eddie had parked The Late Chuckie's rat bike behind the trash bin, the only place in the parking lot where the bike seemed in character with its surroundings.

He watched Bobbi stroll past the police car parked outside Whistle's apartment building. She buffed her nails with an emery board, gave a tiny, uninterested glance into the cruiser as she passed, and then walked on, around the block and back to Eddie.

"Just one cop in the car," she said. "He's working on a laptop computer."

"Probably just filing reports," Eddie said. "But he's busy, and that's a good sign. I'm guessing that he's still technically on patrol and not on orders to guard Whistle's place his whole shift."

Bobbi huffed, "Are we supposed to wait here all afternoon for him to leave?"

"Get ready to run."

She looked around, confused. "Why?"

Eddie slammed his palm on the hood of a gray Saab. The car alarm screeched, *Deee-OOOH! Deee-OOOH!*

He smacked a Lincoln Navigator and set off another alarm, the same cadence as the first. He hit an Audi, a high-end Subaru, some little thing by Mazda—anything with a blinking red alarm light inside. Within seconds, a dozen car alarms were howling.

Eddie grabbed Bobbi's hand, sprinted her across the parking lot to the street, stopped, and then calmly crossed while looking over his shoulder at the chaos of electronic screams, blasting horns, flashing headlights and irate people now pouring from the club, barking curses and searching pockets and purses and gym bags for the remote control doohickeys to tame their cars. These people started looking for someone to blame, and immediately began finger pointing and arguing with each other over the din.

"This could turn ugly," Eddie deadpanned. "I hope there's a cop in this neighborhood."

As if on cue, the officer parked at Jimmy Whistle's place hit his blues and decided to drive in for a closer look at the madness in the parking lot.

Bobbi turned to Eddie with a half-smile. "And I thought my husband was the bad boy of the Bourque family," she said.

They hurried to Whistle's building as quickly as they dared. Out of sight from the street, Eddie checked the back yard.

"Jimmy's crappy old bike is still there," he said.

"Who'd steal that piece of junk?"

"The bike was Jimmy's only transportation, which means he was either killed here and dumped at the farm, or he left willingly in somebody else's car."

"Or he took a cab," Bobbi argued. "Or walked someplace and got snatched off the sidewalk."

A devil's advocate—the downside of bringing a relative on a break-in.

"Just open the door," Eddie said.

Bobbi wiggled a Filene's card against the jamb and had the door open in three seconds. "Ooh," she said, "I shouldn't have done that so quick—you're going to get the wrong idea about me."

Eddie laughed and pushed her gently inside. He felt a fluttering sense of danger, like a pigeon flapping inside his chest. They were committing a crime for a noble purpose, but breaking and entering was still a crime.

"Don't touch any lights," Eddie reminded her. "We don't want to advertise that we're looking around in here."

Bobbi stuck her hands on her hips and surveyed the grime left by an old, dead bachelor. "This would go quicker if I knew what to look for."

"A defining detail," Eddie said. "That's what we call it in journalism. Something to show us an unknown truth about James J. Whistle." He stepped to the kitchen.

Bobbi wandered into the bedroom. "Yuck!" she cried. "He's got dirty clothes piled like a haystack. Eew! And I think he liked to eat in bed. This is gross—how did I end up with the bedroom?"

"Can't be worse than this kitchen," Eddie said. "He was keeping an ant farm in here, the free-range variety."

"Ug!"

"Industrious little fellers," Eddie said. "You should see them work this cheese doodle."

Bobbi laughed and made some comment, but Eddie wasn't listening. In the sink were two clay mugs, empty except for one damp tea bag in each. Eddie leaned into the sink and sniffed them.

Chai spice tea.

The kind of tea Lew Cuhna had been making when he was killed. Eddie checked Whistle's cabinets—nothing but generic coffee, matzo crackers, and macaroni and cheese. No tea. He dug through the wastebasket and sent black ants scurrying. Lots of fast food wrappers, no empty tea boxes.

Eddie had long believed that there was no such thing as coincidence.

Lew wasn't making tea for me...

Cuhna had been making tea for his killer. So had Jimmy Whistle.

What did Jimmy Whistle, thirty years locked up, know about chai tea? The killer had brought his own tea bags. He had asked Whistle to brew it, had even shared some with old Jimmy. Then he persuaded Whistle to go for a ride, eventually to his old lady's farm.

Eddie shot a hard glance at Jimmy's kitchen table, a little square of black Formica. There were two chairs, chrome and padded with pink vinyl. Eddie's imagination put the man in the ski mask in one of the chairs.

You were here.

Jimmy had known the killer well—but not well enough to suspect he was to be murdered.

Eddie walked back to the living room, his eyes combing the clutter and trash. There were no bloodstains, no obvious signs of struggle. The soda cans Eddie had noticed last time he had visited were still upright on the coffee table. The lone picture of Jimmy junior was still on the wall.

Bobbi shouted from the other room: "Is it all right I turn on the closet light? I doubt anyone would see it, and there's a lot of junk in there I can't make out." The bedroom was at the back of the house, away from the street.

"Yeah, that should be safe," Eddie answered. He couldn't look away from the photo of Jimmy junior. Whistle had nearly blown off his hinges when Eddie had reached for the picture. He lifted the frame off its nail and studied it.

The shirtless little boy throwing the ball in the snapshot had little tan lines at his collar and his upper arm, where the sleeves of a t-shirt would be. He was still training his muscles to work together to throw, and his face showed supreme concentration.

Eddie slid the backing off the frame, to look for a date on the photo.

Underneath the picture of Jimmy junior, Eddie found a second photograph, a four-by-six of a man in a business suit—in his mid-thirties, probably—reading the *New York Times* at an outdoor café, apparently unaware that he was being photographed. The date stamped by the processing lab on the back of the picture was three months ago.

Eddie studied the face. The man was a stranger, but Eddie sensed that he knew the guy... something about the chin, the way it tapered and then suddenly squared off.

It's Jimmy.

Naw, couldn't be... Eddie double-checked the date on the back of the photo. This was a recent shot. But the resemblance was unmistakable—the guy in the picture looked like a younger, healthier, broad-shouldered James J. Whistle.

Hmmm... Eddie compared the photo with the picture of Jimmy junior. Same widespread, sad eyes. Same pointy uptick in the middle of the upper lip. There could be no doubt—the man in the picture was the full-grown Jimmy junior. It was impossible to tell where the photo was taken; a city, obviously, with sidewalk cafés. He was reading the *Times*...Manhattan, maybe?

So Jimmy had lied to Eddie about his son. He *did* know what had happened to Jimmy junior, and by the looks of the younger Whistle—healthy, well dressed in a charcoal suit, peach-colored dress shirt, and dark tie—the kid had fared well while his father was in the penitentiary.

"Eddie?" Bobbi called. "I got something here, a picture."

She appeared in the bedroom doorway.

"I got one, too," Eddie said, holding up the photos. "Jimmy Whistle's son!"

Bobbi's face was blank.

"A new picture of him, all grown up," Eddie explained in excitement. "When I first met Jimmy, he told me he hadn't seen

Jimmy junior in thirty years. But he went through some trouble to get this candid shot of his kid having lunch, so he—*what? Why are you looking at me like that?*"

Bobbi looked to the photograph in her hand. She reached it toward Eddie and held it there.

Eddie hesitated, and then took the picture. It was an instant camera snapshot, the kind that developed by themselves. The picture had been taken in downtown Lowell—Merrimack Street at lunchtime, judging by the crowded sidewalk. Eddie recognized himself in the picture coming out of the bookstore, newspaper under his arm and a paper coffee cup in his hand. He was wearing his gray sports coat, white polo shirt, and no tie.

Somebody had used a grease pencil to circle Eddie's head in the picture. Above the circle was a blood red "X."

Eddie could hardly wrench his eyes off the red X over his own image. He said in a whisper, "I can't believe that the police missed something like this. Where did you find it?" He looked at Bobbi.

"Between the mattress and the box spring," she said. "Same place my first husband used to stash his titty magazines." She patted him lightly on the shoulder and nodded to the photo. "Do you know when this was taken?"

He shrugged. "I go there a lot, nearly every day. But that's a summer jacket I just rescued from storage in the basement the past couple of weeks. I think this was a day last week."

"It looks like Jimmy Whistle had his eye on you."

Eddie glanced to the drawer in which Jimmy Whistle had kept his pistol. He had been convinced that Jimmy had only meant to scare him—here at Jimmy's apartment and then later at Eddie's place—but this picture…

Bobbi said, "I don't like that red X."

"It doesn't make the least bit of sense," Eddie said. "Jimmy didn't even know I existed until I tracked him down here to ask him about Henry."

"He must have known more than he let on."

"I came here to interview him. If Jimmy wanted to kill me, I gave him the perfect opportunity."

"Maybe not," she said. "What was Whistle supposed to do? Kill you in his own living room? Throw your corpse over his handlebars and pedal you to the river? He must have been *quaking* inside when you interviewed him." She flicked a fingernail against the photo. "The guy who took this picture helped lock your brother away for life. He might have figured you'd be coming after him. Maybe he was planning to strike first. Or maybe he wanted to get back at Henry for some grudge he nursed for thirty years, and thought he could hurt Henry by hurting you."

Eddie felt a flash of defensive anger at Jimmy Whistle, and then a smear of some darker emotion…satisfaction over Jimmy's death. Whatever wickedness Whistle had been planning against Eddie, he had missed his chance.

"What are you going to do with it?" Bobbi asked.

Eddie wiped the photo on his sleeve and then held it only by the edges. "Keep your fingerprints off it, and put it back," he said. "We've learned all we need to know—Jimmy Whistle knew last week that I was going to come looking for him. Which means the cagey bastard was playing me for an idiot, steering me down the wrong path on purpose. He was using me."

"For what?"

"I don't know."

To stir things up? To ferret out information? To distract the asshole in the ski mask, so Jimmy could operate in the shadows?

"Whatever it was, he was already planning it before Roger Lime's photo turned up." Eddie juggled the facts in his mind. Something was still missing.

What was your angle, Jimmy?

Eddie laughed. Bobbi raised an eyebrow at him.

"It's just nerves," he explained. "I get tense, I laugh."

"I get tense, I eat," she said, patting her own rump. "I need to calm down while I can still fit into my jeans."

They both laughed, nervously.

She looked up at him sweetly, "Thanks, little brother," she said in a hoarse voice, as if speaking past a lump in her throat. "I came here not even knowing if you'd open your door for me, and here you are—risking your life to investigate. Even breaking into a house with me. All for Henry's sake, and you don't even know him—yet!"

"I've gotten to know my brother through you," Eddie said. "Thirty years is a long time to lose, but I'm not going to cry about it. My optimistic side says that Henry could be acquitted by reasonable doubt in a new trial, based on what we've already discovered. But I don't want to take that chance."

Eddie found his jaw tensing and his voice growing stern. "My brother didn't kill those men, and I'm going to get him out of there. I couldn't give up now if I wanted to." They had lost *thirty years*...the thought enraged him. Through gritted teeth, Eddie vowed: "I'm going to play a game of chess with my big brother."

She stared at him, her eyes filling with fright at Eddie's sudden burst of intensity.

"Be careful," she pleaded.

Eddie stared back, unblinking. "Fuck careful," he spat. "I'm getting close, and I'll do *anything* to win Henry's freedom."

She stared at him.

He said again, "Anything."

Chapter 25

After seeing Bobbi safely into a cab, and slipping her ten for the fare, Eddie rode The Late Chuckie's rat bike aimlessly around the city. Something about the bike's exhaust stench and the engine noise—like a dragon gargling toxic waste—cleared Eddie's head of stray thought. The bike practically steered itself down side roads, past old tenement buildings with street-level pubs advertising lowbrow beer in neon in every window. He headed deep into the Centralville neighborhood.

Eddie's brain seemed to be split in two. A tiny part of his brain operated the bike, stopped for lights, signaled for turns, swerved around double-parked cars; that was the easy job.

The rest of his brain obsessed over Henry. What Eddie had told his sister-in-law was true: there was nothing he wouldn't do to get his brother out of prison. The problem was, he didn't know what he *should* do.

The tiny part of his brain that was driving steered down a steep hill, in a neighborhood thick with triple-deckers, and no tourists looking for the historic attractions that the city fathers relentlessly marketed. This was not the neighborhood pictured in the travel brochures; this was where real people laughed, struggled, and died. The bike weaved through several more turns and then went down Lupine Road, and the rest of Eddie's brain tuned in to his surroundings. He had been here twice, the first time years ago on a personal pilgrimage along the roller coaster streets etched into the hills, to a writer's sacred site. The second time was four weeks ago, when he brought his journalism class here on a fifteen-minute field trip. His students had been bored blind—they didn't notice a single interesting thing about the place; none of them could provide a passable description when they got back to class and Eddie had bushwhacked them with a pop quiz.

Two students had dropped the class the next day.

Eddie slowed the bike and looked over the second-to-the-last house on the left.

Kerouac's birthplace.

Lowell's greatest writer was born there, on the second floor of a non-descript multi-family home, mud-puddle brown with yellow trim. There was a little chain fence out front, short enough that you could almost step over it, and a couple windowboxes on the porch rail sprouting unknown greens that had either passed their bloom or hadn't reached it yet. The building's trim needed paint, the lattice that kept the cats out from under the porch was missing some slats. The shades were drawn; there was no life.

What always surprised Eddie about the house was its anonymity. There was no bronze plaque, no sign he could see, nothing to mark the manger in which Lowell's literary savior was born. He wondered if the people who lived there even knew about Jack Kerouac. Could anybody in the neighborhood point out the place Kerouac was born?

At the end of the street he turned left, hit the throttle, roared up a hill and headed back toward downtown.

Kerouac's birthplace was anonymous because it was hidden in plain sight.

He thought about Lew Cuhna's riddle in the same way. Eddie had come to believe that it wasn't a complicated encryption; it was probably the kind of puzzle that became more difficult the harder you thought about it.

He had committed the riddle to memory.

I trust only journalists. Left the key with the two giants, you know the duo. Don't send the cavalry; follow the Union rider to General Lee's surrender.

What bothered Eddie about the clue was that Cuhna had trusted "the key" to two other people, but had expected Eddie Bourque to track it down and get it from them. Why? Especially if Lew only trusted journalists.

Unlesss...

The two giants *were* journalists.

Eddie let the thought simmer. Coffee would help him think, he decided. He crossed the steel Ouellette Bridge, and passed the minor league baseball stadium that vaguely echoed Baltimore's Camden Yards because it was designed by the same architects. He motored toward downtown, and the Perez Brothers diner.

...you know the duo.

Who were the giants of journalism? A "duo" that Lew Cuhna had assumed Eddie would know.

Eddie knew of many famous journalists, but not duos. Journalists were mostly solitary, like baseball players who each helped the team by succeeding as individuals.

Except, well, Woodward and Bernstein, of course. The *Washington Post* reporters who broke the Watergate story were the most famous reporter duo modern journalism had ever known.

Traffic backed up at a red light in front of City Hall. Eddie waited, straddling the bike, twenty car-lengths back from the light. To his left was the library, which Henry had jokingly suggested Eddie visit to solve Cuhna's riddle. It was one of the most impressive buildings in Lowell, a granite-block fortress of turrets and towers that looked like it could repel the assault of ten thousand barbarians. The upper windows were stained glass, half-moon shaped; the roof slate, elegantly trimmed with tarnished copper.

Eddie had not been to the library in years and was not well schooled in the building's history, but he knew it was old. More than a hundred years, for sure. Along with Lowell City Hall next door, the library was one of the few downtown buildings unchanged by renovation during the three decades Henry had been in prison.

Eddie concentrated on a relief sculpture, high on one of the library's main front turrets. He was dazzled by it. A sculptured horseman rode out of the granite, like a rider escaping a bank of impenetrable fog. A scabbard dangled from the rider's hip. On his head, a Civil War soldier's cap.

Don't send the cavalry; follow the Union rider to General Lee's surrender.

"Son of a bitch!" Eddie shrieked.

The bike's tires squealed on the pavement. The motorcycle squirted across the street, up the sidewalk ramp to the library's front steps. There, Eddie killed the engine and stared up at the rider. Now he remembered—the library had been built as a Civil War memorial. The relief sculpture was *a Union rider.* Henry wasn't jerking Eddie around on the phone; he was being literal. You want to find Lee's surrender? Go to the library! Eddie slapped himself on the head, hurt his hand, took off his helmet, and slapped himself again. He left the bike in the sidewalk, parked about as illegally as possible, and dashed up the stairs, through a heavy wooden door, into a foyer of dark wood, lively reddish walls, and gently curving archways.

Beyond the archways, the library's main floor was a large, impressive space of dark wooden pillars, many more arches, circular alcoves, and a high ceiling crossed by heavy ornate wooden beams. It looked antique and distinguished, like someplace where the old Continental Congress might have gathered to decide the future of the colonies. The only obvious compromise with modern times was the glass lamps that hung from the ceiling like mushrooms growing upside down.

A few patrons passed with armloads of books; others lounged with magazines. Eddie hurried to a woman sitting alone behind a reference counter. She was about thirty, with a light complexion, shiny black hair in a bob cut, and lava-red lipstick. She was on the phone, speaking haltingly in a Southeast Asian dialect, which Eddie did not recognize. She raised her eyebrows at him, as if to say, "I see that you need help...give me a moment." Then her eyes narrowed as she inspected the purple bruise around Eddie's throat.

Eddie shifted impatiently from one foot to another, like a little kid outside the bathroom door. Finally, the woman hung up. She asked Eddie in English, "What are you looking for, sir?"

What *was* he looking for?

He hadn't even thought about it.

"I need a book—uh," Eddie said, his eyes darting around the room, "by…Woodward and Bernstein!"

The names did not seem to register for her. She turned to her computer, asking: "Fiction or nonfiction?"

Is she kidding?

"Nonfiction."

A few keystrokes brought up one title: *All the President's Men.*

Eddie nodded like a madman. "I'll take it!"

She paid Eddie's enthusiasm no notice, took a scrap of paper from a stack and wrote the book's six-digit identification number: three-six-four point one-three-two. "It's in the three hundreds," she explained. "That's on the second floor, the stacks on the right. Way in the back, past Lee's surrender."

Eddie was speechless. *Lee's surrender?* He snatched the paper scrap from her, spun and sprinted up wide pink marble stairs.

The second floor was a huge space painted mint green and cream, a more sedate color scheme than the floor below. The ceiling looked to be twenty feet high. Lots of windows brightened the room. It held study tables and orderly rows of short book-shelves. The room also had two large rounded alcoves, opposite each other on the far walls. A gigantic curving wall-painting decorated the alcove to Eddie's right. In the picture, larger-than-life men in blue and gray uniforms gathered solemnly around a table draped in red.

Eddie didn't need to read the plaque beneath the painting; he knew the painting to be the surrender of General Robert E. Lee.

He passed through the doorway to the right of the painting. It led to a bright room with creamy yellow walls and tall steel bookshelves. He quickly found the Woodward and Bernstein book, a hardcover, protected by one of those clear plastic dust-covers librarians liked to use.

What now, Lew?

Eddie looked around, saw that he was alone, opened the book's front cover, and leafed through the pages. Nothing unusual...no handwritten message.

He slipped off the dustcover.

On the book's spine, a two-inch piece of masking tape fixed a short brass key to the book.

Left the key with the two giants.

Eddie's hand trembled as he peeled off the tape. He inspected the key. Tiny lettering on the side read: *U.S. Post Office, Lowell.*

There was also a four-digit number stamped on the key—a post office box number. Eddie slid the book back onto its shelf, pocketed the key, hurried back downstairs and checked the wall clock.

Five-forty-five in the evening. The post office was closed until morning.

Eddie walked slowly from the library, the key in his pocket feeling like a boat anchor.

Chapter 26

General VonKatz met Eddie at the door. He scratched Eddie's shoes to say, "Welcome home!" and "How was your day?" and "Is there food for me in that shopping bag?" Then the cat detected the scent of hot rotisserie chicken. The General whined like an ambulance and walked figure eights around Eddie's feet.

"Keep it down," Eddie said. "The neighbors will think I never feed you."

"Mwaaaaaa! Mwaaaaaaa!" said the General, which, like everything in the language of cats, loosely translated to: "Me! Me!"

"You want somebody to call the SPCA? All right, take it easy, I'm cutting it right now."

The General sprang to the countertop to make sure Eddie was properly cutting the bird. He pushed his head against Eddie's elbow. Some people have rules forbidding pets on the kitchen counter, but not Eddie; a cat doesn't care about your rules, so why give yourself a reason to get mad at it?

Eddie put the General's plate of minced chicken on the floor, and watched the cat leap from the counter, race to the plate, stop, carefully sniff, sniff, sniff, and then eat, swishing gray tail mopping a swathe of Linoleum.

Eddie ate the rest of the chicken, and then cracked a Rolling Rock.

He shoved the sofa against the door, sat, drank beer, and looked at the key Lew Cuhna had left for him. He could not imagine what waited at the post office in the morning. He felt a whoosh of anticipation. He fantasized about breaking and entering to use the key during the night...hmmm...naw. It would be there in the morning.

He was *so close* to some answers, and he started to get excited.

Wrong frame of mind, he reminded himself.

Lew Cuhna died for whatever is in that post office box.

The phone rang.

Mid-term exams were due. Probably another student's grand-mother was about to recline upon the satin pillow.

He smiled, reached for the phone and then suddenly stiff-ened.

In his home, on his sofa, drinking a beer—what could feel safer? And that was the feeling the killer in the ski mask had warned of; the killer had pledged to appear the moment Eddie felt safe.

He closed the key tightly in one hand. With the other, he lifted the phone to his ear but said nothing.

After a moment, Detective Orr asked, "You there, Eddie?"

"It's you, Lucy. Okay." He wiped his sleeve over his face. "Sorry, I'm a little jumpy."

"A *little* jumpy?" she mocked. "Yeah, and my office is a *little* small."

Eddie snickered. He had been afraid to mention the size of her office, but if Orr was making a joke about it, the topic was in play.

"I heard that your office used to be the broom closet," Eddie joked, "until the janitor bought a second broom."

Silence.

Oh boy. Eddie cleared his throat. "Anyway, you called—what can I do for you?"

"Your sister-in-law hasn't returned the messages I left at her hotel. I'm beginning to worry about her willingness to be inter-viewed."

"She's willing," Eddie insisted. *That sounded defensive.* He added, "I mean, I asked her to call and we talked about it. I vouched for you." He thought back. Did Bobbi ever say that she *would* call?

"If she's willing to call but hasn't, then it's my job, considering the circumstances, to worry about her well being," said Orr. "When did you see her last?"

"Today. Um. Earlier."

When we distracted your law enforcement colleague by creating a false disturbance, and then broke into a dead man's apartment and ransacked his stuff.

"This afternoon?"

"Yeah."

"Specifics!"

"Mid-afternoon, uh, from around two-thirty to four, give or take," Eddie blurted. What was it about Detective Lucy Orr that reduced Eddie to a blabbering knucklehead? "I can't pinpoint the time. I didn't wear a watch."

"What were you two doing?"

Uh-oh.

Eddie might lie to a police officer by necessity, but he didn't want to lie to a friend. Maybe Lucy Orr and he were too close to be interviewer and interviewee. In journalism, it's trouble whenever reporters write about their friends, so the practice is banned by newsroom ethics. *Your college buddy just got elected state rep? He has a hot tip? Great, let's get somebody else to write about that.* Eddie wondered if cops had a similar code.

"I'm not going to tell you what we were doing," Eddie said.

She made a grave little moan. "I can ask Detective Brill to conduct this interview if that would make you more comfortable."

Was that a nod toward Orr's friendship with Eddie? Or a veiled suggestion that Eddie might have shagged his brother's wife today?

"My conduct with Bobbi was not *immoral*," Eddie said, choosing the words carefully.

Detective Orr got the message. She asked, "Was your conduct illegal?"

"Am I qualified to say?" Eddie answered. "I don't have a copy of the Massachusetts General Laws at my fingertips, and I'm not a lawyer or a law enforcement officer, such as yourself."

"I'm closing my notebook," Orr said.

Eddie relaxed. "Thank God," he said. "Sorry about the crack about the size of your office. At least you have an office. Mine is a briefcase. I lecture my students under a sewer pipe, and, judging by the mid-term papers, I teach worse than I golf."

"Do you really think you can get your brother out of prison?"

Her abruptness startled Eddie. He pulled the phone away from his head, looked at it a moment and then pressed it back to his ear, saying, "A jury might find reasonable doubt, if Henry could get a new trial."

"Because two of the former witnesses against him are dead?"

Eddie hadn't thought about it that way. Dr. Crane and Jimmy Whistle had provided the bulk of the evidence against Henry thirty years ago. He said nothing. General VonKatz hopped onto the sofa, walked two tiny circles and then settled on his belly, next to Eddie.

"I checked the files," Orr said. "The physical evidence in the case against your brother no longer exists. Destroyed twenty years ago, when the warehouse flooded."

"Aw, Lucy, that sucks."

"Does it?"

"Sure it does," Eddie said, sharply. "Henry could have filed a motion to have the blood evidence tested for DNA. The results would have excluded him as the killer, and there would be no need for another trial."

"You're so sure he didn't do it."

So that's what this is about.

Eddie grew defensive. He said, "I believe in him."

"Following your gut?" she said. "Our guts can lead us dangerous places."

"He's my brother," Eddie pleaded. *Can't she see?*

"Don't split the facts," she said. "He's your brother, and he's doing life for murder."

She's blind.

"What do you know about my family?" Eddie shouted. The General scrambled away. "Or personal relationships? Or following your gut feelings? Christ, Lucy! Do you even *know* anybody outside of the concrete coffin you work in downtown? Do you ever do *anything* but work?"

Eddie switched tones, to quiet sarcasm. "Have you ever had fun?" he asked. "Do you know what fun is? Every time I see you, you're snooping around, asking embarrassing questions, writing it all down in your little notebook."

"That's what you do, too," she calmly reminded him. "Aren't you a reporter?"

Goddam. Fallen into my own word trap.

Eddie felt ridiculous. It was hard to get angry with Lucy Orr. She didn't reflect his anger back at him, so that it just died when it hit her.

"And I do have fun," she assured him. "I'm chair of the police windsurfer's club. There are a dozen of us. We do exhibition races for charity. I'd spot you fifty meters and still beat you across the Merrimack any day." She laughed.

She was absorbing Eddie's anger like light into a black hole, destroying it as fast as Eddie could produce it. He couldn't think of anything to say.

"I don't know about your family, but I know of mine," Orr said. "The lessons are universal."

It was the first time Orr had ever mentioned her family to Eddie Bourque. Eddie had trouble imagining Lucy Orr as a child; he had come to think of her as a policing machine that had been created as is.

He asked, "Were you born and bred to be a cop?"

She paused a moment, smacked her lips. "My father was a police officer," she said. "In Delaware, where I was born. Thomas Orr was chief of his department."

"Ha! I knew your accent was wrong," Eddie said. "It's ninety-percent New England, but once in a while an R slips through."

Eddie laughed, realized he was laughing alone, and then gave his instant analysis of Lucy Orr:

"So your pop was the top cop," he said. "Impressive. You grew up in his gigantic shadow—it's probably been hanging over you your entire career. And when you went into law enforcement, you found the old man's shoes hard to fill, so you convinced yourself you gotta work twenty-four/seven to live up to your father's standards. Because you want to be like him. Right? Right?"

"Is that what your gut says?" she asked.

That sounded like a trap. But Eddie could hardly back down now. "That's how I see it."

She began: "My father used his connections as chief to provide free prison labor to the city councilor who had cast the deciding ballot when my father got his job. Apparently, this was a deal they had worked out before the vote. This councilman owned rental property. My father had inmates painting his buildings, doing odd jobs, saving the guy thousands in maintenance costs. Then he falsified his reports to say that the inmates had been cleaning the highways."

Eddie felt like an ass. His analysis of Detective Orr had been exactly wrong.

"Oh, Lucy," he said. "I'm sorry."

"When the scandal broke, he resigned in disgrace. Never got charged or did jail time, but the city revoked his pension. It was all over the local paper. The talk shows called him 'Tommy Orr the political whore.' "

"Ouch."

"Painful," she agreed, "but not inaccurate."

"And all these years, you've been trying to erase what he did by working so hard."

That ruffled her. "For your information," she informed Eddie, "I *like* what I do. I like solving crimes. I like taking predators off the street. And I'm not so foolish to think that I can undo the past. Neither should you."

Eddie unclenched his hand and looked at the key. It shone with sweat. The key had left a jagged red indentation in Eddie's palm where he had been squeezing it. "This is different," he told Orr, softly. "I'm close to breaking this." He stuffed the key in his pocket.

"Bring me in on it," she said.

"Soon."

She started to argue but Eddie cut her off, saying: "For thirty years I tried not to think about Henry's sins, the shame of it, and the fear—what if I was like him? I didn't want to be capable of murder, but if my brother was, who's to say?"

Eddie's voice cracked. He felt the pinch of emotion on his windpipe, and swallowed hard. "In my case," he continued, "I *can* undo the past. Henry didn't kill those people, so the last thirty years have been an illusion, just a bad movie that I thought was real. I'm going to shut off the projector. Then I'm going to get my brother back."

He was close to crying, though he knew he wouldn't. He didn't want to cry and Eddie never cried unless he wanted to.

She sighed, saying: "I could have you picked up on an outstanding warrant, to keep you out of trouble."

"Like a paperwork error?"

"Probably would take the courts forty-eight hours to sort it out. You'll get your belt and shoelaces back, and maybe even an apology."

"I won't stop until I reach the truth," Eddie promised. "I'll do anything to get my brother back."

"That worries me," she said, suddenly sounding cold, as if Eddie had tapped her in a place outside their friendship. "Promise you'll call me before you get killed."

He thought about being deadpan. *How much notice do you need?* But he heard himself answer, "I swear it."

Chapter 27

The night passed in choppy, sleepless chapters.

First there was an hour tossing on the bed, watching the digital clock's hovering red numerals as they slowly ticked off the progress of the passing night, like the scoreboard of the world's most boring basketball game.

At midnight, Eddie slipped out of bed. He liked to change his environment when he couldn't sleep, but on this night, the sofa was no better. The change disturbed General VonKatz, who felt the sudden need to run from window to window, looking for squirrels. Eddie dozed in short fits. Every noise from the neighborhood piqued his fight-or-flight instincts, like when he tent-camped in grizzly country. He listened for the white van, driven by the man in the ski mask.

Shortly before dawn, a car slowed outside Eddie's house. Eddie tensed, until he heard his *Washington Post* hit the sidewalk. The car sped off. The newspaper reminded Eddie of Lew Cuhna's key, still in the pocket of his jeans, which were still on Eddie's body. There was nothing in the world more important than the key.

What if he comes for me tonight?

Eddie got up. It was quarter-to-four. He put on his running shoes, went back to his bed, and slept.

He woke at five o'clock. Five-zero-zero, exactly—what was the chance he would have woken right on the hour? Hmmmm…One chance in sixty? No…if he considered the possibility of sleeping later—say, until eight o'clock—that would be one chance in one hundred eighty. Wouldn't it? The clock turned to 5:01. Eddie realized he was wide awake.

"Uhhh!" he cried, yanking the pillow over his eyes. *I gotta get to sleep!*

He had left his computer on. The cooling fan hummed harmless little white noise. Eddie let the hum fill his head.

Then the computer said *DEE-do,* the chirp it made when an email arrived over the broadband.

Probably spam, Eddie thought.

Leave me be! I don't want generic painkillers, I don't want to refinance my home or spy on my neighbor with a secret camera, and I prefer my penis the way it is.

He squeezed the pillow over his head.

He caught himself wondering who else might have emailed him so early in the morning. What were the chances that he would have been awake when the email arrived….Hmmm, one chance in sixty?

"Aw, Christ," he cried, sweeping the comforter aside and rising from bed.

General VonKatz had been sleeping in Eddie's desk chair. Eddie snapped his fingers and pointed to the floor. "I need my chair," he told the cat.

The General looked Eddie up and down, rose with a shudder, bowed his spine, kicked out one hind leg a moment to stretch it, then kicked out the other one, yawned, licked a paw three times, hopped down and moseyed away, nails clicking on the hardwood.

"Thanks for rushing," Eddie said. He dropped into the chair, rapped the keyboard to dispel the screensaver and then called up the email.

Oh, the missing mid-term, the last one, from Ryan. Later than the rest, but under the deadline—the way Eddie wrote his news stories. He was about to return to bed when he decided to inspect the paper, to make sure it had arrived intact. He read the top:

> LOWELL—Sharon Matthewson gets to hear free live music three nights a week.
>
> Trouble is, it's usually when she's trying to sleep.
>
> The Board of License last night reviewed Matthewson's noise complaint against her neighbor, Kara's Irish Pub, 670 Hubbard St., which is known throughout the Merrimack Valley as an incubator of new rock'n'roll and heavy metal bands.
>
> Pub ownership claimed last night that they are operating within the rules of their entertainment license, and have already gone beyond what is required to satisfy Matthewson by installing a new vestibule to contain the sound when patrons come in and out.
>
> The board put the complaint on hold for two weeks, to allow commissioners time to schedule a site visit to the club...

Eddie read the story to the bottom. All the relevant facts were there. The top was engaging, even funny, while still respectful. The outcome of the hearing was clearly stated high in the story. And Ryan had added context with just a few words, describing the club as an "incubator" for new acts, which quickly characterized the garage bands that jammed there.

This is good journalism.

It was good enough to be published in any community newspaper. Eddie printed a paper copy of the story and then grabbed his red pen. With a few constructive edits, Ryan's story would really sing, and then Eddie could get back to sleep.

The clock said five-thirty-one. Eddie sighed. It was time to give up on sleep. He set the paper aside for a moment and brewed himself a ten-cup batch of double-strength Sumatra.

Eddie watched it drip, rubbing the key in his pocket.

Chapter 28

The Late Chuckie's rat bike glug-glugged over the bridge. Eddie looked downriver, where the Merrimack widened and became shallow. Patches of yellow-green grass sprouted from little almond-shaped islands where the water parted around sloping mounds of muck. The morning was bright, cloudless, hot. The wind from his slow ride failed to dry the sweat that dripped from under Eddie's helmet. The perspiration came from a mix of nervousness and too much caffeine.

The Post Office was a modern building with a sleek design that suggested computer-age efficiency. Eddie left the bike between two yellow lines, patted his pants, felt the key again—still there—left his helmet and goggles on the seat and walked inside.

The building's air conditioning had been set lower than *cool*, lower than *cold*, somewhere near cryogenic sleep. Sweaty after the ride, Eddie felt a deep-bone chill. He was afraid to ask for help finding the P.O. box—why would the rightful owner need help finding it? He browsed the little metal doors until he found the one with a number that matched the stamp on the key.

Looking both ways, feeling suspicious—probably looking suspicious—Eddie inserted the key and opened the box.

A manila envelope had been folded and stuffed inside.

Eddie wrestled it out.

It was nine by twelve, a half-inch thick, obviously containing paper of some kind. The address printed in green pencil was to Lewis Cuhna, at this post office box, Lowell, Massachusetts.

Cuhna had mailed this envelope to his own P.O. address.

Eddie checked the postmark and raised an eyebrow. Dated last spring…six months ago. He double-checked the box. No other mail inside. Weekly newspaper editor Lew Cuhna had taken the trouble of renting this post office box for the single purpose of stashing this envelope.

Eddie stuck the packet in his waistband, pulled his polo shirt over it and walked out, toward the bike. He felt like he was moving in slow motion, almost like he was not moving at all; it was as if the bike were simply getting bigger, until Eddie was standing over it, helmet strap cinched beneath his chin, his shoe stomping the starter. He revved the engine, blasted the coughs from it, and then drove off.

There was no need to think about where he would open the envelope.

◇ ◇ ◇

There was one car parked beside the Grotto shrine, a twenty-year-old green Oldsmobile the size of a tugboat. A plastic St. Christopher statue stood on the dash. Eddie left the bike beside the car.

Nearly all of the two dozen white candles on the shrine's altar had been lit. Somebody had strung Christmas tree lights around the statue of the Virgin. The lights shone feebly under the bright sun.

A car horn blared from the street. Two men argued loudly. Eddie blocked out their conversation and looked to the top of the shrine. He saw no one. For a moment, he thought he was alone.

He pulled the envelope from his waistband, and then walked to the stairs.

An old woman in a long black dress and white Adidas tennis shoes—a nun, Eddie quickly realized from her black habit—knelt on the staircase, halfway to the top. The nun clutched pink rosary beads. Eddie watched her. She grunted in pain as she stiffly climbed on her knees to the next stair, and then began mumbling her prayers.

Eddie held the iron handrail and climbed past her.

"Excuse me, sister," he said gently.

The nun smiled up at him. Her face was wide, tanned and deeply creased with channels that flowed from around her eyes to the corners of her smile. Her skin was shiny in the sun. She was maybe eighty years old, and beautiful.

"*Bonjour,*" the nun said in a high, trill voice. "It is a joy to love in His name."

Eddie smiled and nodded. "*Oui.*"

He climbed to the top of the shrine and sat on the bench there. Through the willows he could see the windsurfers tugging their bright sails over the river. Eddie wondered if Lucy Orr was among them.

He held the envelope and looked over the river. The sun was hot on his face, hot enough to burn his cheeks if he wasn't careful. He could hear the old nun murmuring her prayers, groaning as she dragged arthritic limbs up each stair.

He hesitated, because the envelope from Lew Cuhna was his last hope.

There are no more leads.

If the envelope did not hold answers, then Eddie would have failed.

He traced the Sign of the Cross—seemed like the thing to do on top of the shrine—and then opened the envelope.

Inside, Eddie found three editions of Lew Cuhna's newspaper, *The Second Voice.*

Eddie recognized one of the papers immediately: it was the edition Roger Lime had been holding in the first photograph released by the kidnappers. The front page had a cliché in a banner headline:

```
SHAKESPEARE FESTIVAL OFF
   WITHOUT A HITCH
```

"So what, Lew?" Eddie muttered. "So *what?*"

Then he noticed the gray text under the headline.

It wasn't a real story.

"Dummy text," Eddie said aloud, running his finger up and down the columns.

It was all computer-generated nonsense, random letters grouped into unpronounceable words. Dummy text, such as this, was created by publishing software to permit a page designer to experiment with the page layout without using real news copy. Once the page design was set, the real news copy would be flowed into the columns to replace the dummy text.

Eddie turned the page—nothing but dummy text, and fake headlines, too. Not one real news story in the entire paper.

He stared at the top half of the front page and tried to make sense of it.

The page looked *just like* the edition that Lime had been holding in the kidnapper's photo, except that this edition wasn't dated; *this* wasn't a real newspaper.

It's a mockup.

Why did Lew want Eddie to see it?

He put it aside and looked at the next paper Cuhna had left in the envelope.

It was another mockup—all dummy text. The front page had been designed to look *identical* to the first mockup, except that the headline was different:

SHAKESPEARE FESVITVAL
IS MARRED BY RAIN

That made no sense.

The weather had been ideal for the Shakespeare festival. No rain at all.

Eddie set that paper aside, too, and inspected the last one— also full of dummy text, and identical to the first two mockups, except that its banner headline read:

CANCELLED: NO SHAKESPEARE
FESTIVAL THIS YEAR

That headline was just idiotic. The Shakespeare festival had been held the same weekend in late July every year for the past two decades. The outdoor festival was a Lowell tradition.

Eddie's head snapped up with a sudden revelation.

He stared blankly at the river for a moment, thinking, thinking. Then he flipped through the papers again, re-reading the headlines.

The nun had reached the top of the stairs. She was a dark figure at the periphery of Eddie's vision. She was mumbling the Hail Mary.

Eddie understood everything, who was doing these killings, and why.

Roger Lime. Dr. Crane. Jimmy Whistle.

"Holy fuck," he said under his breath.

Then the larger truth of his revelation thundered down on him. "Oh, God! Noooo!" he wailed. He crushed the papers in his fists and pressed his palms to his eyes.

The old nun appeared in an instant on the bench beside him.

"*Qu'est-ce que se passe?*" she asked. *What is happening?*

Her fingertips touched lightly on Eddie's shoulder. He turned to her, grit his teeth, buried himself in the old nun's loving embrace, and wept.

Chapter 29

The message on the answering machine that evening was from Durkin:

"Eh? Bourque? Tony at the garage says that shitty Chevette is ready and he wishes you'd come pick it up so he can use the parking space for his new Dumpster. So, if that bike ain't killed you yet, give Tony a call. Oh, and he wants his money. Cash."

Eddie smiled. He had made peace with The Late Chuckie's rat bike.

It won't be the bike that kills me.

Eddie had spent all morning at the Grotto, on his knees, wounded inside, as if a little boy.

He had spent the afternoon on the bike, a man, deciding how he would end the drama of the past six days.

On a whim, he had wanted to see the ocean. Eighty-five miles per hour on The Late Chuckie's rat bike was like doing mach-three on hockey skates; it required unbroken focus to stay alive. The bike had taken Eddie to New Hampshire, up the Hampton Beach strip. The strip smelled like fried food, coconut sunscreen and seawater, as it did in Eddie's earliest recollection of a family weekend there, in a two-story drive-up motel with a view of the backside of a three-story drive-up. Eddie had been five years old. That was before his parents realized that Eddie was not his brother, and that they could not erase Henry's murder conviction by starting over.

Earlier today, the beach had been carpeted with reddened blobs of sizzling beach flesh. You could have walked a mile without touching sand—stepping only on the edges of other people's towels. Eddie had stopped the bike and climbed onto the seawall. The tide was low. Four white-haired men, their leathery bodies tanned so dark that they approached purple, had been playing bocce on the hard sand below the mid-tide line.

Behind them, two small sailboats, probably twenty-two-footers, cut silently along the water.

Eddie had sipped Pellegrino water and watched the boats. They gave him an idea, and he understood what he needed to do.

He had gotten home at dusk, his face chapped from the wind and the sun.

His first call was to Bobbi's hotel. The clerk put him on hold for five minutes, playing Sinatra's "It Was a Very Good Year" in Eddie's ear; the wait wasn't too bad.

Sinatra clicked off, the call was transferred, and Bobbi got on the line. "Hey, little brother!" she said. "Was thinking about the best way to reach Henry about getting a good lawyer. You could write him a note—"

"Won't work," Eddie interrupted.

"Oh, don't be modest," she chided. "I've seen your writing. Henry loves the way you express yourself on paper."

Eddie's words came out hoarse: "I've found something, Bobbi. It's…bad for Henry. The court appeal, the new trial…" He trailed off.

She waited, waited. "Christ, Eddie," she said finally. "What have you done?"

"I'm afraid I've wrecked everything," he said. "Before I tell the police about this, I thought I should tell you. You're his wife, and you need to hear it first. Can you meet me tonight?"

"Where? I'll meet you right goddam now."

"No, later. Say, midnight? I've got stuff to do before I can see you."

Her voice softened. "You're scaring me, little brother. What is all this?"

"There's a place off the river, near this religious school. They call it the Grotto. It's secluded. Nobody will be around late tonight. Let me tell you how to get there."

He told her. They hung up.

Eddie's next call was to Detective Orr's cell phone.

Orr must have recognized Eddie's number on her caller ID, because she answered: "I hope you've smartened up."

"I'm afraid that I have."

"You don't sound like yourself, Eddie."

"I've made a plan," he confessed, "and I need your help—but only you."

"I don't like that," she told him. "We could have a dozen uniforms on this case with one phone call. Why only me?"

"Because the plan involves murder."

She said nothing for a few seconds. If she was surprised by Eddie's admission, she didn't let on. She said, calmly: "You can't expect me to help you."

"I expect you to stop me."

The telephone conversation with Lucy Orr went on for hours, interrupted several times so Orr could make other calls, to verify Eddie's facts. When they had finished, Eddie hung up, rubbed his ear, and checked the clock. Ten-thirty.

Eddie brewed a pot of Columbian. But as he went to fill a mug, he impulsively dumped the coffee down the sink.

I need steady hands.

He put on a Sinatra CD, turned it up loud enough to drown out his thoughts, then reclined on the couch and closed his eyes. At the last note of "All Or Nothing At All," Eddie turned off the music, went into the bathroom, and fished Jimmy Whistle's heavy black gun from the toilet tank.

Chapter 30

The pink figurines seemed to levitate inside their wooden boxes, surrounded by black night, lit by their own ruby lights. Eddie released the throttle and let The Late Chuckie's rat bike glide past the Stations of the Cross. He remembered words Kerouac had written about this place:

"The roar of the river, mysteries of nature, fireflies in the night flickering to the waxy stare of statues."

Eddie was fifteen minutes early. Bobbi was already in the parking lot, waiting behind the wheel of an old Lincoln, a pocked and dented sedan rusting around the wheel wells. She checked her wristwatch as Eddie arrived. She had parked the Lincoln facing away from the river. The waxing moon, still a crescent, lit the parking lot gently with distant streetlights and the red glow of the twelve Stations. A breeze swept silently over the hulking shrine, ducking into its shallow cave to tease the candle flames on the altar.

By the time Eddie had shut down the bike and stowed his helmet and goggles, Bobbi was sitting cross-legged on the Lincoln's hood. The car looked tan in this unnatural mix of light. His sister-in-law had worn black jeans and a ruffled scoop-necked top. Most of her hair was tucked under a small leather hat with a thin brim. A few misbehaving wisps hung down over her face. She had the presence of a really good country music singer—attractive, yet beaten around by life. Eddie scanned the parking lot, squinting into the shadows, seeing nobody.

"I got sick of the bus," Bobbi announced, banging a fist on the hood. "Borrowed this thing from the stock-boy at the CVS. This is a test drive. Looks like hell but runs good. He wants six hundred. I might make him an offer."

"It's all bullshit, Bobbi."

She cocked her head and smiled at him, curious but not upset with his language. "What's eating you?" she said.

Eddie stared at her. "From the day I met you, you never stopped saying that the Bourque boys were gullible," he said. "You were right."

Still curious, like she was waiting for the punch line, she asked, "What's this about?"

"Your husband."

"Henry?"

"I should say your ex-husband," Eddie said. "The most recent one."

She shifted on the hood, uncrossed her legs and let them hang down the side of the car. "What do you know about that cheating asshole?"

"More than I had thought," Eddie said. He looked toward the shrine, breathed deep. "But I'll get to that."

She gave him a clenched smile and then a little rat-a-tat laugh. "I'm not following," she said.

"Ralph V. Nicolaidis," Eddie said, studying her face. Her cheek quivered. Eddie smiled. She was a superb actress, but not a perfect one. "He was the driver in the Solomon armored car holdup thirty years ago—the guard who escaped."

"A history lesson?" She shrugged. "So what?"

Eddie sighed and rolled his eyes, a little overdramatic. "The heist was an *inside* job," he said. "Jimmy Whistle planned the robbery with Ralph Nicolaidis—that's how the robbers were able to take the car to the middle of nowhere and open it without anybody radioing for help. The driver was in on it."

She shrugged again. "It's an okay theory, I guess."

"It's more than theory," Eddie continued. "Jimmy brought in Henry to be the muscle, in case Dumas and Forte, the other two guards, put up a fight. I'm pretty sure that Henry didn't know that Nicolaidis was in on the heist—Nicolaidis probably acted like a hostage, letting Jimmy and Henry tie him up in the basement of the old farmhouse in Dunstable, where they held the guards after the robbery."

"Henry's never mentioned that guy—Nicolaidis," Bobbi said, stumbling over the pronunciation.

"Nick-oh-LAY-dis," Eddie corrected, with a wink.

He said, "We may never know for sure, but I assume that Jimmy and Nicolaidis planned to kill Henry as soon as the heist was complete. Why split the dough with the rented muscle? But Henry proved smarter than Jimmy had figured. Maybe he suspected a double-cross. Maybe he was just being greedy. Whatever the reason, Henry hid the gold."

"Your brother did *what?*" she said, gamely sticking to her script.

Eddie ignored her. He felt his excitement building.

"No honor among thieves, ay?" Eddie said, realizing instantly that he had slipped into the French-Canadian accent he had learned as a boy from his aunts. It snuck into his speech sometimes when his mind raced ahead of his mouth.

"Why are you telling me all this?"

After a deep breath to slow himself down, Eddie said: "When the cops were closing in, Nicolaidis faked an escape, hiked through the woods until he was suitably dirty and tired, and then rejoined society, passing himself off as a victim of the crime."

Bobbi frowned. "Not a chance," she said. "If this was true, then Jimmy Whistle knew the driver was in on it. Whistle never said a word about it at Hank's trial."

Eddie rubbed his chin and thought it over some more.

"That bothered me for a while," he admitted. "Then I rationalized it this way—Jimmy had already reduced his sentence by testifying against Henry. Giving up a third suspect wasn't going to help him."

"There's no honor among thieves," she reminded him, sharply.

"But there is practicality," Eddie argued. "When I saw Whistle at his apartment, he told me he had arranged to have somebody look after his kid, Jimmy junior. I'd bet that Jimmy agreed to keep his mouth shut if Nicolaidis promised to keep an eye on junior—the only thing in the world that mattered much to Jimmy."

Eddie thought about it a little more. "It could also be that Nicolaidis threatened to throw junior in the river if Whistle blabbed," he said with a shrug. "Either way, Jimmy and Henry took the fall, and Nicolaidis got away with it."

Bobbi fidgeted and then whined impatiently, "What does this have to do with Henry? How can we get him out of prison?"

"Ralph Nicolaidis went to the police academy," Eddie said. "And became a police officer—a cop friend of mine checked the records tonight."

"So?"

"So he worked his twenty-odd years, maybe grabbed a little cabbage off the poker table when he and his buddies busted an illegal game," he said. "He probably shook down crack dealers for payoffs now and then. Before he knew it, thirty years had gone by, and James J. Whistle was getting out of jail."

Eddie raised an eyebrow at Bobbi and said in a low voice, "Ralph and Jimmy wanted the gold, didn't they?"

She stared at him. "How would *I* know?"

"Six *million* dollars in gold, un-fucking-traceable after it's melted down," Eddie said. He smiled, turned his palms up. "Problem was, the man who hid the gold is in the federal pen—unavailable for comment, as we say in the news business."

"Henry has never said anything about gold."

Eddie laughed. "That was the problem!" he shouted. "And that's where *you* came in." He jabbed a pinkie in her direction. "You got to know Henry, molded yourself into the woman he wanted, and even married him—if only on paper—to get him to spill the location of the gold."

Bobbi slid off the car and stood. Her jaw clenched, she seethed, saying: "I *don't* have to listen to this."

Eddie reached behind his back and drew Jimmy Whistle's gun from his waistband. He leveled the weapon at Bobbi. "Yes," he informed her, "you do."

She leaned unsteadily against the car, lips parted but saying nothing, unable to look away from the weapon pointing to her face.

The gun was cold in Eddie's hand, and even heavier than he had remembered.

"You had studied Henry's case," Eddie said. "You knew the evidence was circumstantial, except for the blood on his shoes. Get rid of the blood and the case would turn to vapors."

Fright stirred in Bobbi's eyes.

"But you never wanted to get Henry out of prison," Eddie said quietly. "You only wanted to give him *hope*. If you could convince Henry that he was just a few good attorneys from being free, then he'd want you to hire the best lawyers money could buy, ay?"

Again with that goddam accent!

Eddie continued, more slowly, "That kind of legal dream-team would cost a fortune. But if Henry *truly had hope*, wouldn't he tell his dear sweet wife where to find the gold?"

Eddie waited in silence.

Bobbi moved her lips to begin to speak, but nothing came out. Her eyes went from the gun, to Eddie's eyes, to the gun.

The weapon grew heavier. Eddie's throat dried out. He coughed and spat on the tar.

"What amazed me," Eddie said after a minute, "is the patience the three of you showed in discrediting Dr. Crane—you, Ralph, and Jimmy Whistle."

She smiled blandly—just muscles flexing under skin, nothing more. "You're crazy," she sputtered.

Eddie had hoped Bobbi would have broken by now.

He would have to push harder to get a confession.

"You kidnapped Roger Lime," he shouted at her. "Then you went to Lew Cuhna—Mr. Small Time Newspaper Editor. You bribed Cuhna, or you threatened him, or probably both, to create *mock newspapers* for Roger Lime to hold in the ransom photo. That first mock paper had to mention an event in the future that was sure to be in the headlines. The outdoor Shakespeare festival was perfect—it's an annual tradition. You had Cuhna print up a few different headlines, to cover yourselves in case the event got rained out or canceled, and then you photographed Lime holding each paper."

Eddie felt sweat gathering on his brow. He kept watch on Bobbi, kept the gun pointed at her, and quickly swiped his forehead against his shoulder.

"That's why the headline was a little off—you couldn't have predicted a drunk driver would have driven into the stage set. The second paper was easy. Cuhna drew up another front page showing Roger Lime holding a story about *his own kidnapping*.

"Once you had the film you needed, one of you *killed* Roger Lime and burned his body beyond recognition."

"No," she said in a tiny voice.

Eddie rubbed his throat. "I'm guessing that Nicolaidis did the actual deed, though you're just as culpable."

Tears gathered in her eyes. Was she acting again?

"Six months later, after the Shakespeare festival, Lew Cuhna completed the scam by designing his real newspaper *exactly like* the mockup," Eddie said. "It's not hard. He probably used the same templates and simply typeset actual news copy in place of the dummy text. After the real paper was on the streets, you sent the cops the six-month-old picture of Roger Lime holding the mockup, and a bank president appeared to miraculously come back from the dead."

"No, Eddie."

"Everybody thought Dr. Crane had fucked up the dental identification of Lime's body. He was discredited. Nicolaidis silenced Crane with that phony suicide, and there was nobody left to vouch for the blood evidence against Henry."

Bobbi looked around, as if waiting for help to arrive.

Why won't she just crack?

Eddie had no choice.

He had to push her some more.

"You were in on this, Bobbi, you had to be," Eddie said, giving her a glum frown. "You were at my place when Lew Cuhna called with something important to tell me. That afternoon, Cuhna got whacked. And it was you who found my photo in Jimmy Whistle's apartment. The police didn't miss that picture—you brought it in your purse to make sure I stayed good and confused. When did you snap the photo? When you were preparing to scam me?"

She said nothing. Eddie screwed up his courage and flexed his hand around the gun. "My cop friend checked the marriage records, Bobbi," he said. "The day before you married Henry Bourque, you got divorced from Ralph V. Nichols."

Eddie had to guess at this next part, but he felt good about his chances: "How long will it take the police to figure out that Mr. Nichols long ago Americanized his name from Nicolaidis?"

A single tear ran down her left cheek. She whispered, "I don't know that man. Why are you saying these things? When will you let me go?"

Goddamit, she had called his bluff.

Eddie had to take the ruse to yet a higher level.

"I wish it didn't have to be this way," Eddie said, blinking rapidly. "But you and Ralph Nicolaidis are the only other people who know the truth about Dr. Crane's death. I can't take the chance you'll tip the cops before Henry gets out of prison."

Eddie spread his feet for balance, gripped the gun with both hands and stared down it at her.

Bobbi's eyes widened with a sudden revelation.

She blurted, "You're not going to *kill* me out here!"

"I said I would do anything to get my brother out of prison, and I meant it," Eddie said. "You and Ralph Nicolaidis are killers. You deserve whatever you get—it's justice. Why shouldn't I get my brother back?"

She shrank against the car and slid to the pavement. Against the front tire, she huddled like a frightened animal. Softly, she said, "You need to put the gun away, Eddie. I'm your *family*."

She's not going to break.

Bobbi wasn't buying Eddie Bourque as a vigilante killer. Eddie couldn't blame her. He wouldn't have bought it either—not yet.

"Put down the gun, Eddie!" a voice called out.

Eddie whirled.

Detective Orr, prompt as always, stood beside the shrine. She wore a Lowell police department sweatshirt, gray sweatpants, wet below the knees, and her gunbelt.

"I've been tailing you, Eddie," she said, walking toward him, shooting a quick glance toward Bobbi. "When I saw your bike coming this way, I took the bridge to the boathouse, and then rode my windsurfer here. I came up the riverbank and hid behind the shrine. I heard everything."

"Get outta here, Lucy," Eddie ordered.

She continued walking toward him. "The law will sort this out, Eddie."

"Get away from me."

Detective Orr drew close and reached a hand for the gun.

The weapon spit fire and thunder, a low *boom*, like a giant knocking two boulders together.

Lucy Orr spun, clutched her chest and fell convincingly enough. Maybe too convincingly—when Eddie turned the gun back to Bobbi, it was shaking in his hand.

"Oh Christ, no!" Eddie cried.

He lunged one step toward Orr on the ground, and then abruptly spun back toward Bobbi. He panted for a few seconds, to let her process the scene, and then growled, wet and throaty: "See what you made me do? She was my *friend*." He sighted down the pistol. "You're evil…and you're going to pay."

She cracked.

"Do you know how many times I saved your fucking miserable life?" she snarled.

So the tears had been part of her act.

"You didn't save anybody," Eddie said.

"Ralph thought you might have seen him at Crane's place, and decided to take you out with the van," she said, angrily. "He never consulted me. When he saw that you had gotten away, he was enraged. But I persuaded him that you could be useful with your pigheaded brother. I convinced him to hold off until I had approached you, to see what you knew about Crane and Roger Lime. As it turned out, you hadn't seen a thing at Crane's garage."

She held eye contact with Eddie and pushed herself back to her feet.

"You can still help us," she said. She nodded in an exaggerated way. "I can control Ralphie. Help us with Henry and we'll split the gold three ways." She waved her hands at him; it was an odd and distracting motion, like she was about to do a magic trick. Eddie focused on her face.

"Where," Eddie asked, "is Ralphie?"

"I'm here, asshole."

A chill passed like a cold blade through Eddie's gut.

Slowly he turned toward the familiar voice.

Even without his ski mask, Eddie recognized Ralph Nicolaidis, a bull in human form.

The Bull was standing with Lucy Orr. One of his powerful hands held Orr by the hair, drawing back her head, exposing her white neck, at which his other hand held a bayonet. Moonlight flashed off the blade.

Eddie saw Orr's throat ripple as she swallowed.

Orr said slowly, "He got the drop on me. He was in the trunk."

Eddie's eyes flashed to the old Lincoln's trunk, which gaped open a few inches, bouncing slightly in the breeze. He gripped the gun in both hands and aimed it at the Bull's head, a big square block of boney brow, military-style haircut and droopy walrus moustache. The Bull pressed its head close to Orr, like her conjoined twin.

Eddie was six feet away. Down the sight of the gun it seemed like sixty.

"Tut-tut-tut, you wouldn't want to hurt the lady cop," warned the Bull. "Like you said, she's your friend. She must be, to go along with an act like you pulled tonight." To Bobbi he ordered, "Get in the car, babe, we're getting the fuck outta here."

In his periphery, Eddie saw Bobbi climb into the car. The door slammed. "Ralphie," she said out the window, "what are we gonna do?"

Never taking his eyes off Eddie, the Bull answered, "We're going to take the lady cop for a ride, so your brother-in-law knows not to follow, or call the cops."

The gun in Eddie's hand wavered. It was getting heavier, as if nature had turned up the gravity.

Orr wheezed, "Shoot him, Eddie."

"Shut up," ordered the Bull.

"You can do it, Eddie," said Orr.

Eddie willed the gun to be steady. Why wouldn't it listen? *Why won't you fucking listen?*

The Bull looked at his big hands, both occupied holding Orr. Then he glanced down at Orr's gunbelt. "Take out your gun and hand it to me," he whispered to her. "I want it."

Orr didn't move. The Bull squeezed her. She gasped. Her eyes closed.

"Do it!"

Eddie watched Orr's hand move slowly toward her pistol. *No Lucy...if he gets your gun...*

She slid the holster guard aside, gripped the handle with a thumb and forefinger and slowly withdrew the weapon.

"That's it," said the Bull. "Bring it up so I can reach it."

Orr paused, looked at Eddie, blinked once, and then with a sudden flick of her wrist flung the weapon away. It clunked and skidded into the darkness.

The Bull squeezed her again and pulled the dagger tighter to her throat. "Bitch!" he croaked. The blade drew a dribble of blood. Orr grimaced.

Sweat ran like acid into Eddie's eyes. The acid mixed with tears. Lucy Orr had defied the Bull to save Eddie—*with a bayonet at her throat.* Eddie's breathing was loud and irregular. He held out the pistol. He blinked away the tears, saw the Bull's head moving in and out of his gun sight. The muscles in Eddie's arms burned under the weight of the impossibly heavy gun.

The Bull grunted. He looked to the car, then back at Eddie. "Let's go," he whispered to Orr, and stutter-stepped her toward the Lincoln.

Eddie panned the gun toward them as they moved. The trigger seemed to push back against his finger with irresistible force.

"Shoot him, Eddie," Orr said, tension rising in her voice.

"Shut the fuck up!" said the Bull.

"Imagine the Lone Ranger," Orr said. "Shoot him where the mask would be. He won't even flinch."

"He's not shooting anybody," said the Bull, as he backed up against the car. "Get the door, Bobbi."

The door opened. The Bull pulled Orr toward it.

Blood dripped down Lucy Orr's neck from where the blade had broken the skin. She closed her eyes, gasped, and then looked fleetingly toward the shrine, eyes huge in the moonlight. "Eddie," she called out, "if he gets me in this car, I'm dead!"

The Bull stopped pulling and looked at Eddie. "Ahhhh," he purred. "I know your little secret. In your one-act play a few minutes ago, that gun fired *blanks.*" He grinned, the way he had in the old well. It was his killing grin. Lew Cuhna had seen it. Dr. Crane, too.

But not Eddie's friend Lucy Orr. She would not see it.

I have another little secret.

Only the first round had been blank.

Boom.

Eddie killed him.

Chapter 31

The parade of government cars passed for hours by the Stations of the Cross.

Eddie tried not to listen when Bobbi called his name as the cops placed her in the back of the squad car. He looked away when the coroner's long gray station wagon arrived. Investigators showed up. Evidence gatherers. Crime scene photographers. Blood splash-pattern experts. Ambulances. Fire trucks. Last to arrive were the politicians—who had come to tell everyone else how to do their jobs.

The sun had barely cleared the triple-deckers to the east, and it was already hot at the Grotto. From the bench atop the shrine, Eddie sipped a Dunkin Donuts hazelnut that one of the cops had brought for him, at Detective Orr's urging.

The Merrimack River ran steady, not in any rush this morning. A hot breeze blew. It seemed like a fine day to take up windsurfing.

"Eddie? Eddie? You're not paying attention," Detective Orr said.

"Sure I am," he told her. "Just not to your questions." He smiled so she would know he was kidding, and then said, "Haven't we covered it? I've told you everything I know."

She looked out to the river, nodded, slipped her notebook in her waistband and sat down next to Eddie. She fiddled with the white gauze around her neck. It had been a shallow cut, no stitches. "You're right," she said. "Enough for now."

They watched the river for a minute. Then Orr said, "Why do you think they killed Jimmy?"

Eddie sipped coffee. "Just being practical," he offered. "They knew I'd be bringing the police to the farmhouse after I got out of the well. The property deed for the farm leads right back to Jimmy's mother, and to Jimmy. Better to silence the old convict, before you and Detective Brill hauled ol' Jimmy to an interrogation room and stuck a bright light in his face."

"We don't do interrogations that way."

"Or put him in thumbscrews or clamped jumper cables on his nuts—whatever," Eddie said. "Nicolaidis probably called Bobbi from his van, and had her pick up Whistle and bring him to the farm. The son-of-a-bitch probably made Jimmy dig out the bones before he killed him."

"Which reminds me," Orr said, pulling out her notebook and flipping through it. "Tyngsboro police found the van, abandoned down a dirt road. The VIN number matches a van reported stolen six months ago in upstate New York."

"Seems about right."

"They say there's an odd little coffee table inside—shaped like home plate," she said. "I could probably get it for you, if you wanted it."

Hmmmm. Eddie didn't want Henry's table destroyed, but did he want it in his house? "Let me think about that," he said.

They watched the river a little longer.

Orr said, "That's a lot of bodies, even for a thousand pounds of gold. Four men dead."

Roger Lime. Dr. Crane. Jimmy Whistle.

Who else?

Oh, of course, Eddie thought with a shake: *Ralph Nicolaidis.*

"Plus don't forget Dumas and Forte, the other two guards," Eddie reminded her. "They were killed thirty years ago for that gold."

She cocked her head. "Yeah, what about that? How do their deaths figure? I mean—knowing what we've learned?"

Eddie's phone buzzed. He checked the caller ID number: Ryan Daniels, the only half-decent student in Eddie's class.

He answered, "Hey Ryan!"

"Whoa—you're psychic, man!" Ryan said. "You're the coolest teacher *ever!*"

There was no way Eddie was going to disagree with *that*. "What's up, Ry?"

"Uh, Professor Bourque," Ryan said. "I'm afraid I have to drop your class."

"What? Hold on." Eddie covered the phone and said to Orr, "Teacher-student conference."

She nodded, hint taken, and walked off.

To Ryan, Eddie said, "You can't leave now—you're the first one who's actually starting to *get it*."

"Oh, yeah, dude, I know—I mean, Professor Bourque," Ryan said. "That's why I'm dropping the class. I'll be working nights, covering concerts as the new full-time music writer for *The Second Voice*."

The phone squirted from Eddie's hand. He grabbed for it, batted it twice into the air before snatching it. He said, "Lew Cuhna's old paper? Ryan, that's great."

"Yeah, man, thanks," Ryan said. "Um, it's a small staff, as you know. So I gotta do some cop coverage, too. You know? And I heard about you on the police scanner this morning, and I was wondering if you could help me on my story, gimme a quote or something."

Eddie laughed. "Tell you what, at the police press conference today, ask the chief to explain how this incident is related to the kidnapping of Roger Lime. Watch him pop an artery! Blam!"

"Whoaaaa. No shit?"

"Good luck, man. You know more about reporting right now than I did in my first job."

Chapter 32

Eddie arrived in upstate New York tired and wind-chapped, sunburned and bow-legged, with an aching back and a sore ass. He left his helmet and goggles on The Late Chuckie's rat bike, took a thin cardboard box from the saddlebag and went inside the prison.

The guard's eyes narrowed at the box. "You can't bring anything into the visiting room," he informed Eddie.

"Call the O.I.C.," Eddie said, using the slang for officer-in-charge.

The guard pressed the phone to his head, shooting Eddie glances as he spoke. He hung up and shrugged. "You got friends in high places. You're all set."

Eddie didn't bother to mention that he had a friend in Congress, who happened to sit on a House committee with the congresswoman who represented this section of the Empire State.

The guard looked in the box, to make sure it did not contain a machine gun or a grappling hook. Satisfied, he led Eddie into the visiting room.

"Sit at number five," he advised. "The phone's busted at six."

Eddie sat. Waited. Checked the clock. Waited.

There's so much to say, hardly any time.

No, Eddie thought, there *was* time. This was a marathon. You don't win a marathon in the first hundred yards. The two brothers had the rest of their lives to get to know each other.

A door beyond the glass opened and Henry came out, cuffed and shackled and looking precisely as he had before. He nodded at Eddie, smiled, and sat.

Eddie took the phone.

Henry did not.

He stared at Eddie for a minute, a little smile at the corners of his mouth. Henry looked to the telephone, and then nodded toward the guard's station, the next room over. Then he pantomimed listening to a telephone with his hand over the mouthpiece.

He was pretending to eavesdrop. *So the guards eavesdrop.*

Henry smiled and nodded as understanding spread over Eddie's face. Then Henry mouthed five words, slowly so that Eddie could read his lips:

"Do."

"You."

"Want."

"The."

"Gold."

Eddie had expected the question. He had spent the past two weeks, after the confrontation at the Grotto, rationalizing about all the good Eddie Bourque could do with six million dollars in gold. But he couldn't take it. He could melt down the gold and recast it into any shape he liked, but he would never strain out the blood.

"No," Eddie mouthed back.

Henry laughed without sound on his side of the glass, and then picked up the telephone.

"You got my letter?" Eddie asked.

"Next time include beer."

"I'm sorry about your wife."

"Marriage isn't prison."

Eddie looked for pain in his brother's face. There was thirty years' worth. "I'm taking some time off," Eddie said. "For the mountains. I thought you could pick one you'd like to visit. I'll camp there, make some notes, tell you about it."

Henry nodded. "I killed those two guards," he said.

"I know."

They met eyes, understanding each other. Eddie had dreaded this moment. He was glad when it was over.

"You could still file motions for a new trial, or for clemency," Eddie said. "It's been thirty years."

Henry shifted in his chair, looking uncomfortable. "Maybe some day," he said. Looking away, refusing to meet Eddie's eye, he added: "I need to be sure it would never happen again."

A lump grew like a tumor in Eddie's throat.

"Maybe some day," Eddie repeated at a whisper.

Henry switched the phone to his other ear. "I've done what you asked—petitioned for a transfer to a state pen in Massachusetts, maybe Gardner—that's not too far from you."

"Naw, just forty-five minutes. That would be perfect."

"Probably take a few months, but I'm first on the list when a bed opens up. Next time somebody gets shanked, I'm in." He made a bright, hopeful face and held it, batting his eyelashes.

Eddie couldn't help himself and burst into laugher.

"You're good at puzzles," Henry said. "Their whole plot was based on misdirection. You cut counter-grain to solve it."

"I get lucky sometimes."

"Are you going to try to solve any more puzzles?"

Eddie shrugged. "If any come up."

"I have a lot of time to think about puzzles."

"I could use the help." Eddie was beginning to learn how Henry communicated. Keep it moving. Henry had not even glanced at the box on the counter on Eddie's side of the glass. Eddie patted the box. "This is for us." He took from it a small black-and-red checkerboard. He set up the plastic chess pieces— white for Henry, black for himself.

"I've been playing chess every day since you wore diapers," Henry warned, a little smile on his lips. "You can't possibly beat me, not in a hundred tries."

"You're probably right," Eddie said. "But prepare yourself for that glorious day when your little brother learns to kick your ass. Now move!"

To receive a free catalog of Poisoned Pen Press titles, please contact us in one of the following ways:

Phone: 1-800-421-3976
Facsimile: 1-480-949-1707
Email: info@poisonedpenpress.com
Website: www.poisonedpenpress.com

Poisoned Pen Press
6962 E. First Ave. Ste. 103
Scottsdale, AZ 85251